Available from HQN and

CAROLYN DAVIDSON

Nightsong
Redemption
Haven

Other works include:
Harlequin Historical

*Edgewood, Texas
**Montana Mavericks
†Colorado Confidential

CAROLYN DAVIDSON

The Bride

HQN™

ISBN-13: 978-0-373-77220-9
ISBN-10:   0-373-77220-3

THE BRIDE

Dear Reader,

While traveling through the great southwestern part of our country, my husband, children and I drove through New Mexico. Going from north to south, we went the length of the state, and this author was fascinated by the vivid scenery and the wonder of the area. My mind immediately went into writing mode and I thought those magic words: "What if?"

As every writer knows, that simple thought can set into motion any number of brain waves, which in some cases lead to a story. A story we hope will gain readers' attention and involve them in the wanderings of our imaginations. Such was the case with this book. For several years I thought of what might have happened over a hundred years ago, what sort of man and woman might be involved in this story. And then, a year or so ago, I put it all together in my mind and on my computer. The result was my story of a captive bride, and the man who won her heart.

My hope is that my readers will enjoy their trip into the world of the 1800s and the Territory of New Mexico, where Isabella and Rafael found their future together.

Carolyn Davidson

This book is dedicated to those who married in earlier times, back when life was perilous and every day was an adventure. It is, more important, dedicated to the memory of my parents' marriage. They were born very near the time this story takes place. Theirs was a wedding between two strong, independent individuals who sought the joys of wedded bliss and found not only that, but the trials and tribulations of two very different, stubborn people in the midst of a changing world. The life they lived gave to the children they raised a legacy. It was one that inspired their offspring to seek and find marriages containing love and fidelity, enough to last for a lifetime.

So to Mother and Daddy, whose memories will be alive in the thoughts of those who loved them, this book is dedicated.

And, as always, my words are given with love to Mr. Ed, who loves me.

The Bride

PROLOGUE

The Territory of New Mexico
1890

Isabella Montgomery trembled as she stood before her father. Feeling compelled to state her case she forced words from her throat, well aware that she risked, almost invited, her father's anger. "I am fourteen years old, Father. I know that there are girls of my age already married, but I fear I'm not ready to become a wife." Her voice broke as she considered the man her father intended for her and revulsion filled her mind. "Juan Garcia is as old as you are. How can you think of giving me to him as a bride?"

And even as she spoke, she knew her plea would be in vain, for her words would not be heeded by her father.

Charles Montgomery was a man of mixed heritage, who saw before him the means of his own upward climb into society, and his eyes were dark, dull orbs as he considered the female before him. Given his mother's Spanish aristocratic background, he would have been of exalted heritage, had not that woman been seduced by an Irish immigrant and given birth to a child who looked like a throwback to the Spanish grandees, yet bore the name of an Irish potato farmer.

Now he aimed higher, aware that wealth might also be his, even though it was at the price of his daughter's future. A small thing to be sacrificed, for of what use was a daughter, anyway? But, for some reason, his child was worth more than he'd imagined, and this was an opportunity he would not allow to slip through his fingers.

"You will marry the man chosen for you, Isabella." His eyes were hard, seeming to be made of onyx, so harshly did they glitter in the lamplight. "I have educated you with the finest of tutors, readying you for your position in life. Be happy that I am willing to give you time to become a woman first. You are small, not fit yet for a wife's duties, and your body has not shown signs of maturity. You may find that the convent will suit you. The sisters will guide you, teach you womanly ways, and in two years or so, you will be a fit wife for Juan Garcia."

"He is an old man." Her words were harsh, scornful and without respect for the man who had set her destiny.

With a blow she had expected, she was dashed against the thick wall of her father's parlor, her cheek bleeding from the signet ring he wore. And yet, she could not have accepted his will for her life without protest.

If nothing else, Isabella was destined to be a woman of great pride. That she would also be possessed of great beauty her father had long since decided was a given, for she wore the face of her mother, a woman lauded for her beauty and figure. A woman whose death had followed the birth of Charles Montgomery's only child. That the child was a girl was a tragedy, but one he bore up under. For even a girl child could be made into an asset.

At fourteen, she carried the promise of great beauty, and, catching the eye of a man who collected objects of distinction, an offer was made for her. It was more than Isabella's greedy father could resist. Perhaps a period of time might bring about an even larger amount of cash from the man whose greedy eyes claimed the girl, whose avid lust seemed to know no bounds. For Isabella, as he might have predicted, was not agreeable to an early marriage.

Juan Garcia had been persuaded to wait for her body to ripen, and the Sisters of Charity would see to it that Isabella did just that in a climate guaranteed to protect her from outside influences. Two years in the convent would make her fit for marriage, the sisters teaching her the duties of a woman. This marriage would bring honor to her father, the joining a link between two wealthy families, providing Charles Montgomery with grandchildren to inherit his holdings.

With bitter tears and a sorrow too heavy to be borne by a child, Isabella was sent away from the only home she'd ever known, to live in almost silent seclusion with the Sisters of Charity. Their kindness was given to the poor of the community in which they lived, leaving the confused child whose presence provided their convent with funds for her keep a modicum of attention. For though they were not unkind, nothing could replace the mother's love she so desperately needed.

Her father died when she was sixteen and the lawyer provided funds for her to remain at the convent for two more years. At the time of her father's death, she'd been told of his passing, of the sudden illness that had claimed his life. She'd mourned not for the man he'd been, but for what might have been had he honored her as his daughter, had he offered her the love of a father. And then, with barely a pause in her daily schedule of work and prayer and faithfulness to the nuns, who gave her what attention they could, she faced her future, a future that seemed insecure, living one day at a time, never looking beyond the sunset, but thankful for each morning's dawning. Thankful for the day-to-day schedule that took her time and attention. For each day had seemed to solidify her position here at the convent.

SHE'D RECENTLY LEARNED that Juan Garcia was growing angry with the wait for the claiming of his bride. He'd told her father's lawyer that he would be coming to claim her. So for now, she existed in a vacuum, for she could not face her future.

Stepping carefully, Isabella sought a path of least resistance, whispering prayers, attending chapel services, bowing her head in submission to the rules of the convent and, in all ways, seeking to be invisible.

All to no avail.

CHAPTER ONE

Convent of the Sisters of Charity
The Territory of New Mexico—1894

THE GIRL WOULD NEVER BE A NUN. Whether she was here by her own volition or that of another, the outcome was obvious. And if she was the one he sought, freeing her from the convent was of immediate necessity. Even if she did not answer to the name of Isabella Montgomery, she had answered the call of his sensual nature.

For one glimpse of that face, that portrait of innocence personified, would be enough to bring the most stalwart saint to his knees.

And Rafael McKenzie was no saint. Therefore, his perception of the female he watched was, of necessity, tainted by his carnal nature. He was a man who had, early on in his life, set himself up as a judge of womankind, his decisions based on an early brush with the evil inherent in many women of great beauty.

Not that beauty itself was evil, but that the quality of perfection might be used for a woman's own gain. Thus, the temptation to profit by pleasing features and a body that matched the same description might be overwhelming to a woman of less than stalwart principles.

He'd heard of her, this woman who lived in a convent, adhering to a lifestyle that was almost guaranteed to oblige a woman to live within moral boundaries. The absence of men in her vicinity made it probable that she was a virgin, a woman untouched, more than fit for his wife. He had no illusions about marriage, for he'd seen a great variety in his life, and none of them had inspired him to that fate. Only the need for a bride offered the incentive now to seek out a candidate.

That she was pledged to another man was well-known in the community where she had been born and raised. Until she'd been sent, on the brink of her womanhood, to the convent of the Sisters of Charity, where she would be taught the ways of a wife. And now, four years later, she certainly must be more than prepared for such a life. And so he had sought her out.

The Diamond Ranch needed a woman to sleep in the massive bedchamber belonging to the master of the domain, the man who was due to inherit the thousands of acres making up the most successful ranch in the territory. A woman to grace the table in the enormous dining room, to sit before the parlor fireplace in the winter months and blossom, eventually, with a child beneath her skirt.

A wife for the man who was about to step into the position of master of all he surveyed.

And Rafael McKenzie was that man, inheritor of

Diamond Ranch, a man whose father would soon leave him his inheritance with but one stipulation. He must find a bride, must bring her to this house where no woman had been in residence for a number of years. Oh, there were maids and cooks, those who did the everyday chores that ran the house in a smooth manner. But there was no regal beauty to carry on the fine bloodlines of the McKenzie name.

And so, if he was to inherit the ranch, if the wealth of his father was to become his, he must find a woman fit to take on the task of mistress of the Diamond Ranch, in a timely manner. For the will stipulated that he could not wait to be married for more than a year after his father's death. Once the days of mourning were past, he must marry. And to that end Rafael McKenzie lent his intelligence, for losing the inheritance was not to be considered.

Marriages were occasionally made in heaven, he had heard; but he was only too aware that, more often than not, a match between two people required a more earthly approach in order to achieve any degree of success.

He'd observed that the most beautiful women rarely made the best wives. Sad, but true, he thought. Yet, looking once more at the vision who sat in a pew at the front of the small chapel, he decided that he would be willing to bend his ideal to suit the female he'd sought and found. For there were compensations to be found if the woman in his marriage bed were to be the one he saw before him now. He could tolerate much for the joys inherent in bedding the woman known as Isabella Montgomery.

She'd been described as a beautiful child, and the words still fit her. For she had grown to be a magnificent woman. From this angle, it was hard to judge entirely the degree of beauty she possessed. Hair hidden beneath a starched arrangement of white fabric, a scarf of sorts, and body almost entirely enclosed by a gray serviceable dress, there was very little of the girl exposed for a man to look upon.

But her face alone, he decided, was worth his best effort. To that end, he took careful note of the pure line of her forehead, the wide-set eyes, the high cheekbones that told of some long-ago ancestor whose bloodlines were not of common descent. Skin so translucent it might have been spun from silk, fragile and delicate features, cheeks that begged a man's touch, eyes that looked out upon the world with a sadness equal only to a bereaved mother whose child has been stricken. She was a woman unequaled, if just her beauty were to be considered, but as a female in this setting, her beauty was not the first consideration. For her position here was of prime import.

As a nun, a teacher or nurse, perhaps, she would be a resounding failure, if he were any judge of such a thing. For what schoolboy could look upon that face without losing his heart? What man, nearing death, could look into those eyes without regaining his strength and vowing to live and exist simply for the opportunity to woo and win her?

And what man of the cloth, the most stalwart leader in the church, could see the expression of pure innocence on those pristine features and not be stricken by the beauty she owned? Would not toss his vows to the four winds in order to claim her as his own?

Rafael was not even faintly related to any of those vulnerable male creatures who had raced through his mind. His thoughts were neither youthful nor pure, his intentions probably better not spoken aloud and his mind not closed to temptation of any sort.

Particularly not the enticement now set before him.

The black-garbed priest at the front of the small chapel droned on and, never a man to listen overmuch to a listing of his sins, Rafael managed to put the sermon from his mind and concentrate instead on the best way of removing the girl from her circumstances. That she would take his hand and walk willingly from this house of worship was a scenario he could not hope for, one he was not about to risk.

Perhaps he could announce to those in charge that he had come to claim a missing heiress and proclaim to one and all that she was indeed that treasure—if, indeed, she proved to be the fabled Isabella Montgomery. Identifying her might be simple enough, but claiming her would pose a problem.

For he was not the man who had been chosen for her to wed.

A fact that garnered many thanks from his arrogant soul, for the person of Juan Garcia was not to be envied. A man who was without honor, thinking only of himself and his cravings. A man who had numerous bastards strewn about the countryside, results of his tendencies to plunder the poor families of their women. He was known as a man without the personal habits of a gentleman.

In plain language, he was not a man well liked by anyone who knew him. His only claim to fame was the betrothal agreement that would allow him to claim Isabella Montgomery as his bride on her eighteenth birthday, a day but a week away. Though he had come from a good family, the lines had become flawed as they applied to the man. He'd attained a degree of wealth, but land was more to be desired than mere money, and in that vein, Garcia was lacking.

An agreement such as that written between Garcia and Charles Montgomery for the hand of his daughter would not hold water if the girl were claimed, married and bedded by another. A man might be obliged to offer recompense, but the bride herself would be considered damaged goods.

She would be ruined in the eyes of Juan Garcia, unfit for marriage. And if Rafael McKenzie had any luck at all in this venture, Juan Garcia would never get his hands on the maiden.

The idea of claiming a missing heiress was certainly enticing, but then, who would believe Rafael McKenzie had any right to such a woman? Certainly not the flock of black-garbed nuns and the white-haired priest who seemed to be the guardian of said flock, for he would warrant they possessed more than their share of intelligence. And so it seemed he must take matters into his own hands and solve the dilemma himself.

The mass appeared to be at an end, for, arms outstretched toward his small congregation, the priest uttered words of blessing. At least, that was the general consensus of the worshipers surrounding him, for they stood and shuffled slowly and ceremoniously from the chapel.

Not willing to be conspicuous by his deviation from the expected, Rafael followed the three men who had shared a pew with him, and managed to keep a watchful eye on the woman he believed to be Isabella. She was alone, not by choice apparently, but by purpose, for even as she made her way down the aisle, she walked alone, segregated from the others who had attended early mass.

Once outside the door of the chapel, Rafael stood to one side, watching as the girl walked sedately down the two steps and onto the path that led to the larger building to his right.

Last evening, upon his arrival here, he'd found a beautiful oasis in the midst of the surrounding arid countryside, and inside a dormitory of sorts he'd been given a small room in which to sleep. Hidden in a veritable Garden of Eden, the buildings, the bare dormitory and the stark, almost unadorned chapel, were simple, in a setting worthy of more ornate structures.

Perhaps a cathedral, he thought, his mind wandering as his gaze focused on the figure that walked away from him. *She* would be more suited to a cathedral, a setting that would enhance her beauty.

But not as a nun, not as a Sister of Charity, which was what she appeared to be on the verge of becoming, here in this dingy bit of solitude. Instead, he could envision her walking down a long aisle, her garb that of a bride, her hair long and lustrous beneath a veil, for surely they had not yet cut that glorious mass from her head. Her body adorned in a white gown of silk, sewn to fit the perfection of her form, completed the vision he wove, wishing that even now he could see through the gray garb she wore.

He almost laughed aloud as the thoughts flitted through his mind. She might very well be far from perfect, for her form was not to be seen beneath the all-enveloping folds of her garment. Yet, he knew. Knew with a sense he could not explain, that the woman he watched was perfection personified.

Woman? Perhaps. Or a girl just hovering on the brink of womanhood, a virginal beauty who waited only for the proper man to toss her over the brink into the settled, safe world of marriage. Or failing that, perhaps the swirling waters of sin.

And at that idea, he cleared his throat and consciously drew his features into a solemn visage of a man contemplating his final resting place. Surely the sermon just delivered in the chapel behind him was meant to put even the most jaded man on the straight and narrow.

Not that Rafael was jaded. Only weary of the effort to find a virtuous woman, one who would fit the formula set forth by his family for the future mistress of the Diamond Ranch. Virtuous women were not difficult to find, for he'd seen them in every town he'd passed, usually left on the shelf when the plum choices had been scooped up by more discerning men.

Virtue was not what he sought. He would accept it as a bonus, but his thoughts were more on a woman— a girl, perhaps—who had a face he would welcome in his bed. Not in the dark of night, but in the light of morning, when only the clear, honest eyes belonging to a woman he could live with for an eternity would look up from the pillow beside his and meet his gaze.

Unless he took a hand in things, such an outcome was not likely. He was sought after by the mothers who wanted their daughters to make a fine marriage, who knew he was a man of wealth, of good family, a trophy to be proud of should their female progeny be adept at snagging his attention.

Even his own mother, before her death, had pushed him in the direction of several such young ladies, creatures he had shunned with barely any effort, knowing they would not measure up to what he wanted in a woman. And so he had followed the tale of a sequestered woman, a story told by men who had caught sight of her as a girl, here in her present setting. Kept from public view, she had become a legend of sorts, a woman who lived in a convent, yet was not a nun. Perhaps intending to form such a vocation, but as yet, simply a resident.

Now that he'd seen her for himself, he felt a sense

of exultation. For the woman he'd dreamed of had become a reality. What he wanted was even now walking before him, heading for the building where he suspected she also lodged.

He would see to it that she was not left here to become another one of the creatures who walked solemnly to and fro, hands folded and eyes lowered in a pose of sanctity and prayer. She would not be wasted thusly. He had decided it would not be, and those who knew Rafael would not have expected any less from him, than that he rescue her from her fate.

No matter that it might be her own choice that had brought her here.

He walked slowly toward his destination, intent on gathering his clothing, his pack of belongings and seeking out Isabella's whereabouts. The cell where he'd slept was small and unadorned, a stark example of the usual accommodations here, he was certain, for every room he passed seemed to be formed of the same components as his own private cubicle. And such was no doubt the type of place where the object of his search slept. He envisioned her in a white gown, engulfed in yards of cotton fabric, lying on a virginal bed, probably not any softer than the one he had arisen from just an hour since. She slept alone, of that he was certain. For the look on her face was that of a woman unawakened.

The long hall leading off to his right was the dining room, he recalled, and thinking of the breakfast that would fill the empty place in his middle, he went through the doorway and found a seat at the end of the table. The front of the room seemed to be reserved for those who lived in this place, the robed figures looking much alike to his undiscerning eye.

Except for the girl who sat across the table from him, perhaps twenty-five feet distant, hands folded in her lap, eyes downcast, as if she prayed for the food she hoped to find before her.

His own bowl of porridge arrived within minutes, and he looked around for guidance as to whether or not he should commence eating or perhaps wait until some robed figure would pronounce his food fit for consumption. Saying grace over his food was not unknown to him, for his parents had duly blessed each and every repast that graced their dining room table in his youth, and he was not averse to such a thing taking place now. Except for the fact that the porridge bowl already felt barely lukewarm, and as such, did not merit a prayer spoken over its contents. Aware that his thoughts were not suitable here, he sought to tame their wayward direction and concentrate instead on the goodwill of those who had allowed his presence here last night. For though they had demanded, and received, a suitable recompense for his stay, he had not been turned away, but treated as any other traveler seeking lodging for the night.

Rafael was not any other traveler, but a man who had sought out this convent with purpose in his mind. A man who owned the loyalty of three men who even now watched from a wooded area close by, awaiting a signal from him.

A signal that would prompt those men forth to assist in his mission of taking Isabella Montgomery from this place. She was a rare combination of Irish and Spanish descent, the last of a long line of Spanish aristocracy, the female who held within her the possibility of a child who would take up the reins of his family's holdings and become a man of wealth and the founder of a dynasty. A woman who might be persuaded to take her place at the Diamond Ranch, where bloodlines were strong and children were born to inherit.

But to bear such a child, the woman in question would first need to be mated to a man of strength and honor. A man who stood to come into a great inheritance, one which would provide him and his children with wealth and honor.

Rafael was such a man.

CHAPTER TWO

AN ASSORTMENT OF TRAVELERS sought out their various modes of transport in the morning light. In the courtyard, men mounted horses, climbed into carriages and left the gates of the convent. Leaving behind their coins, most of which would find their way into the pockets of the priest, with only enough gold provided to ensure that the women who labored there were decently fed and clothed.

Theirs was not a life of luxury, but of service, and as such, they did not complain, but lived in anticipation of a future reward.

Isabella was not among those who had such high-flown ambitions. Her future stretched out before her, a blank page on which she hoped to write a vision that included a home and family. But Father Joseph had told her just recently that she was destined to be a nun, and she had nodded readily, lest she be confined to her cell, from which she might never find escape. And perhaps becoming one of the sisters here would be her chosen fate, for anything would be preferable to marriage to the wrong man.

From the narrow window through which she observed the courtyard, her eyes sought out the man who had spent the night in a room in the corridor of guests. A tall man upon a dark horse with silver on bridle and saddle alike, who had scorned the lukewarm bowl of porridge served for his breakfast. A man of dark hair and eyes, a man of masculine beauty, his features sharply honed. Garbed in black, his trousers and shirt of some fine fabric, his hat molded by strong hands before he placed it on his head, he was by far the most interesting part of her week. Perhaps her year, she thought with a smile. Would that Juan Garcia's looks might match this man.

His gaze touched upon the building from which she watched and his eyes flashed as they narrowed on the empty windows of the long series of cells, then settled on the space behind which she stood. With a start of recognition, she caught his change of expression, the almost imperceptible tightening of his lips, the hardening of his jaw.

He looked upon the men who readied their horses for travel, who led pack animals from the barns into the area where their leaving would take place. Then, with a swift glance that touched upon the narrow slit of her cell window, he looked through the open gates, toward the woods just beyond the convent proper, and nodded his head.

A message to someone waiting there? A warning, perhaps? With a casual movement he looked back to where she stood within her cell and his eyes lit with a message she had no chance to decipher.

She was still, silent, almost forgetting to breathe as she watched his approach, saw the tightening of his grip on the reins that lay across his horse's neck. It was a moment of anticipation so great she could scarcely stand quietly where she was, knowing he saw her, aware of his questing gaze upon the place where she stood.

Another man approached him, riding through the gate, then angling his mount to approach and converse with the tall stranger. With a nod, as if accepting a mission, the second man rode to the door of the convent. Dismounting, he strode to the portal and rang the bell. It resounded through the halls, announcing a visitor, an event not unheard of in this place where travelers often found their rest.

But not in the middle of the morning.

The door was swung open, and Sister Agnes Mary stood framed in the archway, her mouth dropping open in shock at whatever words she heard spoken by the man before her. Stepping back, she was followed by the messenger, even as the man who had given him his instructions watched, sitting tall and silent atop his horse.

And then he moved, his horse following some unseen signal, walking directly across the courtyard to where the window of her cell exposed her to his sight. She stepped back, but he only smiled, an arrogant arrangement of his lips that held a measure of amusement. Unnoticed by the men milling in the courtyard, he directed his mount to stand beneath her window and his voice was low, but commanding, as he spoke a few words.

"I am Rafael McKenzie. Be ready."

Her lips moved, but her words were silent. *Ready for what?*

That his charge was directed at her was without question, for his gaze touched her, seared her with heat and beckoned her to listen.

"The door of your room will open," he said, his lips unmoving as the sound of his words reached her. "Go with Manuel. He will bring you to me."

She stood transfixed by fear, or perhaps hope. If this man, this stranger, could free her from this place and from fear of Juan Garcia's arrival, she would go with him. Whatever the destination he planned for her, she would ride with him through the gates of the convent, then down the road and past the town of San Felipe to the open country beyond.

The door to her cell opened silently, only a slight draft from the corridor giving notice that someone stood behind her. Turning, she looked into the eyes of Sister Agnes Mary, those kind, calm windows into the soul of a nun dedicated to her calling.

And then the man in the shadows spoke. "I am Manuel. You will come with me."

Without hesitation, Isabella reached for her shawl, a luxury she used at night when the air was chilly, one she felt might be a necessity today. Sister Agnes Mary lifted her brows in silent query as she stepped into the small room, but the man behind her did not make any explanations for his act, only pushed her with a gentle hand toward the narrow cot.

"Sit, Sister," he said, his voice soft, almost kindly, as if he respected the woman's position here. Without repeating his command to Isabella, he held out his hand to her, fingers long, straight and clean, and she gripped it with her own smaller hand, feeling her bones engulfed in his greater strength.

Leaving the room, closing the door with an almost silent click of the latch, he led her from the building, his steps long and swift, hers—of necessity—quicker, lest he drag her across the floor. The soft slippers she wore kicked up clouds of dust behind her as she walked, and Manuel looked down at them, as if judging them not sturdy enough for the events of this day.

The outer door stood open and they crossed the threshold, where the tall stranger awaited them. With little finesse, she was lifted by the man who led her, her waist seized in his grip as he stepped closer to the black horse, giving her over to the hands of the man whose words she had obeyed.

Go with Manuel. He will bring you to me.

And so he had. Brought her to this man who gave her no promise of safety, but with whom she felt secure, whose firm touch she trusted, whose dark eyes she met calmly, her whole being filled with trembling anticipation. She knew her shivers were obvious to the man beside her, who lifted her so easily, and was even more aware that her quaking flesh was readily felt by the man who received her into his hold atop the dark horse.

He settled her across his thighs, holding her firmly, carefully, as if he would not insult her by careless handling, and she felt herself leaning against him without hesitation.

"Good girl." The words were soft, spoken in the same dark voice, again carrying no farther than her hearing, as if they existed in a place where no other could interfere.

"Where—" The word was whispered, then silenced by his hand against her waist, offering a compelling tightening of her diaphragm that forbade speech.

"Silence." Again he spoke, the single word touching her ear as a whisper, and she was mute, not out of fear, but with acknowledgment that he was to be respected and obeyed. His arms around her were long, his hand lifted the reins easily from where they had been left over the saddle horn. His fingers twined in the leather in an automatic gesture, and the horse moved toward the gate at some unheard signal.

The wooden sign that designated this place as the Convent of the Sisters of Charity swung in the breeze over her head as she found herself passing beneath it. With a sidelong glance, she watched as two other men emerged from the wooded area to join the horse she rode upon, and noted the dull gleam of rifle barrels that were slung over their saddles. Her own mount, the horse she shared with the stranger, carried a leather scabbard that bore its own weapon.

Leather holsters were tied to the men's thighs, their contents looking dangerous and worthy of her respect. Two men rode abreast, then behind them her captor, his mount elegant in black leather tack, silver gleaming from saddle and bridle.

Manuel fell in place as the rear guard, a position he apparently took pride in, for his own weapon was a mark of his role, lying across his thighs, ready for use. His hat was pulled low over his forehead as he searched the horizon and then turned his horse to check from whence they had come. His appearance was that of a trusted man, one who could be relied on to do his master's bidding without hesitation. One who would stand at his master's back, defending the man he served.

She watched the men who surrounded her, for the first time in years in close contact with the other half of the world. Men, the species almost unknown to her... For at fourteen, she had been but a child, almost unaware of the staff who worked and lived at her father's hacienda, all but the cook, who treated her as a child of her own.

Now the horse beneath her moved briskly, silently, only the sound of leather creaking and the low whinny of one of the packhorses filling her ears. The woods surrounded them—ahead lay the road to the village, behind them the convent, and here, riding a black monster of a horse, she was at the mercy of a man whose instructions she had followed as a child might obey a parent.

At that thought, she almost laughed, swallowing the unexpected mirth that begged to be spilled from her lips, recognizing her position as being far from that of a child. She was a woman, perhaps not in experience, but certainly in years, for at her age many young women had wed and produced a family.

The changing of her body had been gradual over the past years, but definite. No longer a child of scrawny proportions, she bore the attributes of a female approaching adulthood. Breasts that seemed too large for her slender body, a smattering of body hair in various places that made her wonder at its appearance and the monthly cycle that the nuns told her was the proof of her fertility.

She had been taught well by the nuns, told of the use of her various body parts, and the reason for the changes she wondered at. And had sometimes thought of her father's plan for her future. With his death she'd initially felt a sense of relief that she no longer would face marriage to a man thirty years her senior, a man who had looked at her with eyes that burned and searched out her secrets.

But now, she feared Juan Garcia's arrival. So long as he did not know where she had gone, she was safe from him.

"Did Garcia send you?" she asked, as that unwelcome thought entered her mind.

The man behind her laughed, a harsh sound, and his firm, negative word of reply somehow reassured her.

But, she realized, she lived now with a danger that

might prove even greater than that of Juan Garcia. The man who held her against his body was the present. The future was yet to come. And with a sudden burst of insight, she recognized that her future might not be set in stone…yet. Though her captor might consider her his property, she was a free woman, until such time as he delivered her to the destination he had in mind. If she could find a way to escape him, she might yet choose her own way, might even find a life that would be pleasing to her.

A life of her own. One not dictated by the strong arm that held her against her captor. Her captor? Or perhaps the man who had rescued her from the certainty of marriage to Juan Garcia, unknowingly giving her the opportunity to seek another fate.

The rider ahead of her, on her left, a man Rafael had called Jose, turned his horse to the side as they reached the center of the small village, and the other two horsemen continued on without him. She was silent, not wanting to be hushed by her captor's stern voice, should she be so bold as to ask their destination.

As if he sensed her need, the man who called himself Rafael bent his head and whispered words against her ear. "We will stop just ahead, to eat. Jose will bring food from the general store in the village."

She nodded. They had traveled only an hour, perhaps two, for the village was more than five miles from the convent, and she felt the need for sustenance. The breakfast porridge had been bland, almost tasteless, and the milk warm, not fit for consumption.

Sister Ruth Marie had told her only a week or so ago that she must eat more, for her clothing was loose and in danger of falling from her without the aid of a braided rope about her middle. Apparently the goal of the sisters was to make her as round and rosy as they all appeared to be fashioned beneath their robes.

But no longer. Now she would eat as she pleased, as much or little as suited her, and the sound of that silent vow of independence pleased her, as she straightened in the grip of her captor.

Another mile or so found them within a grove of trees, and she looked about her at the shaded clearing where the sun did not shine. Overhead, the trees lifted heavy branches to the sky and only an occasional bit of glittering sun peeked through the leafy roof.

She lifted her chin, daring a look at the man who held her. "Who are you? How did you know where to find me?" Surely that was not her voice, that low, sultry sound that pierced the silence.

He bent his head to her and his eyes traveled over her face, past the pale skin of her forehead and cheeks to the barely exposed flesh of her throat. She felt the piercing of his dark gaze, knew a moment of fear as his mouth tightened and his jaw clenched.

"More importantly, who are *you?*" he returned, his tone one she could not deny. "I came to the convent seeking you out, for you are a woman I'd heard of, and I would know if you are the one whose name is Isabella Montgomery."

"Yes, I'm Isabella," she said, wondering as she

did so how he had heard of her. And somehow, she found the courage to ask him the question that begged an answer.

He listened to her halting query and smiled, an expression that softened his features and brought a strange beauty to his face. "I've heard, over the past year, stories of a young girl whose beauty rivals that of the loveliest of women, a virgin who was being readied as a bride. There were travelers who had slept in cells at the convent during their journey, men who spoke of a young woman they had seen. I listened to several such men, heard their tales of a fragile girl who would be given to an old man, whose father had sold her betrothal to gain a fortune. And I could not bear that such a thing would come to pass, Isabella. I knew I must see for myself the creature described to me as a young woman of good family, a girl with beauty and grace, one fit for the task of becoming mistress of Diamond Ranch."

Her chin tilted upward, a defiant signal that gave him pleasure. "And you felt it was your right to claim me? Even though I was not free to be your wife? Knowing that I was betrothed to another, you took me from the convent and now you will force me to be your wife?"

She thought he looked relieved, pleased perhaps, as he spoke again. "You have courage, Isabella, to speak to me with such a lack of fear. And yet, even knowing that you would will it otherwise, I have to admit the truth of what you say.

"I was told you were a beauty, a woman untouched, meant for marriage to a man who will no longer be able to claim you."

"Who told you all these things?" She felt her breath catch, stunned that her name had been bandied about in the hearing of strangers. Wondering that Juan Garcia's claim on her was of such general knowledge.

"That's not important for now," he said, lifting one hand to touch her cheek, as if testing the skin, then brushing against her temple, leaving a heated memory behind as he dropped his palm to rest against her thigh.

"You haven't the right to touch me," she said, looking down at the tanned hand that lay against her habit. Never had a man been so familiar with her and she felt a strange, heated curiosity at his presumption, acting as though he had the authority to lay his hand against her if he so willed. She turned her head to look up into his face, aware of the harsh lines of his jaw, the firm set of his mouth and the heated intensity of his eyes as they met hers.

"I think you have little to say about what I do, Isabella Montgomery. I'm the man in charge here, and if I desire to touch you, I will." He allowed his hand to squeeze gently against her leg, fingers pressing into the tender flesh, and she winced.

He laughed, a soft sound that mocked her reaction. "I didn't hurt you. Don't pretend that I did. I only made you aware that I answer to no one. You are mine and I will control what happens to you."

"I'll have bruises to show for your hands upon me,"

she said, and for the first time felt a harsh pang of fear strike at her depths. He might give her more than a few simple bruises, he might rob her of her most cherished possession, with not a thought of the consequences to her future. For the nuns had told her that her chastity made her of great value to her future husband.

Ahead of them lay a clearing, where a bend in the road swerved to miss a stand of trees. Just beyond the oak grove, he turned his horse toward a grassy expanse. The sun shone down on the sylvan glen with a brilliance she suddenly craved to feel against her skin. Perhaps only the skin of her hands and face would be exposed, but she would revel in the warmth.

The other men joined him, one of them turning to take her weight in his able grip. He was a big man, not a Mexican, as were the other two, but red-haired, with freckled skin. He was unsmiling, but nodded as she was lifted from the perch she'd held over the past hours and lowered into his hands.

"I'm Matthew," he murmured quietly. "Don't be afraid. I won't drop you." His voice was low, his words reassuring, as he set her on her feet and held her immobile for a moment, until she could catch her balance.

From above her, the man still in the saddle cleared his throat. "Turn her loose, Matthew. She can lean against the horse if she feels wobbly."

She thought Matthew's hands left her reluctantly, and as he stepped away, she detected a look of apology on his face. And then her thoughts were taken up with the weakness she felt in her legs, the ache in her back from the unnatural position she had held for the past hours. She looked up quickly as the man above her moved.

"I've got you." Rafael McKenzie touched the ground with his left foot, dismounting from his horse, and reached to steady Isabella. His hand gripped her shoulder and she tensed against his fingertips. "I'm not going to hurt you," he told her firmly. "All you have to do is behave yourself and you'll be fine."

She turned her head, her eyes dark brown, looking to him like a fine piece of velvet. "I resent you telling me to behave. You've taken me against my wishes, and now I'm supposed to be agreeable to it."

"You didn't fight me off when I sent Manuel to get you. You were agreeable enough then." His smile was amused as he looked down into her puzzled expression. "Why all the fuss now?"

Her eyes glittered with anger and he admired her spirit, even as he recognized that she stood no chance of fighting against him, especially not with three other men along to help him keep the peace.

"You've never heard a fuss raised, mister. I'm trying to be polite, trying not to get you angry enough so you'll beat me or—"

Her voice broke off, as though the words she'd thought to toss in his face were unspeakable, threats of such a vile nature, she could not stand their flavor on her tongue.

"If you want me to raise a fuss, I can do that," she

said after a moment of silence, during which he watched her complexion redden with fury and then, as if she recognized her helplessness against four men, her voice failed, her mouth thinned and a waxen pallor touched her features.

If he knew anything about women, she was about two breaths from a dead faint, and he found himself almost wishing unconsciousness might claim her, at least until he could determine his strategy.

For, truth to tell, his trek to the convent had been one of impulse, his aim that of a man in search of a bride. That she was not being readied to be *his* bride was a small matter, one he would tend to when the time came.

And the time had come. His father had smiled at his words of intent, perhaps remembering his own marriage, one he'd forced upon a woman who later formed half of a perfect union. At any rate, he'd been pleased at Rafael's plan to claim his bride in such a fashion. And Rafael was certain that his choice was right for him.

For at first glance, he'd known that she was what he had yearned for, what his hungry heart had craved through all the weeks of searching in small villages and larger cities in his quest for the perfect bride.

That this particular female was possibly designated to be a bride of the church was a minor thing, a challenge he was more than prepared to take on. Let the women who stood no chance of marriage tend to the church's business. Teaching and nursing and tending to the poor.

Isabella Montgomery was not such a female. Such a woman had a higher calling, for to his way of thinking, there was no greater value of a woman than that of being a wife and mother. And he would see to it that she had the opportunity to fulfill the promise he saw in her, a woman fit for the master's bedroom at the Diamond Ranch.

CHAPTER THREE

ISABELLA WAS SETTLED on a small bit of blanket before the fire, leaning to the warmth automatically as the air became chilled with overhanging clouds. Food was doled out to the men who sat nearby, speaking among themselves, laughing at small jokes and dutifully ignoring her presence, as if their leader had deemed it to be thus.

A napkin lay in her lap, its contents representing her share of the food. The bread was torn from a loaf, apparently a knife not being judged necessary for the task. Beside it, a large chunk of yellow cheese tempted her. Cheese was a luxury in her diet, for the milk from the convent was turned into butter to be sold in the village. Now, to be offered cheese and fresh, soft bread was a treat indeed. Someone had taken this loaf from their oven only hours ago, she decided, for the bread still retained a suggestion of warmth as she picked it up and held it to her mouth.

Automatically, her eyes closed as she offered up a prayer of thanksgiving for the food—a sincere prayer, for she anticipated the treat with relish. She bit off a piece of the cheese, then bit off some bread, and chewed them together, the flavor tempting her into another tasting of the food she'd been offered.

"I'm sorry we can't give you a better meal," the man said, settling beside her on the ground. "We'll be home in two days' time and the table will be laden with good things."

"Home?" She looked up at him, noting the harsh sound of his voice, even though his words were merely conversational, not threatening in any way. "I thought the bread and cheese were wonderful. Can your home offer better fare?"

"It doesn't take much to please you, does it, sweetheart?"

She winced at the endearment, one she'd heard in days long ago, from her mother. "Don't call me that, please," she said softly. "My name is Isabella."

"I know your name," he said with a smile, one that crinkled the corners of his eyes and made him seem more approachable. But he was a man, and therefore not to be spoken to as an equal. Men, the padre had said, were to be looked up to and honored. Women were merely put on earth for the birthing of children and the work of slaves. Then there were those who were chosen to do the work of the church. Such women were servants of the Almighty and were to be honored.

She'd seen examples of the work women were expected to perform. Indeed, she had done much of the work herself, scrubbing and cooking and pulling weeds in the gardens. The younger women, those not yet a part of the community of nuns, were given the most taxing of the chores and she wore blisters on her knees from the flagstone kitchen floor, where she had learned the meaning of scrubbing her fingers to the bone. Not literally, perhaps, but close enough to bring open sores to her fingertips.

The lye soap did not lend itself to soft skin, and her hands showed the results of frequent exposure to the strong stuff. She looked down at the dry, chapped skin that covered her hands, noting the split corners of her fingers, where occasionally blood had run from the tender flesh.

Her fists clenched, lest others might see the shameful results of hard labor, the marks that scarred her hands. She would never boast of the work she had done, but consider it her due as a woman that she be but a servant to others. A woman must at all times be silent and, as much as possible, melt into the walls, so as not to be noticed.

She'd heard the words over and over, had listened well to the women who taught her the daily lessons. A woman's worth was gauged by the number of children she could produce for the church and give as a token of her appreciation to her husband. Her honor lay in the cleanliness of her house and her ability to be silent and do as she was told.

Now, this man who had taken her prisoner taunted her by calling her his *sweetheart*, a term she could never hope to attain as her own. She felt mocked by his words, and she felt resentment rise within her at his treatment.

"Isabella." He spoke her name slowly, as if the syllables rolled over his tongue, and were relished as being of good flavor. "Bella, I think I shall call you."

"Who are you?" she whispered, her pride seeking to know the name of her captor. "Why do you take me with you from the convent?"

"I'm Rafael McKenzie," he said, pride touching the name as he spoke the words. "I have need of a wife, and I think you will be able to fill the place in my home that is empty."

"A wife? What foolishness. I've been spoken for already. From my early years, I've known that my father gave me to another man and he may even now be seeking me out."

Rafael McKenzie laughed as if her words were not of any value. "I know about Juan Garcia, my dear. But he will not have you. By the time he finds you, I'll have established you in my home, as my wife, and he will have no chance to take you from me."

"And if I don't want to be your wife? What then?" Even as she spoke the words, she felt his anger touch her across the narrow space between them.

"I'm not offering you a choice. You made the decision yourself when you left with me. By that action, you gave yourself into my care, and I have chosen to make you my wife. I'll take you to Diamond Ranch and marry you there in front of my people."

She felt the food she had eaten rise up in her throat to choke her. Without warning, she knew her stomach would empty itself and rather than be shamed by such a thing, she rose and ran from him, seeking shelter in the trees that formed a canopy over them.

He followed fast on her heels and his hand touched her shoulder as she reached the privacy of the low bushes she sought. She jerked from him, falling to her knees as her stomach emptied itself on the ground before her.

His hands were gentle now against her shoulders. Then one slid to her stomach and she bore the indignity of his support as she bent over, her face only inches from the ground. He lifted her as the spasms ceased and held her against himself, her back warmed by the heat his body radiated. Her head fell back and touched the support of his shoulder, and she closed her eyes, feeling only the shame of her body's betrayal.

His hand touched her mouth, a piece of fabric held against her lips and she took it from him, wiping the residue of her disgrace from her skin. Again her stomach revolted and another spasm tore through her, but he would not let her go, simply holding her securely in his embrace as she bent and spat upon the ground.

"Take a drink of water," he said, holding a cup to her lips, and she opened her eyes to Manuel standing beside her, apparently having offered the cup for her benefit.

"Thank you." She whispered the words beneath her breath and her fingers clenched around the rough metal of the cup. A sip of water bathed the inside of her mouth and she leaned forward to spit it upon the ground, then drank again from the vessel, this time swallowing the cool liquid. A shudder gripped her body and she felt herself slipping to the ground, but a strong arm wrapped about her waist held her upright and she dangled there in his grip.

"I've got you, Isabella. You're all right now." His whisper was one of reassurance and she could only nod as she heard his words. Her eyes were closed, the cool air seeming to revive her, for she had felt the darkness of a faint hovering over her. It seemed he would not allow her to escape him in that way, for he turned her to face him, lifting her chin a bit and then waiting for some response from her.

She resisted in the only way she could, her eyes refusing to open, her body stiff and unyielding.

"Look at me," he said, and his voice was harsh now, as though he had lost patience with her. He drew her closer against himself, and lifted her until her feet were inches above the ground, his arm firm about her waist as she felt herself pressed against his body.

"Please, put me down," she said, the demand sounding to her own ears more in the nature of a plea. One he heeded, for she felt the earth beneath her shoes and opened her eyes so that she could balance herself and regain some semblance of strength.

"I won't let you go," he said softly. "I don't want you to fall. Just be still and take a deep breath, sweetheart."

She found herself obeying his dictates and felt a gradual return of her usual stability, holding herself a bit apart from him. He would not loosen his firm hold, but gave her the space to move, as if he would let her find her feet and regain her pride.

"I'm all right now," she whispered, bowing her head again as she knew a moment of uncertainty. This man had seen her weak and ailing, had held her despite her body's rejection of the food he'd offered, and now he simply gave her the support she needed.

"I know you are. You're a strong woman, Isabella. You've had a long ride this morning, and what with being taken from the only home you've known for a matter of years, you're weary and confused. And then I've forced you to ride before me, forced you to allow my touch on your body. Something I feel you have not experienced before." He bent to her, tracing the lines of her forehead with his lips.

"I've given you a bad time, haven't I?"

"I'm glad you admit at least that much," she said with a trace of haughtiness she hadn't known she possessed. Gone was the weak-willed girl who had disgraced herself just moments ago. She felt now the strength of a woman pouring through her veins, and she stood erect, as though she had been offered a chance at freedom.

"I came with you willingly, but only because you seemed to offer the best chance I had at leaving the convent, lest the arrival of Juan Garcia should occur, for I knew he would be coming for me. The convent is my home and I would have become one of the Sisters of Charity were things different." She looked up at him, meeting his hard gaze with certainty. "I am not ready to be a bride. I won't marry anyone. Not you, not Señor Garcia. I couldn't face the thought of speaking marriage vows with him almost five years ago when I entered the convent, and I still can't."

"Ah, that's where you're wrong, my love," he said mockingly. "You will say your vows in the chapel at Diamond Ranch. Whether you feel ready for it or not, you'll marry me. And before Señor Garcia can claim you, you will be my bride, my wife."

And I will cherish you, body and soul. He pondered the words that begged to be spoken to her, wondering for a moment where such poetry had come from. For Rafael McKenzie was not given to spouting words that described soft emotions. Yet, this girl, this woman he had claimed as his own, had already forged a place for herself within his life.

Rafael inhaled her fragrance and knew it for what it was—a combination of soap and fresh, clean skin. And beneath it the underlying aroma of woman; that sweet, sometimes pungent scent that lent tenderness to his touch, desire to his thoughts. He was not a stranger to desire or passion, but felt now a softer strain of the emotions he associated with the females he had known.

For Isabella aroused in him the knowledge that she was what he had yearned for, that her flesh would be like nectar to his senses, her skin softer than any he had touched. Her mouth would give him pleasure, her arms a refuge against the harshness of life and her body would offer itself as a vessel for his sons.

No matter that he married at the behest of his father, that the ceremony was a necessity before he could inherit his destiny, he would have chosen Isabella Montgomery from all the women in the world, once he had seen her, once his hands had held her finely boned form in his grasp. She appealed to the depths of his soul, the part of him that sought out beauty and purity. For she was clean, fresh and all that was lovely.

The task of winning her heart would not be without difficulty, but the arrogant soul of Rafael McKenzie soared as he thought of the path he would take to accomplish that end. He would use kindness as a tool, tender touches as a means to an end and his natural urges to conquer would be held in abeyance, his desire would be curtailed until she was his bride, his wife.

And then…and then, he would claim her, know her in the most intimate sense, and she would be his.

He bent closer to her and his whisper was soft, coaxing in her ear. "You will be mine, Isabella. My bride. My wife."

My bride. My wife. The words resounded within her and Isabella found them unacceptable. The movement of her head was a rebuttal of his words, one that seemed to amuse him, for he laughed aloud. "You have no choice, sweetheart. Once you're mine, once I've taken you to my bed, the fine señor will no longer be interested in you. He bargained for a young girl, a virgin. And you will no longer be able to claim that title."

"I've known no man," she said quietly. "My virtue is to be given only to the man I marry, the man I choose."

"You chose me when you walked out of the convent," he told her, and the words rang with conviction. "You will be my wife."

"Would you take a woman to your bed who is not willing?" she asked, daring a look into mysterious eyes that seemed to search her secrets out.

He smiled darkly, and yet she caught a glimpse of warmth glittering in those black eyes that met hers. "You will be willing. I guarantee it." He pulled her against himself, her head cupped in his big hand, pressed tightly to his chest. "Rest easy a moment, and then I will give you something to drink that will settle your stomach."

She breathed deeply, fighting the incipient dizziness that gripped her. "I must sit down," she whispered. "I feel faint."

Her lifted her instead, carrying her to a rude shelter formed by tree branches that bent to afford a private place. He leaned forward to deposit her slight form on a blanket, a folded bit of fabric, perhaps a shirt, placed beneath her head, and then hovered over her, this man who had so changed her life in the past hours. He brushed back stray wisps of hair from her forehead, his fingers tangling in the covering that hid the dark locks of hair from his sight. With a gentle movement, he pulled it from her, tossing it aside, leaving her hair open to his view. Even tangled and matted against her head, it captured the light and glowed with a deep beauty he admired.

His fingers raked through its length, and he gentled

his touch, fearful of pulling it and causing pain, but she lay quietly beneath his hands, her eyes half-open, yet her gaze never leaving him, watching him closely, as if she would shield herself from his presence. Beside him, Manuel appeared, holding forth a cup, tendering it to Rafael with a look in her direction, as if he would beg her to accept his offering.

Rafael took it from him and his query was silent as he looked into her eyes. She read it clearly in the questioning look he gave her and nodded, a slight movement of her head. With a smile, Rafael bent closer.

"Thank you, Manuel. This isn't too hot for her, is it?" he asked, lifting the cup to his own lips before offering it to Isabella. He tasted it as Manuel shook his head, and then handed it to her. "It won't burn you, sweetheart. It's coffee. Drink a bit."

She wrinkled her nose at the scent of the strong brew. "I'm not fond of the stuff," she said. "Do you have tea?" And then she almost laughed as she thought of the foolishness of her request. "No, of course you don't," she whispered, reaching to touch the cup he'd offered.

A small sip passed her lips and she swallowed it obediently as he urged her compliance. It lay strong and warm in her stomach and she felt a bit of the heat travel through her, as if she'd been chilled and now was being warmed from the inside out. Another swallow followed the first and she leaned her head back, away from the cup as he would have urged her to drink more.

"Enough for now," she murmured, inhaling deeply and finding herself leaning against him, his arm beneath her shoulders, his body hovering over hers.

"We'll stay here for a bit, give you a chance to rest," he told her, and she only nodded, unable to speak the words that would have rushed from her lips.

Where was he taking her? Why did he want her…why her and not any other woman? She heard the words in her head, but found them impossible to speak aloud, and only shivered as she delivered herself into his hands.

Rafael watched her slip into unconsciousness, not a faint as he'd feared, but a sleep that seemed to claim her suddenly, as though she could not face the next moment of her future without her body's natural sleep to give her strength. She breathed deeply, her muscles limp against his support, her head falling to one side, her neck appearing as a slender stalk. He touched her cheek with his index finger, brushing a bit of dust from the fragile skin, and then he bent to brush his lips over the same place, tasting the fine-pored texture with a whisk of his tongue.

She was sweet, untouched, a woman of virtue, and he felt exultation sweep over him as he considered what her presence would mean in his home. She would bear children to fill the empty rooms, she would be at his side, night and day, and she would be a proud, beautiful addition to the Diamond Ranch.

His venture had been successful beyond his wildest dreams, for she was his now, his possession, the woman he had sought for so long.

THEY SET OFF AGAIN late in the afternoon, a time when they should have been seeking shelter for the night. They would ride until dark, then find a shelter, she'd heard Rafael tell his men. Silently, she sat before him on the big horse, riding easily, her weight against his thighs, her waist encircled by his arm.

His stallion had an easy gait, one she found no difficulty adjusting to, for she had ridden during her early years, her own horse a mare, much smaller than the mount she traveled on today. She thought of the small bay mare now, wishing for a foolish moment that she might be even now in her own saddle, heading for the hacienda where she'd spent her childhood.

But no longer would she live there in the shadow of the mountains, where cattle spread across the acres of her father's land. The land that was perhaps under the guidance of another. With her disappearance from the convent, her father's lawyer would be in the midst of a dilemma, for he had no idea where she was. Perhaps this man, this Rafael, would contact the lawyer and she would be able to claim the land left to her. All it had gained her thus far was the knowledge that some small part of her father's legacy had been spent on her care at the convent.

She yearned now for the familiar place where she'd been born, where her childhood years had been spent in the company of Clara, the cook, the woman who had loved her and tended her after her mother's death over ten years ago. She recalled those days of her childhood, remembering the faint images of her mother that still lived in her mind. The times she had spent with the woman who had borne her and loved her.

For hours on end her mother had told her of her future, the man she would come to love, the family she would have, the children her husband would give her. It had been a much-loved story, one she had dreamed of as a child, living on the ranch, growing up there.

Amazing that even as a child, such a life was all she had ever yearned for. That the thought of marriage had so appealed to her, with an unknown man, sharing his home with her, his love for her already taken for granted.

It had not come about as her mother promised, for now she was still a girl, not yet twenty, and the man who held her against himself was a stranger, certainly not a man her mother would have chosen. And for a moment, Isabella was glad that her mother was gone, for her plight now would bring only heartbreak to any mother whose child was in danger.

The horses slowed their speed, their canter changing to a trot, which left Isabella in discomfort, for she could not adjust herself to the harsh gait without anything to steady her in the saddle, only the man's right hand on his reins, his left arm snug around her middle.

"We'll stop before long," Rafael said, his voice low against her ear as they turned from one road to another, this one more of a trail, with only two tracks forming the way. There were tracks where buggies or wagons had traveled through the mud of the rainy season, making deep wedges in the dirt.

His horse walked now, on the grass at the side of the double track, his men following his example, one of them calling out suddenly as he pointed to the west.

"Over there, Rafael. There's a barn for shelter. Perhaps not in good shape, but fit for a night's stay."

"Yes." With but a single word, Rafael agreed to his man's signal and turned his stallion toward the building that sat on the horizon, alone in a place where there should have been a house, perhaps, or outbuildings of some sort. As they traveled closer, Isabella saw the reason for the barn's singular desolation, for the burned ribs of a house stood beyond the dilapidated building, and several smaller sheds stood empty between the barn and the former house that had long since burned.

"There's no one about. No one to ask permission of, so we'll just camp here," he said to his men, slowing his stallion as they rode ahead and dismounted before the barn. One opened the big door, a task almost too much for one man, for the door seemed to have been in its tracks for a long time.

Yet, once it was opened, a cat strolled out from the dim depths of the building, as if she'd been disturbed from a nap and had come to greet the newcomers.

"At least it should be relatively mouse-free," Rafael said with a smothered laugh. He rode past the gray-and-white creature who had paused to wash her paws in the middle of the doorway, and grudgingly moved a bit as the big hooves of the stallion stirred up the dust beside her.

"You don't frighten her," Manuel told the horse, rubbing the long nose with a gentle hand. "She's a spunky one."

"Very like the one on my lap," Rafael told him quickly. His arm tightened as Isabella jolted angrily at his gibe.

"Let me down," she said cuttingly. "I need to find some privacy."

"Sorry, sweetheart," he said coolly. "Privacy is in short supply. You can look for a corner to use, but in my sight."

She shivered at his words. "You don't mean that."

"Ah, but I do," he answered, loosening his arm from her middle as he slid from his saddle with an ease of movement she envied. Her legs were stiff, her back sore from forcing herself to sit upright for hours on end, and she wasn't sure she had any feeling in her feet, so numb were they from hanging loose on either side of his stallion.

He reached for her and lifted her down, standing her upright before himself, not releasing his hold on her until she jerked from his touch.

"I don't want you to fall," he said quietly. "Don't push me away."

"Just turn me loose," she said, her words a plea, as she looked about the interior of the barn, seeking a spot where she might find privacy. A back door hung ajar, opening onto a flat area, perhaps a corral, she thought, so she began making her way in that direction. His hand held her arm and he walked beside her, closely, as though ready to catch her if she should falter.

Not willing to show a sign of weakness, she tossed him an arrogant glance and pulled her arm from his fingers. "I want to go outdoors by myself, please."

As if her final word, the small courtesy she'd offered touched him, he paused, looking beyond her to where the twilight had fallen, where the open space beckoned her. "I'll stay by the door," he said, moderating his stance a bit. "Don't go out of sight."

She walked with him to the opening, pushing the door aside, its one connecting hinge squeaking with a noise that startled the cat, who had trailed after Isabella. The small creature jumped atop a musty stack of hay and darted behind it, hiding herself from the watching men who seemed amused at her antics.

Isabella stood alone in the opening, Rafael behind her, his warmth tempting her as the wind caught in the high rafters of the loft above and whistled past them through the opening in the low ceiling. She peered out into the dusk and spotted a small building just beyond the corral fencing.

"I'll walk over there," she said, pointing to where the ramshackle structure stood at a lopsided angle.

"I'll be sure it's safe," he said, walking ahead of her and looking within the door that hung ajar. "It's empty," he said, pushing the door open farther so that she could enter more readily.

With a look of clear warning in his direction, she entered the dark, dingy shed and found a modicum of privacy there. The knowledge that he stood just outside the door should have bothered her, she supposed, but somehow his presence gave her a sense of security and she ignored her natural inclination toward independence. If the man wanted to watch over her, so be it. She'd choose a more important fight, somewhere down the road.

And she realized as she left the crude shelter that she'd already accustomed herself to the presence of Rafael McKenzie in her life.

CHAPTER FOUR

THE LOFT IN THE BARN held a sparse amount of hay, left from another year's harvest, but with a few industrious swipes of a broken rake, the men managed to scrape up several piles around the edges of the floor. It was to one of these that Isabella was led, just as dark enveloped the earth and the barn was thrust into a midnight hue.

She stood before the sparse bed he'd offered and looked up at Rafael. "Surely you could locate a feather tick?" she asked tauntingly. "Or at least a blanket to cover the hay?"

"Your wish is my command, fair lady," he said, sketching a salute in her direction and tossing down the blanket she had used during her nap earlier in the day. He stood watching her, hands on hips, his mouth grim, his eyes searching her as if he sought some form of acquiescence in her stance. She would not give him that for which he seemed to be looking, and she bent to straighten the blanket, then lay in the center of it and pulled both sides over her for warmth.

"You send a very definite message, Isabella," he said harshly. "I assume I'm not welcome to share your bed."

"You assume right," she said, a haughty tone painting the words. "I am a lady, even though the circumstances don't seem to give me that place in the general scheme of things. I'm being treated like a woman of ill repute, handled without care and given no more respect than a woman of the tavern might be shown. I reserve the right to sleep alone, Señor McKenzie." And with those well-chosen words, she turned on her side and curled her arm beneath her head, in lieu of a pillow.

He laughed. To her chagrin, he chuckled aloud, mocking her with his amusement, not allowing her even the semblance of privacy as he lay on the hay next to her blanket. His body was warm, curled up beside her, his heat radiating through the blanket she held tautly over her shoulder. Behind her, he settled himself for the night. Then, with a swift motion, he slid his arm around her waist and pulled her closer to his share of the bedding he'd provided.

She was stiff, her body held rigidly against his touch, her heart beating rapidly as if she feared his next move. But he merely held her, breathing deeply and relaxing, well on his way to slumber. Around them the other men sought out various piles of hay, two of them covering with a bedroll, the other— Manuel, she thought—standing near the window that looked out over the yard behind the house.

"He is on watch," Rafael told her quietly as if he'd noted her looking at the man who did not take to his bed. "In four hours, another will take his place. You can rest easy."

"That's a matter of opinion," she said sharply, rolling even tighter in the blanket she clutched to herself. Behind her, she heard a muffled chuckle and then he took the edge of the blanket that almost covered her head into his hand and tugged it downward, exposing her face as he lifted himself on one elbow. In the rays of moonlight slanting through the big door across the loft, she knew her features were exposed to him, that the faint light illuminated her, and she lay silently before his scrutiny.

"You're a beautiful woman," he muttered, softly so that his voice did not travel beyond her hearing. "I wanted you the moment I saw you in the chapel. Even with your hair covered and that gray rag you wear surrounding you with the sanctity of the church, you touched me."

She inhaled sharply. Surely he did not mean to seduce her? Not here, in this place where his men kept watch, where the moon showed their movements if anyone should want to watch them. She turned her head, seeking his eyes, trying to gauge his mood. For if he merely teased her, she could close her eyes and ignore him. If, on the other hand, he tried to bend her to his will, attempted to touch her more familiarly with those elegant hands, she would fight him, no matter that it would be a losing battle.

"I'd like to sleep." It was a statement of intent, and as such, she felt he must either ignore it or make a move to involve her in his plans.

She heard another soft laugh, a mocking sound that

chilled her, and then he tilted her chin up with one long finger beneath it, turning her face to meet his gaze. "I'd have a kiss from you, my dear," he said quietly. "I think such a thing is proper between two people who are on their way to their wedding."

"I'll not marry you." It was as plain as she could make it, and she was proud that her voice did not waver on the words.

"Ah, but you will. And if I must make you mine before the fact, I will. One way or another, you'll be my bride."

Her quick mind caught the message he gave. Either she stood before his priest and said the words of the marriage ceremony willingly, or she would approach the chapel as a ruined woman, with only her pride to hold her erect. He was determined to have her, and she felt the violation of his words strike deeply within her soul.

"You would take my body without marriage?" she asked quietly, muffling her words so that they could not be heard by the man who watched the yard below.

"Not unless there is no other way to force this thing. I'm not in the habit of hurting women, especially not ladies like yourself. But I am a determined man, Isabella, and I will have my way in this."

She turned her head away in silent protest, but to no avail, for he touched her cheek once more and turned her toward him, her body obeying his greater strength. He lifted over her and his head lowered, his eyes dark as they looked deeply into hers. "I'm going to kiss you now, Isabella. Don't make a fuss, for I'll not hurt you, only give you a kiss of commitment, a promise of what is to be."

His lips touched her, dry and warm against her skin, and his mouth opened a bit over hers, the damp touch of his tongue against her soft flesh a shock. She fought to escape, and her hands came up to press on his shoulders, then slid to gain space against his chest, trying to force him from her. The struggle was silent, for she would not be shamed by his actions, and should the men be watching they would know of her defeat at his hands.

He levered her farther into the hay, his body upon her, his lips invading the soft tissues of her mouth, and a sound of fury caught in her throat, one he heard, for he shushed her with a soft whisper.

"I'll only kiss you, for now," he said, his mouth open over hers, his tongue forcing its way past her lips and teeth, exploring the wet places she tried to keep from him.

"No." The single word was more of a plea than an order, and he heard it with ears that knew of her fear. Inspiring fright was not his intention, but the girl seemed not able to accept his hands and mouth upon her flesh, and he knew then that she was indeed untouched by any man. For she shivered beneath him, her body chilled by her fear, and the trembling of her hands against his chest told him she was filled with terror.

He would not have it. Would not tolerate her hatred, for that was what he sensed in her twisting, flailing body. She fought to release herself from his touch, as if the very terrors of hell were threatening her, and he knew a moment of regret that he had so caused her the shame she knew at his hands.

He lowered his weight upon her, holding her against the hay, almost burying her in the mass beneath her, and his mouth rested against her ear. The words he spoke were soft, endearing, meant to offer her an apology, but she shuddered, twisting her head to dislodge him from his place atop her.

"Isabella. Listen to me. Don't fight me, for it won't do you any good. I don't want to hurt you, girl. Lie still now and I'll leave you be. If you'll just settle down, I'll lie behind you and keep watch for the night."

As he spoke, whispering the same words over and over again, producing a litany of comfort he had not intended for this night, she quieted, her breathing became slower, less agitated, and her movements ceased...until she was still beneath him, until he could feel each curve against his body, until her breasts were pressed against his chest, and she had regained some bit of sanity.

"Please." She spoke only one word, but it was enough. He touched her lips with his, a soft caress that asked for nothing, but gave a silent assurance of his presence. "Please." She repeated the word, and he felt her hands pressing against his chest as he lay upon her.

"All right." His whisper was soft, barely discernible in the silence of the night. "Don't fight me, Isabella. Just lie quietly now."

She took several deep breaths as if she could not find enough air to fill her lungs, and then she subsided beneath him, her breath coming in soft sobs, as if she could not halt the tearing ache that rent her body, that made her tremble and shiver in his arms.

He rolled her against himself, and cocooned as she was in the blanket, she might have been a child, so carefully did he adjust her against himself, with no trace of masculine satisfaction as he held her trembling body next to his.

Surely she could sense his need for her, certainly she knew that he had clamped an iron hand on his desire, that he would not harm her, nor cause her shame before his men. And to that end, he whispered soft words again, assuring her of his care of her, promising her safety and the shelter of his arms against all harm.

Isabella was held for the first time in her life by a man whose aim seemed to be the conquering of her body, yet he gave her vocal assurance that he would not harm her, but keep her safe. And she believed him for this moment in time; she heard his words and trusted that he would do as he said.

If he'd threatened to take her body as a man takes a woman, she would believe that also, for he was a man who spoke his thoughts aloud, and she knew that sometime in her future, he would claim her as his woman. But not tonight. Not here in the silence of the hayloft, where other men slept and watched for intruders. Where he had set up a form of protection for her until the morning.

It was with a shattered sense of security that she slept. And in her dreams, she knew a man was nearby, knew the warmth of arms about her, sensed the long length of his form beside her and his breathing touching her face in the night hours. She closed her eyes, whispering a prayer that she might be safe until morning, that the night would not bring a terror to engulf her, that her captor would not turn against her and use her for his own pleasure.

THE SUN SHONE IN THROUGH the open window, scattering its warmth on the men who lay on piles of hay, on the woman who was wrapped securely in a blanket nearby, the man beside her awake and waiting till she should stir.

She slept deeply and he was pleased, for had she not felt secure with him, her sleep would have been broken, her eyes wild with fear, and he would have fought for the whole night to keep her quiet and secure in his arms.

Now a lone rooster crowed, his voice seeming rusty, as if he were not accustomed to serving as an alarm to nearby sleepers. Rafael rolled from his place, rose and stalked to the open window, looking down on the yard below. Three hens and a red rooster pecked in the dirt, seeking out a breakfast that promised to be scant, given the sad state of affairs on this abandoned farm. Again the rooster crowed, tossing his head back and issuing his call to the morning.

Behind him, Rafael heard the rustle of the hay, the

murmur of a woman's voice as she left the darkness of sleep and fought to face the new day. He turned, his eyes caught by the dark hair that was revealed by the blanket that fell to her waist, hair that had been bound yesterday, but now had escaped its bondage and spilled over her shoulders and down to the hay behind her, forming a frame for the delicacy of her face and throat. She was fine-featured, her eyes were large and dark, with violet shadows beneath. And yet she seemed rested. He knew she had slept well, for he'd held her throughout the night, had heard her soft murmurs as she dreamed, knew when she'd been tortured by a nightmare. He'd inhaled deeply, intrigued by the fresh scent she bore, that of clean skin and hair, and more importantly, the aura of femininity that surrounded her.

Now he went to her, squatting beside her as she attempted to awaken, rubbing her eyes with long, slender fingers, then, threading those same fingers through her hair, bringing it to some semblance of order. "I have no brush and my clothing is soiled," she said softly. "Is there any way I can find something clean to wear?"

He wished for a moment he could wave his hand and create all she needed, bring to view the clothing she might wear, the hot water she might use for a bath. But there was no point in being foolish, he decided, for this morning was reality and what he considered was but a luxury he had no way of providing.

"We'll stop in the next village and find you something to wear," he said, compromising a bit. "There should be a general store, somewhere we can find food, perhaps a hotel or restaurant of some sort." He bent to her and pulled the blanket from her, revealing the gray dress she wore, rucked up now about her thighs, exposing her legs to his view. She flushed, her hands moving quickly to pull the fabric down, unwilling to allow his eyes to dwell on her limbs.

"I'll help you up," he offered, clasping her hands in his and pulling her to her feet, rising before her as he did so. She swayed for a moment, and he held her firmly, lest she fall. "We'll go downstairs into the barn, and I'll send Manuel to see if the pump works at the watering trough."

She only nodded, as if speech were beyond her this morning, and turned to climb down the ladder to the floor below. He followed her, watched as Manuel grasped her arm, helping her down the last rung of the ladder. Noting his quick look of reproof, Manuel shot him an apologetic glance and backed away, bowing a bit.

"I'll see to the pump." Scooping up a canteen from his saddle, Manuel went outdoors to where the pitcher pump was bolted onto the end of the trough. He allowed a cupful or so of water to trickle into the opening at the top and then took the handle in his other hand and put his strength behind his actions, pumping vigorously for a moment. In less time than she'd expected, Isabella saw a stream of water run out into the trough, and heard Manuel's shout of success.

She went across the yard, bent low to scoop the water that flowed into her hands, then brought it to her mouth, drinking deeply of the clear liquid. Again she waited as a double handful filled her cupped palms, and again she drank. A third time, she bent low and splashed water over her face, running her hands through her hair, dampening the waves and curls to discourage their tendency to fly free of restraint.

With quick movements of her fingers, she braided the length of hair, twisting a bit of twine around the end of the braid. Her clothing was splattered with water, but she cared little for appearances, noting that clean water would certainly not harm the dirt she'd accumulated over the past twenty-four hours. Her habit was soiled, wrinkled and not fit to wear, but it was all she possessed for the moment, and until Rafael McKenzie could find something else for her use, it would have to do.

From the barn behind her, the men led their horses, saddled them quickly and waited for Rafael to mount his own stallion before they took their places. He swept himself up into the saddle easily, then looked to where Isabella watched him, her eyes wary of the horse who pranced and tossed his head.

"Come." He held out his hand to her and waited. Lest she make him angry, she walked closer to the horse, leaving room for a quick escape should the animal offer her any harm. "Give me your hand," Rafael said, the words an order he obviously meant for her to obey, for his own gloved hand reached for her.

He'd buried his head in the watering trough, and the result allowed her to see clearly the shape of his skull, the dark hair fitting closely to each curve of his head, his face gleaming in the sunshine from the water he'd splashed on every available surface he could reach. His sleeves were rolled up to his elbows, his arms still damp from the bath he'd given himself, and she thought he was a man to be feared, his face sharp and graven, his jaw firm, his eyes deeply set and flaring with messages she did not comprehend. He wore a rough beard, showing no signs of a razor this morning, and she remembered the feel of his face against hers during the night, when he'd bent low and brushed her cheek with his own, his whiskers scratching against her skin.

A blush covered her cheeks, and she felt its heat sear her flesh, knew his amusement was directed at her as he snapped his fingers and held out his palm in her direction. "Come to me, Isabella. I grow impatient."

Lest he be angered, she lifted her hand to his and felt his grip on her wrist. He lifted her, his other hand reaching to hold her waist, and with an easy shifting of his body in the saddle, he lifted her to sit before him, in the same position she had endured the day before. She moved a bit, trying for a softer place for her bottom, but there was no pillow of softness between her and the tough muscular legs he offered as a lap.

With a sigh of resignation, she leaned back against his chest and rested there as he would have her. A sound that might have signified satisfaction breathed in her ear and he picked up the reins, his horse moving to walk down the lane to where the tracks led to the next village.

He seemed to know where he was going and she decided there was no point in making a fuss today, or she might not find herself the possessor of clean clothing or food for her breakfast. If he'd left her at the convent, she'd have fresh clothing on today and have already partaken of the lukewarm porridge at the table with her peers. Now, it seemed she was a whole lifetime away from the convent, and the thought of what lay ahead of her today caused a chill to travel the length of her spine.

CHAPTER FIVE

"You're quiet, Isabella. Have you decided to be a good girl today?" She thought his words were deliberately snide and glanced back at his face, hoping to catch a look of superiority on it. No such luck, she thought glumly, for he only smiled at her and squeezed her with his left arm around her waist.

"I'm hungry, and my clothing is dirty, and being a *good girl* is beyond my capabilities right now," she said, as if it were his place to supply her needs and cater to her moods. And indeed it was, so far as she was concerned.

Ahead of them lay a quiet village, smoke rising from chimneys, the small houses lining both sides of the road as they neared the area where dogs and horses, accompanied by the men who owned them, lined the boardwalks before the stores. Hitching rails were handy and the reins of several horses were twined around the simple accommodations.

"We'll go into the general store," Rafael said quietly. "I expect you to mind your manners and be silent," he told Isabella, lifting her down from his saddle and following her as she smoothed her skirts and tried without success to brush away some of the wrinkles. "Can I depend on you to not make a fuss? Or shall I leave you out here with Manuel?"

"You take a chance either way," she answered, glaring at him. The man was treating her like a child and she was becoming more angry by the minute. "If you don't take me into the store with you, I'll make a fuss out here that will bring the law down on you, and you'd better believe me. I'm at the end of my rope and I don't care what happens at this point."

He bent his head and spoke softly, so that only she could hear his words. "You'll behave yourself, or I'll treat you as I would a child, and you'll find yourself turned over my knee and your bare bottom will feel the flat of my hand." He held her shoulders in his harsh grip and she lifted her gaze to meet his, finding no sign there of the man who had been so tender during the night.

"Do we understand each other?" he asked, and she could only nod.

Her eyes filled with angry tears and she shed her fear of him in that small movement. "I doubt that anyone has ever felt such hatred for you as I do now," she whispered. Her shoulders straightened and she held her head high, almost as if daring his reprisal. It was not to be.

"I'll take you with me, Isabella," he said quietly, one hand on her forearm, holding her before him. "We'll find clothing for you and food to last until tomorrow. Don't make me regret trusting you this far." He paused, his gaze sweeping over her face, noting the tears that still left runnels down her cheeks. One hand lifted to touch the salty drops and he wiped them with his index finger. "I think you cry from anger. Am I right?'

She pressed her lips together, fighting the recurrence of the tears that plagued her. Her head nodded once, a brief acknowledgment of his words.

He smiled, a compassionate expression that warmed her, and then he turned her to the double doors that opened into the general store. She stepped up onto the sidewalk and walked beside him, her arm in a grip that promised retribution should she not cooperate.

Rafael opened the door and she walked over the sill, his big body pressing against her back, then taking his place at her side once they had gained the open floor leading to the counter. A man stood there, his eyes half-lowered, his mouth pursed as if he did not like the looks of his customers, but was too smart and anxious for their coin to make a fuss.

"What can I help you with?" he asked, his voice gruff, his eyes intent on Isabella, no doubt wondering at the soiled and wrinkled clothing she wore. "Something for the lady?"

"My wife needs some clothing. We left her case behind and she has need of a skirt and blouse, or perhaps a dress." Rafael, not at a loss for words, lied fluently, his smile obliging as he held Isabella close to his side.

"Any particular color, ma'am?" the storekeeper asked, his gaze still intent on Isabella and her dull gray garb.

She shook her head. "Anything will do. Just something comfortable for me to change into."

He reached behind him for a glass bin, one containing dresses of various colors. One, a medium blue with white lace and a heavy flounce around the hem, was on top of the stack and he picked it up and shook it out before him.

"Looks about your size, ma'am," he said nicely. "Would you like to try it on?"

Isabella shook her head, and held out her hand for the dress. Without argument, the storekeeper gave it to her and she held it up before herself, holding the waist against her middle and looking down to gauge the size.

"This one will do," she said quietly. "It may be a bit large, but that's all right."

"Let's see another in the same size," Rafael said sharply. "She'll need more than one dress."

Without pause, the storekeeper brought out another dress, this one made of medium green fabric, with flowers scattered across the skirt and bodice alike. It had short sleeves and a full skirt, and Isabella nodded to Rafael, agreeing to its purchase.

He motioned toward Manuel. "Wait over there, please, Isabella," he instructed her, nudging her in the direction he'd chosen.

Without pause, he drew a leather purse from his pocket and paid what the shopkeeper asked, speaking quietly as he watched the man fold the two dresses neatly and wrap them in a length of brown paper. Without pause, the storekeeper reached for another glass bin and slipped a garment from it, stowing it between the dresses before he tied the bundle with a bit of string.

"Now, food for our travel, if you please," Rafael said, pointing at a large round of cheese on the counter. "Give us three pounds of the cheese and some of the smoked sausage in that glass jar. A couple of pounds will do." He looked around at the food displayed on the countertop and motioned toward loaves of bread. "Three loaves of bread and that box of cookies next to the bread."

"Mrs. Hancock bakes the cookies for us twice a week. Mighty good cook, that Mrs. Hancock," the storekeeper said cheerfully. "Anything else, sir?" He finished wrapping the bread and tied the bundle off neatly. The cheese was wrapped in a bit of cheesecloth and then in a towel, and the sausage was put into a metal tin.

"Coffee," Rafael said briefly. "A pound or so."

He watched as the man measured out the ground coffee into a white cotton bag and tied the neck with a string.

"That'll do," Rafael said, paying again from his leather pouch.

From across the room where she waited with Manuel, Isabella shifted and tugged to free her arm from the other man's grip. He looked down at her with a glance of warning, and as if Rafael saw and deciphered the small altercation he called out to her. "Did you want something else, sweet?"

She ceased her struggle and shook her head. "Just something to drink. I'm thirsty."

"I've got sarsaparilla in bottles," the storekeeper said helpfully. "Maybe the lady would like that."

Rafael looked across at Isabella and she nodded. In moments, he'd offered it to her and she held the brown bottle in her hand, her brow furrowed with puzzlement. Smiling with understanding, Rafael took it from her and lifted the cap with a twist, then handed it back. She drank from the bottle—obviously something to which she was unaccustomed—and her tongue licked the final drops from her lower lip.

"Should have put it into a glass for you," Rafael whispered in her ear, bending over to take the bottle from her and lifting it to his mouth for a swallow. "We'll share," he said softly, and his eyes sparkled with mischief as he drank from the place where her lips had so recently touched.

Isabella reached for the package with her dresses inside and Manuel was there before her, lifting it gently from her hands with a murmured suggestion. "May I carry it for you, señorita?" Without awaiting a reply, he held it and turned to the doors of the general store, picking up a second package before he left the counter. A second man took the rest of the purchases and together they left the store.

"Anything else you'd like?" Rafael asked her

quietly, his hand still firm on her arm. He stepped away from the counter for privacy's sake and turned her to face him. "Don't make any mistakes at this point, Isabella. We'll leave quietly if you don't need anything else. Don't make me draw my gun against the shopkeeper."

She slanted him a look of scorn. "I don't doubt you'll do it," she said bitterly. And then she looked down at the floor. "I need nothing else."

"We'll take our leave, sir," Rafael said, turning Isabella to the door and pacing her steps as she walked beside him.

Behind him, the man uttered a casual word of farewell, and they left the store, heading quickly toward their horses. Beside the tall horse Rafael rode, Isabella came to a halt. "Can I ride behind you?" she asked quietly.

"You don't want me to hold you in my arms?" Rafael asked, his voice teasing, his eyes gleaming as he surveyed her form.

She felt limp, weary from the riding, yet the thought of his strong arms holding her fast before him made her hesitate. "Does it matter what I want?" she asked bitterly. "I didn't think I had any choice in this whole thing."

He nodded, considering her bowed head. If the woman thought he was going to let her ride behind him when holding her on his lap had provided the only distraction on this whole ride, she was mistaken. "I'll keep you where I can see you, Isabella," he said, not releasing her arm until Manuel came to their side.

As Rafael mounted, Manuel took Isabella's waist between his hands, and in a moment had lifted her up, placing her carefully, gently, on the solid width of Rafael's thighs.

As she settled into a comfortable position, Rafael's relief was great. For had she begun shifting and twisting on his lap again, he might have suffered as he had earlier, his manhood pressing against the restriction of his trousers, her every move against him an agony in frustration.

He wrapped one long arm around her waist as they backed from the hitching rail and she held herself stiffly in his embrace. "Let go, Isabella," he whispered against her ear. "I won't hurt you, I'm just holding you close, lest you fall from the horse."

Her shoulders eased their stiffness and she leaned back a bit, her head next to his shoulder. He caught a waft of her scent, a clean, fresh aroma that told him she was a woman who valued herself, who kept her body clean and her hair washed frequently. Not for Isabella the slovenly habits of so many women, those who were careless with their bodies. She might be wearing clothing that showed the results of hard travel, but beneath the rough, homespun dress she wore was a body that had not gone more than a day without a thorough cleansing.

A woman fit to rule the home waiting to welcome her, where the servants would greet her with smiles and respect, for he would allow no other option. As his bride, Isabella would be the mistress of Diamond Ranch, and due the honor owed her as Rafael's wife.

THEY HALTED FOR FOOD shortly after the sun hit the sky directly overhead, and Isabella staggered as she was lowered from the horse. Rafael dismounted quickly, reaching for her. "Are you all right?" he asked, his frown showing a concern she hadn't expected. He held her loosely, but seemed to fear her balance if he should turn her free of his touch.

"I need to find a private place, please," she whispered, fearful of the other men hearing her request. She felt the heat of embarrassment creep up her cheeks as Rafael looked down at her and she dropped her head.

"I'll take you into the trees," he said quietly, handing his reins to Manuel and turning her toward the grove of trees where they had halted. The other men spread a blanket on the ground and made haste to open the food they'd purchased, ignoring Isabella and Rafael as they went a short way past the tree line.

A tall willow tree stood near a small stream and Rafael took her in that direction, ducking his head to step beneath the drooping branches. "This will offer privacy enough, I think," he said. "I'll be over there, Isabella, but I'll turn away."

She looked around at the verdant area, where willow branches trailed to the ground all around the big tree. "Thank you." Then, waiting until he passed again through the sheltering branches that surrounded her, she watched until he paced to a nearby patch of bushes and turned aside.

In moments she had relieved her distress and rearranged her clothing, just as he spoke her name. She looked up, sighting him through the branches, and headed to where he waited. "I'm finished," she said quietly. "Is there any water I can use to wash my face and hands?"

"The stream looks to be clean, or else you can use water from the canteen." She motioned quickly at the flowing stream before them and he released her hand, allowing her to kneel at its banks. She splashed water over her hands and arms, washed her face and dampened her hair before she rose again.

He led her back to the place where the men had settled down to partake of the food. They'd left a good portion of the blanket empty for her use and she nodded at them as she sat down, arranging her skirt around herself. From his horse, Rafael brought a canteen of water, offering it to her. She drank deeply, the water relatively cool and fresh from this morning's pumping.

She looked up to find Rafael's gaze on her, his eyes half-shuttered, his nostrils flaring. Water dripped from her lower lip to her bodice and she lifted a hand to wipe at it, unable to take her eyes from his.

"Let me have it," he said, taking the canteen from her and lifting it to his lips, his eyes never leaving her face, as if he would imprint upon her the pleasure he found in her taste on the metal container. He stood, hanging it on a branch, then settled beside her, lifting a piece of cheese cut from the wedge they'd purchased. The bread had been sliced by one of the men, the slices ragged and thick, but welcome.

Rafael lifted the towel holding the bread and Isabella took a piece, inhaling the fragrance as she took a bite. "She must have baked this today, probably this morning," she said. The piece of cheese Rafael had chosen was placed in her hand and he added a length of the sausage before he settled beside her.

"Eat well, Isabella. We'll not stop again until nightfall." His eyes scanned her face and he smiled gently. "I hope the food will not overtax your stomach. I want you to hold it down this time."

With his warning ringing in her ears, she ate the cheese, then wrapped the bread around the sausage and took a bite. From his saddlebag, Rafael had brought forth another bottle of sarsaparilla, and offered it to her, removing the cap first. She drank deeply, then handed it back to him. The other men had already raided their own saddlebags and were enjoying the cool drink, their attention on their food, their eyes carefully focused on all else but the woman who shared their blanket.

Rafael wrapped four cookies from his stash in a bit of the cheesecloth and handed them to Isabella. "You're in charge of these. We'll eat them as we ride, a bit later on."

She tucked them into the front of her dress where they would not be crushed or dropped from the horse, and nodded her agreement.

"Do you want to change into one of your new dresses?" Rafael asked as he pushed himself to his feet. "We can wait until you change, if you like."

"No. I'd rather wait until I can wash up well. There's no sense in wearing clean clothing on a dirty body." It was something that had been drummed into her in the convent, where she had bathed daily, then donned clean clothing every morning. The nuns were clean, their habits healthy, and she had enjoyed what sparse pleasure she gained in the bath she took every evening.

"Your body is far from dirty," Rafael said, bending to speak in her ear, lest any of the men should hear him.

He was rewarded by a smile from her soft lips and he felt a shaft of pure desire touch him from the top of his head to his toes. The knowledge that he would soon own her as his wife, that her body would be his, gave him a pleasure beyond description and he bent a look of possession upon her.

Her eyes widened and she spoke but a single word, yet it was readily understood. "What?"

That she had caught his look and deciphered it accurately was no surprise to him. Isabella was a woman of intelligence, and it wouldn't take an inordinate amount of that quality to figure out that he was claiming her as his own, and his eyes were merely registering the fact.

She stood, brushing crumbs from her skirt, and waited for him to mount the black horse he rode. The men folded the blanket and gathered the remains of the food, wrapping it and settling it into a saddlebag, where it would be handy when they stopped again.

Manuel stood beside her, a silent figure of a man, as if he knew his assignment was to watch over her and keep her where she belonged while Rafael made ready for riding. Once her captor had settled himself in the saddle, she was again lifted and placed across his lap, his hands pulling her dress to cover her legs. But the breeze thwarted his intentions, blowing the fabric aside, revealing her calves and ankles. The soft slippers she'd donned upon leaving the convent were wearing fast, their fabric better suited to the hallways and chapel of the convent than the rough country they traveled through.

"We'll get you some decent shoes as soon as we get to Diamond Ranch," Rafael said, looking down at the thin covering she wore on her feet. "You'll have bruises on your feet from walking on stones and harsh ground."

"I've been bruised before," she said tautly, only too aware of his gaze resting on her feet and legs. His hand reached to smooth the fabric of her dress over her legs and she flinched from his touch.

"Do you fear me?" he asked quietly, as if the gathering of herself as his fingers measured her legs beneath the homespun fabric had bothered him. "Don't draw away from me, Isabella. I have no intention of hurting you. All you must do is cooperate and do as I say. We'll live through this long ride, and you'll have a soft bed to rest in tomorrow night. I don't want you to suffer because of me."

"I don't fear you, Mr. McKenzie. Only what you will do to me when we reach your home."

He looked puzzled at that, she thought, for his forehead puckered a bit and he looked down at her with a question in his eyes. "What do you think I'll do to you? Beat you or treat you badly?"

She bit at her lip, not wanting to answer his query, yet unwilling to back down from this encounter. "I fear you taking me to your bed."

The words lay between them, the color leaving her cheeks as she spoke, his own eyes seeming to become warm and searching as he sought out her face, one hand tilting her chin upward, the easier for him to look into her eyes. "I'll not hurt you, Isabella. I'll marry you before I touch you, before I make you my wife. Has no one ever spoken to you of this?"

She laughed bitterly and opened her eyes fully, the better to see his puzzled look as she spoke taunting words. "And who would speak to me? Perhaps Sister Agnes Mary? Or the Mother Superior? Should they have told me what they have experienced of marriage and the taking of a woman's innocence at the hands of a man?"

"You know nothing of being a wife, do you?" He seemed to be bothered by this, she thought, as if he wished for some woman of great wisdom to properly tutor his bride-to-be.

"Nothing." The single word was spoken in a hushed manner, and Rafael looked down at the girl he held. Old enough already to be wed and perhaps more than old enough to have already borne children, she seemed today to be but a child herself. A creature of innocence, of purity, not meant for the marriage bed. And yet, she was far from what he'd expected a nun to look like. At his first glimpse of her, Isabella had given him pleasure, her face and what parts of her form he had seen. She was beautiful, serene and quiet, a woman fit for the position he would offer her.

Still, his heart stuttered when he thought of the days to come, the wedding to be organized, the great bedroom where she would sleep for the rest of her life, in the bed where he'd been born.

For now, the man who had fathered him lived in a room closer to the kitchen, where his needs were easily attended to by the staff who cared for him. Where his nurse's call could be heard should he need help. The man owned a heart that refused to supply blood to all the parts of his huge body. A stubborn man who would only be limited in his activity by the frailty of his body, no matter what the doctor told him. A man who would soon find his place in the family graveyard, out beyond the orchards.

And to that end, he had demanded that Rafael, his only son, find a bride, a woman fit to carry on the McKenzie name, bearing sons to inherit the land and the enormous ranch that supported a dozen families.

Wanting to please his father, partly because of the love he bore the man who had sired him, Rafael had set forth to do just that. And had found the woman of his heart, a woman who would grace his table, reign over his kingdom and in his bed would give him the fidelity and honor he expected of a bride. She would want for nothing, would live as a princess in his home and only be expected to give her husband the gift of her body and the promise of sons and daughters.

Now he'd managed to find and claim the woman he wanted. Whether by fair means or foul he'd captured the prize, and was almost home with her in his arms. Not happily, perhaps, but he had enough confidence in his own skills as a man to convince her of the wisdom of his choice. Enough knowledge of the female form to woo and win her to himself, given the opportunity to do just that.

But first, he must make certain that she knew what her limits were, what boundaries he would set for her, here in the place where he took her. A home close to a hundred miles from her own father's ranch, and half that distance from the convent where she had spent the years of her girlhood.

She must be made to understand that as the bride of Diamond Ranch, she had a definite place to fill, not only on the ranch but in the community of ranchers that surrounded his homestead. He ran a thousand head of cattle, a large herd of horses and grew field after field of oats and wheat. Diamond Ranch was prosperous, and without pride, he knew that he was responsible for a good share of the profits it had gathered over the past five years.

His father's health had deteriorated rapidly with the onset of heart disease, and Rafael had assumed the reins once it became apparent that the elder man would be an invalid. Another attack had weakened him considerably, and by that time the men recognized Rafael as their source of authority and power. He'd worked hard for the past years, and now the time had come to reap the rewards, to become the head of the family, to occupy the master's bedroom with his bride.

On his lap, Isabella stirred, her bottom wiggling over his thighs, her back stretching a bit, then settling once more against him. "Are you weary?" he asked, his mouth against her ear.

"My body is. I feel that I've been sitting forever, and my legs are going to sleep, my back is aching and the sun has made my head hurt." She looked up at him, a sidelong glance that pleased him, for he saw the strength she exhibited, the aching muscles ignored as she shifted again to settle herself more comfortably.

"We'll stop soon," he said, nodding at Manuel, who had cast him an inquiring look. "We need to make a pot of coffee and heat the rest of the sausage over a fire. You'll feel better with some food in you and the ground under your feet."

She sighed. "I don't mean to complain, even though it serves you right. Any man who would steal away with a woman deserves all the complaining she can come up with."

"You've been surprisingly short on complaints," he said. "I expected you to be moaning and groaning all day long. Most women would have given me hell for putting them through what you've had to endure."

"I learned early on in life that complaining doesn't solve the problem. Usually, I manage to handle any situation without calling for help."

He turned her a bit in his arms, revealing her face to him fully. "What kind of problems did you have as a child that caused you to develop so adult an attitude?"

She only shrugged and grimaced. "Just the usual childhood upsets. I didn't have a mother to go to, so our cook heard a lot of my woes, until I found that I was more adept at solving the problems than she. I was standing on my own by the time I was ten or twelve."

"And why were you sent to the convent? Did you so badly disrupt your father's household that he wanted to get rid of you?" His voice was gently teasing as he spoke, but Isabella heard a note of concern through the query.

"I went to the convent because I wanted to," she said firmly. "Father tried to talk me out of it. He wanted me to be married to Juan Garcia just after my fourteenth birthday, and when I refused, he lost his temper with me."

"How did you win that battle?" The thought of a mere child of fourteen being married off to a man like Juan Garcia was enough to make his blood run cold, and Rafael felt anger rise in him at the thought.

"He agreed to let me stay at the convent and learn the skills of a wife until I was sixteen, and when he died that year, there was enough money left to keep me there for another few years. I'd about decided to become a nun by then, for I knew that anything was better than marriage to Señor Garcia." She shivered against him as she spoke, and a flood of respect for the young girl who had fought and won her freedom washed over him.

"Señor, there is a spot ahead where the water is fresh and the area is defensible." Manuel rode beside him and spoke welcome words, for the man seemed to be aware that Isabella was weary and more than ready for sleep.

"Tell the men to stop where you say and set up camp," Rafael said easily. "Isabella and I shall be with you momentarily."

Manuel nodded and rode to speak with the other men, leading the way to the chosen spot, an area not more than five hundred yards ahead. Slowing his stallion to a walk, Rafael spoke softly to Isabella, words aimed at soothing her and assuring her of her safety.

"We'll stay in my small tent tonight," he said easily. "I'll find enough supple branches to make a bed for you, and there is enough food to fill your stomach until morning."

"I'm not hungry," she said, sounding a bit pouty to her own ears. "I don't mean to be any additional trouble to you, señor, but I'm only tired and ready for sleep. I don't care if I have food or not."

"You will eat, Isabella. I won't have you sick

before I take you to my home. We'll have a hard day's ride tomorrow, and I want you to feel well."

"Then leave me be, and give me a blanket to cover myself with. I don't need your tent or a bed to rest on."

Rafael laughed, helpless to conceal his amusement at her. "You have no choice, my love. You will sleep in my tent on my blanket and you will eat first. I can be stubborn when it pleases me."

"I've noticed," she snapped, sitting upright and leaning heavily on a part of his anatomy that protested her weight.

He shifted her to one thigh and held her there, unwilling to tell her what she had done to cause him such discomfort, but she stiffened in his grip and twisted from his hold.

"You are a burdensome woman," Rafael said, bringing his stallion to a halt and lowering her to the ground. One of the men drew near to keep an eye on her as Rafael dismounted easily, and at a nod from Rafael as he claimed Isabella with one hand on her waist, his trusted man turned and walked back to the camp they were busy forming.

A fire was already laid, the wood piled neatly with kindling beneath it, a pot of water already hanging over it on a hook. Even as they watched, Matthew opened the sack of ground coffee and measured an amount into the waiting water.

"I know you had coffee before when you were not well, but do you normally drink it?" Rafael asked Isabella, settling her beside the fire that awaited a match. She perched on a cushion one of the men had placed there for her, and she looked at the others who worked silently around her, wondering which of them had thought of her comfort in such a way.

"I can tolerate it, though tea is preferable, but it was only available on occasion. The Mother Superior said coffee was not a healthy drink and she forbade it to be purchased for the convent kitchen, except in small amounts."

"You may have whatever you desire at our home when we arrive there," Rafael told her. "You may have anything it is in my power to provide for you."

She looked up at him in surprise. "Why are you so generous with me? You just told me I was...what was it you said? Oh, yes, you told me I was burdensome. Not a flattering description, to my way of thinking."

"I thought of something entirely different when I told you that," he said with a laugh, a sound that was echoed by Manuel, who had apparently noticed his employer's discomfort while riding during the last hour or so.

"I haven't tried to be a burden to you. But then I haven't put forth any effort to make your life easy, either. I suspect you'll just have to put up with me the way I am."

"I'm looking forward to just that," Rafael said, bowing his head as if in tribute.

"My father used to tell me I was a troublemaker when I was a child. But our cook defended me. She said I was too smart for my own good, and my father did not understand me."

"I'll be sure to work at that, Isabella. Understanding you will be my priority for the next fifty years or so."

CHAPTER SIX

THE FOOD WAS MORE of the same, less palatable than he would find at his table on the ranch, but the men didn't seem to find it without value, and Isabella ate what was put before her. A thick piece of bread, a length of sausage—held over the fire until the skin split from the heat—and a chunk of cheese made up her meal and she dutifully chewed and swallowed until it was gone.

Two of the men had worked at setting up a small tent for her use. Hers and Rafael's it appeared, for his saddlebags were placed inside the flap, and his blanket roll was spread on the ground, taking up over half the space available inside the small structure.

It was fully dark, the moon hung low on the horizon and the sound of night birds in the forest played a mournful melody in her ears as Isabella was led to the tent and instructed to crawl within. She sent Rafael an imploring look that was archly ignored as he held the flap wide enough for her to affect easy passage. She crawled to where his blanket roll lay and took one of his coverings for herself, spreading it beside his and settling herself on it, wishing for another quilt of some sort to keep out the night air.

Once the sun had set, the wind picked up and the tent did little to keep the cold from her. She slipped her tattered slippers off and lay down, curling to face the outer wall, drawing her feet up under her dress to keep them warm.

Outside, Rafael spoke to the men, instructing them as to their turns at watch, and then he crawled in beside her. The tent suddenly seemed to shrink in size and she felt her chest tighten as if her breathing were restricted by his presence. He whispered soft words of instruction to her, telling her to scoot closer as he lay down behind her, and when she patently ignored his words, he reached one long arm around her waist and tugged her to rest against himself.

Whether his arm was too tight or she was tense at his familiarity, she felt surrounded, swamped by his nearness. No matter the reason, her breath caught in her throat and she shivered against him.

"Are you cold?" he whispered, holding her close, sliding his left arm under her head to provide a pillow of sorts. His right arm encircled her, the heat of his body warming her back more than she would have thought possible.

"I'm not very warm," she said shortly. "I thought my cot at the convent was hard and uncomfortable, but this is even worse. I believe there's a rock right under my hip."

He laughed and moved her back a few inches.

"Would you like to lie on top of me? It might be softer, but I'm not sure you'd like the end results."

She felt a blush climb her cheeks at his words. "Don't say such things. Please try for a little restraint, señor."

"You have no idea how much restraint I'm suffering under, Isabella. I've seldom been so uncomfortable in my life. Sleeping with you and not being able to turn you to face me is trying my patience."

"Why should you want to turn me to face you?" she asked, wonder alive in her words, for she honestly could not understand his meaning.

"It would be easier to kiss you that way. Now I'm settling for the back of your neck and the side of your throat," he told her, demonstrating his problem with a brush of his lips across her nape.

Again she shivered and he laughed softly, aware of listening ears. "Don't worry, love. I won't do anything to frighten you tonight. I want you to trust me, and if I allow my hands to roam over your body the way I'd like them to, you won't be speaking to me by morning."

"I don't know what you mean," she whispered, her voice a soft whimper.

"I know you don't, and that makes it even more difficult for me to behave myself. I'd like to hold you close and touch all the soft curves that make up your body. My hands itch to touch your breasts, Isabella. They are heavier than I had first thought and feeling their weight against my arm is a torture I hadn't planned on."

He moved his arm a bit and she recognized that it was firmly placed just beneath the line of her bosom, and indeed, her breasts were supported by its firm, muscular shape.

"Please, Rafael." She couldn't speak the words that begged to be uttered, and her plea was seemingly enough to arouse his pity for her fast-fleeing innocence.

He bent over her and his kiss touched her neck, just beneath the curl of her ear. "I won't hurt you, Isabella. Not here where the other men could hear if you cried out, nor would I cause you shame before others." He rocked her against himself. "Rest easy, love. I'll only hold you close and keep you warm."

THE SUN WAS BRIGHT, rising over the eastern sky, bringing new life to the clearing where they lay asleep. The birds chattered in the trees overhead, the small animals ran to and fro without fear and the horses stomped their feet, anxious for their morning's feed. The men rose quickly, and one of them put a pot of coffee to boil over the fire.

Inside the small tent, where she'd slept better than she'd expected, Isabella blinked her eyes and realized that sometime during the night she'd indeed turned to face the man whose arms enclosed her. She breathed against the skin of his throat, her eyes trained on the whiskers that had grown even longer during the night hours. His arms tightened around her and his whisper was low.

"I didn't force you to turn to me, Isabella. But I'm

glad you did. Your soft parts were welcome against my chest, and I enjoyed the feel of your hair against my hands. You have beautiful hair, my love."

"Don't call me that," she protested. "I'm not your love, only the woman you've captured and taken prisoner."

"You're the woman who will marry me within a week's time," he told her, his voice not allowing for argument.

WITHIN AN HOUR, they were once more on the road, in this case a narrow lane where only one buggy at a time could be accommodated, or two horses were able to ride abreast. Should a traveler meet another, one would have to pull aside, onto the verge, where trees grew close to the rider as he passed by. Sunlight filtered through the trees, leaving patches of gold on the ground through which they passed. And for those brief moments they felt the heat of the day beneath the overhanging branches.

Isabella rode again on Rafael's lap, across his thighs, becoming used to the warmth of his limbs beneath her, the strength of his arm surrounding her waist and the heat of his breath on her nape as they traveled. He spoke but seldom, seeming to be in deep thought this morning. It was almost midday before he spoke his mind to Isabella, after having heard the grumbling of his men, speaking loudly of food and needing a chance to rest their bones for a bit.

"We'll be home before dark," he murmured softly.

"You may want to wash and change your clothing before we get there. I'll try to locate a good spot by the river for you to have privacy. I have soap with me, and you can use one of my shirts as a towel if you like."

"Does your family know you're bringing me with you?" And if they did, what did that tell her about this man who had taken her by force? Would his family approve his method of gaining a bride? Another thought brought her up short and she twisted against him, turning to watch his face as she asked the question that had entered her mind more than once during this long ride.

"How did you know enough to seek me out? You knew when you arrived there at the convent that I was living with the sisters, didn't you?"

He nodded shortly, his mouth firm, his eyes dark and searching as he looked down into hers. "I told you before, Isabella, that I'd heard of a beautiful woman, sequestered among the Sisters of Charity, a girl taken from her home at a young age, pledged to marry a man of whom no good is spoken. Juan Garcia is a man known for his cruelty to both man and beast. He thrives on devising methods whereby he can rule those who work for him, whose destiny he controls.

"I knew that any woman fated to be his wife would face a lifetime of misery. That alone was enough to send me north, riding for almost fifty miles, to find the girl who was being trained for a place in his hacienda, where she would be less than a servant to his desires. I had heard the tale of a woman whose beauty rivaled the loveliest flowers in nature, whose face and form were beyond description, for you were seen and noted by travelers in that area." He paused in his descriptive phrases to look deeply into her eyes, a slash of color across his high cheekbones, his nostrils flaring as if he scented prey within his reach.

"I found you there in the chapel, and I knew when my eyes were finally sated with your beauty I would still want you as my bride, no matter how many years we were together. I saw just a trace of your dark hair beneath the headpiece you wore, the curve of your cheek, the flash of dark eyes and the slender form of one who was not a good candidate for the convent. I wanted you, Isabella. Enough to take you without permission. Enough to steal you from Juan Garcia, and make you my own."

"And if I had not been as you'd been led to believe? If my face and form were but ordinary, not the sort to appeal to a man's desire—would you still have taken me with you?"

"That didn't happen, did it? You are what you are, and I am smitten with the woman who is called Isabella. You will be my bride, my wife and the mother of my children. Those who will inherit from me, the sons who will run Diamond Ranch and make it known as the most productive and successful in all of the territory."

"You expect much of me," Isabella said, "and I may not be capable of doing as you have planned. What if I don't have children for you? What if I only have daughters? Will you put me aside and find another woman to fulfill your dreams?"

"You are what I want in my life," he told her firmly. "I knew when I set my eyes on you that I would have you as my own, that you would fill my bed and my house and my life. I have wanted women many times, as a panacea to my body's needs, as a young man seeks pleasure with a woman, but never have I known the need to possess that overcame me in the chapel when I set eyes upon you."

"There is no chance that you will change your mind, that you will set me free?" she asked even as she knew his answer without the words being spoken.

"My father is lying abed a bedroom, even as we ride toward Diamond Ranch. He will not live much longer, and I must have my life well in order before the day of his death. He has bidden me to marry well, to a woman of virtue, a woman who has been gently raised, a woman who can take the reins in her hands and rule over the home I will give her. The home I cannot inherit without obeying my sire."

"Who is there now? Does your father make the rules and give the orders?"

"My father is the final word on anything that relates to Diamond Ranch. So far as the house itself is concerned, my cousin, Lucia, has been in residence for two years, since my father became too ill to function as he should. Lucia is a distant relative, a daughter to a far-removed cousin, but related to my mother's family. She will go back to her family when we arrive, for I will have no need for her there."

Isabella laughed, a bitter sound that rang in the air and brought quick looks of alarm to the men who rode with them. "You'll just send her away, as if you've taken what she had to offer, and now she will be of no further use to you?"

"I've taken nothing from Lucia. She has had two years of training in running a hacienda, of readying herself for a marriage of her own. She has lost nothing, but gained a great deal of experience."

"Why don't you marry Lucia? It would seem she is already trained in the arts of being mistress of a large home. It would have saved you a long ride, a tedious journey with a woman who wants only to escape you."

"Lucia is not the woman I want as my bride. She tends to be bold and outspoken, and is not appealing to me. She will find a man of her own. In fact, her father has already written a marriage contract for her. She will no doubt be married within a month of arriving at her home, even though she is not happy about the marriage." He paused and his voice softened. "You are a woman who appeals to all that is masculine in me, Isabella. It is you I have chosen."

Isabella looked dubious. "Will Lucia greet me with smiles and a warm welcome when I walk into the house she has worked to keep organized and ready for a bride?" Her voice carried a degree of doubt he could not mistake and he curled his arm even tighter about her middle, holding her against his chest with a strength that almost took her breath from her body.

"It is of no concern to me, or to you, either, whether or not Lucia welcomes you gladly. She will be leaving soon after we arrive to return to her family. She has been well paid for her work and time, and is of no importance to either of us."

"You're a harsh man, señor. I'm not sure I can ever like you, let alone respect you as a husband. I will wait for the day to come when a younger, more lovely woman comes into view and you find yourself tired of me, and ready to ship me off to the house where my father was until his death."

His arm tightened again and she gasped for breath. "That will not happen. You will grow old with me, with our children around us and our lives entwined in the life of Diamond Ranch."

"You speak as if your word is law," she said scathingly. "As if you rule Diamond Ranch like a monarch on a throne."

"And so I do," he admitted. "When my father is buried in the family graveyard, the ranch will be mine, every acre will be under my control, as will my wife."

She felt a spasm of fear fill every part of her, from her trembling lips to the toes that were even now numb within the slippers she wore. As if he felt it tremble throughout her body, he bent low and brushed his lips against her ear.

"You need to rest, love. We'll stop here." As if they knew his mind, even without explicit instructions, the men who rode ahead of them found a glade near the narrow road and their horses passed through tall grass to reach the place they had chosen. Aching in every joint, Isabella slid from the stallion's back, only to find herself leaning against the sturdy neck of the horse, her balance undone by the weariness of her limbs.

Behind her, Rafael swung his long body to the ground and his arm circled her and tugged her against his side. "Come, I'll find a place for you to sit. You need to have your feet rubbed to get the circulation going again."

She stumbled along at his side until he found a place he deemed suitable for his purposes and she was lowered to sit in a patch of thick grass where small white flowers bloomed around her. She stretched out her feet before her, wiggling her toes, leaning to rub the aching muscles of her calves and, finally, lifting her knees and bending to rest her forehead against them.

Rafael crouched beside her, his hand covering the back of her head, his long fingers twining through the length of her hair, his touch gentle, as if he would comfort her. "Let me help you, Isabella. I'll only massage your feet, your toes."

She was beyond caring about such things as modesty and the rules of behavior that governed men and women. If the man wanted to place his hands on her feet and bring back the tingling blood flow, she would not argue the matter with him.

"Lie down," he commanded, settling a saddlebag

for her to use as a pillow, then lowering her to rest against it. He sat beside her, his hands reaching for her feet, sliding her homespun garment up to reveal slender ankles and the rounding of her lower limbs.

She watched him from beneath lowered lids and thought he was a beautiful man, with his dark hair askew over his forehead, his black eyes flashing amusement in her direction as if he knew her thoughts, and approved of her interest in him. His jaw was firm, squared and harsh, and his nose was but a sharp blade, much like the Indian braves who had worked on her father's ranch.

Had she chosen a man for her husband, she could not have found a more handsome specimen, nor one more appealing to a woman's baser nature. For she could find no aversion to him as a man. He had a masculine arrogance about him that made her bristle even as she admired his self-confidence. He would have life lived as he pleased, with no need to give way to another's opinion. As a husband he might be a hard man to deal with, but he would not be cruel.

And at that thought, she remembered the harsh look in Juan Garcia's eyes when he had looked at her, his gaze avid, his mouth open with lust as his motivation. Now that she was beyond the schoolroom, she began better to understand that her life as a Garcia bride would have been misery indeed. The thought of having Juan Garcia touch her in any intimate manner was enough to make her stomach roil and lurch.

Yet this man who had held her close for two days

atop his stallion had not given her any feeling of revulsion. He had touched her body, her face, and his hand had been buried in the wealth of hair that hung to her waist. And she was not repelled by him.

As though he knew what thoughts rambled in her mind, he smiled down at her, his clever fingers returning to massage her toes, the arch of her foot and the slender bones of her ankles.

"Is that better?" he asked, his smile arrogant as though he knew what blessed relief he had brought to her aching bones.

"You know it is," she said shortly, as if she would not give him the satisfaction of knowing he had pleased her by his ministrations. It was all she could do not to close her eyes and surrender to the weariness that had overcome her. He leaned over her, lifting her in his arms, and she found herself sitting upright, her bottom planted on his crossed legs, her back to him. As she would have struggled to keep herself upright, he calmed her with hands across her shoulders and his mouth at her ear.

"Shush now. Let me rub your shoulders and loosen the soreness in your back." Before she could find breath to protest, without giving her a choice, he held her before him and his long fingers touched all the places that ached from the tedious hours atop his horse. He ran his hands down her shoulder blades, pushing against the tender flesh, kneading the muscles beneath her skin, bringing ease to the whole length of her back.

And she allowed it without a murmur of protest. Never one to keep her mouth closed when she had a chance to speak her mind, Isabella had had a monstrous time at the convent, learning to be quiet, to speak only when spoken to, learning to keep her opinions to herself. Now, she reminded herself, she was no longer in the convent, no longer forced to keep her mouth pinched shut when words came to mind that she longed to spew forth.

But for some reason, the touch of Rafael's hands on her back, the strength emitted by those long fingers, the soothing press of his palms against sore muscles—all seemed to fill her with a contentment that would not call forth words from her lips, and she was silent. Her eyes closed and her head bent forward as he plied his magic fingers on the long length of her back, and even when he ventured below her waist and his warmth extended to her hips, she held her tongue.

For she could not gainsay him the pleasure he gave her.

"Feel better, love?" He whispered the temptation in her ear and she only leaned back against him, rotating her shoulders and leaning her head against his shoulder.

"You like this, don't you?" His laugh was quiet, his tone amused, and yet she did not take offence at his high-handedness, touching her as he did, speaking with such familiarity in her ear, and she wondered why she vacillated so between modesty and pride.

"When we marry…" His pause was long and she

held her breath, wondering what joy he would promise her upon the day she became his bride. "When we marry, I'll rub your back for you every night."

She shivered at his words, for she had no doubt that rubbing her back would be the very least of his ventures once she was ensconced in his bed. She knew little of the marriage ceremony, never having witnessed one, and even less about the acts committed between husband and wife, only that they were painful for a woman to withstand, and men found great joy in casting their seed hither and yon, with whichever willing females they could seduce to their will.

The women in her father's hacienda had spoken openly about men and the acts they performed on the women of their choice. Unknown to them, Isabella had hidden beneath the table or in the pantry, the better to learn the mysteries of life, as it was lived by those who inhabited her father's hacienda and its outbuildings.

Details were rather sketchy, but she'd heard of men who were worthy of being courted by the women who did such things. Had the cook known of her eavesdropping, she would have been roundly scolded and perhaps felt the touch of a switch against her legs, but even as a child Isabella had known how to blend in with her surroundings, a trait which stood her in good stead in the convent.

She really would have liked the life of a nun, she thought, except for the many hours required of each nun to be spent in prayer. She thought the prayers were repetitious, and had no patience with saying ten Hail Marys for each misdeed she confessed to the priest.

For a moment she was tempted to send a prayer of thanksgiving heavenward, that she had been gifted with the presence of this man, so different from another she might have been forced to marry, this man who seemed to hold her in high regard. At least he wanted to make her his bride, and that was a far cry from being hidden in a hut or shack as had some of the women on her father's ranch. Women to be visited when the urge came upon the men who kept them isolated. Her father had kept a woman for himself in a small house behind the men's bunkhouse.

She cleared her throat and broke the silence. "Do you have a woman hidden away that you visit at night?" she asked, aware of Rafael's silence as he absorbed her query. "I suppose it isn't any of my business, but I just wondered."

"How do you know of such things?" he asked, his voice choked as if he held back some emotion. "Who told you of women kept aside to be visited by their…" He broke off as if he could not think of a word that would be seemly to speak in her presence.

"I heard the house women talking when I was but a child, and though I didn't know why my father had a woman living on his ranch, one he visited at night, I was aware of the existence of such a thing."

"I have no woman at Diamond Ranch. You will not be disgraced by my taking another woman to my bed. I will be faithful to you." He rested his hands on her shoulders and tightened his grip. "Do you believe me, Isabella?"

"I have no reason not to believe you. I only asked because I wondered—"

"Wonder no more," he said forcefully, interrupting her words. "We'll not speak of this again, for it is not fit conversation for a woman's ears, but know that I will sleep only in your bed, once you are my wife."

She stilled, shrinking from him. "And until then? Are you free of your vow until you marry me?"

He made a disgusted sound, turning her roughly to face him. "That's not what I meant. I'll have my ring on your finger within a week, Isabella. I can wait that long to have you with me to soothe my passion. I have a notion you'll be weary of me before you think. You may even welcome my absence, should I not sleep beside you on occasion."

She lifted her gaze to his. "No, that is not so. I would have made a vow to be chaste had I become a Sister of Charity, and now, if we are to marry, I'll make a vow to be…You know what I mean, Rafael. Don't make me say these things aloud. I fear a dark flush will stain my cheeks for the rest of my life if you keep tormenting—"

"That's enough," he said, again cutting her off midsentence. "I'll admit that I'm teasing you and it is not fair, for you are an innocent. And though I'm enjoying your blushes and stammering as you attempt to express yourself, it is not right to take advantage of you. I beg your patience with my arrogance."

"I don't understand you, Rafael. You are one man now and in ten minutes, you will be another. Sometimes you are kind and treat me as a lady, and there have been moments when I feared for my virtue."

Rafael laughed aloud at that, his amusement touched by her honest words. She would be a mixed blessing, that was obvious, for on one hand she would confound him with her innocent approach, and on the other hand he expected she would rob him of his self-control when she discovered the strength of her attraction for him. The woman could lead him in circles, given the opportunity, and he would be smart if he nipped her independence in the bud, and kept her unaware of her ability to influence him.

"Men are designed to be happy with one woman. When he has found the woman he wants to have as his own, a decent man will keep his attentions only on her for all of his life, Isabella. I could take you into the forest right now, my love, and make you mine, take your innocence and use your body. No one would wonder at it, for a woman affianced to a man is as good as his bride already."

She withdrew from him, not a physical action, but one of the spirit, and he felt the absence of warmth as he looked down into her face. "That wasn't a threat, Isabella. I didn't mean it as such. And if we were to be on the road for a great number of days, traveling, sleeping at night in my small tent, I might not be able to take you to my father's house, still a virgin. But as it stands, you will be an innocent on your wedding day."

The men who sat near the fire and drank tin mugs of coffee began to speak of leaving, Jose rising to water his horse, Manuel speaking softly to Rafael, asking for instructions. "We must leave," Rafael said, rising and lifting Isabella from her place on the ground. "It will be past sunset before we reach the ranch, and I don't want to travel in the dark. There are too many dangers in the night hours."

They mounted and made ready to ride on, Isabella again on Rafael's lap, but this time turned so that her legs lay over one side of the horse, and she was held in his arms, secured by his strength against his body.

"Sleep if you can for a while," he told her. "This will be a late night, by the time you are introduced to the staff at the hacienda and we have our dinner. Close your eyes and rest."

Isabella thought him foolish to expect such a thing of her, but to her amazement, she drifted off into a sleep that was neither deep nor restful, but instead one from which she roused frequently, aware of the warmth of his body, the muscular cradle in which she rested and the scent of man that surrounded her.

She felt his lips against her forehead several times, a strangely comforting touch that made her feel safe and secure. And how that could be when she was the captive of this man was more than she could understand.

They rode in silence, their horses traveling at a faster gait than before, as if they knew that the comforts of their home barn and pasture awaited them. The men spoke among themselves, laughing frequently, joking in their own language, one Isabella understood, but did not know the nuances of speech they used.

She closed her eyes, drifting in a place of warmth and comfort, her heart beating at a regular pace that told her of the total lack of fear she felt. And in the midst of her half dreams and moments of waking, she knew a pleasure she had not expected when his lips touched her skin with care and he murmured her name against her temple.

CHAPTER SEVEN

AS PROMISED, RAFAEL DREW the group to a halt an hour before sunset, at a place where a stream of water ran beside the trail they traveled. He took her to the water, shielded by a tall growth of bushes, and walked the bank of the stream, peering down into the brush and across the narrow expanse of water to the opposite bank, searching out anything that might harm her.

"There is no trace of snakes, Isabella, no creatures that will cause you discomfort. I'll leave you with the soap and my clean shirt to dry with. Don't leave this spot, for if you do I will find you, and the results of your disobedience will be painful to you."

"I don't like being threatened by bodily punishment, Rafael," she said, her temper at a high, her indignation simmering as he attempted to intimidate her.

"Then do as you're told and there will be no problem. It is as simple as that."

She undid the belt that held her dress in place, and watched him, waiting for him to turn away. But it apparently was not to be, for his gaze did not leave her.

"May I have privacy?" she asked proudly, her head held high, her cheeks rosy with yet another blush.

"I'll turn my back until you are in the water," he conceded, "and then when you are ready to quit the stream, I'll cease watching you. Other than that, you must put up with my presence here. I find that I'm not sure of your cooperation or your obedience."

She flung him a look of desperate dislike and bent to take off her slippers. Then, as he turned away, she slid from the dirty dress and removed her underclothing quickly, stepping into the stream and wading to the center of it where it was fast-moving and more than a foot or so in depth.

She sat in the water, relishing the cool touch against her flesh, leaning her head back to allow her hair to be cleansed of the dust of the trail. The soap he had given her was brown, smelling much like the lye soap which was made at her father's hacienda when she was a child. It sudsed a bit between her hands and she scrubbed at her hair, cleaning it as best she could. Kneeling in the stream, she used the soap to cleanse her body, rubbing it from neck to knees and back.

Being clean today was a luxury, she decided, for even though she had become accustomed to the nightly bath at the convent, there was no luxury involved in the form of bathing she'd become accustomed to there. She'd been allowed two minutes in which to climb into the tub and wash herself. Usually the fourth or fifth in line to use the water, she never felt totally clean, for she had been washing in the residue of others before her. Then, too, her scrubbing was, of necessity, brief, for by the time her two minutes were up, there was a knock on the door and she was given ten seconds' warning to be out of the water.

Dressing for bed on those nights had been a simple matter, for she'd just pulled the white nightgown over her head and allowed her body to dry on the coarse fabric as she paraded back down the long corridor to her cell.

But this cool brook, and its clean, clear water streaming past her, taking the suds with it, was a wonderful thing. She luxuriated in it, lay flat beneath the water for a long moment, holding her breath, then allowing the bubbles to escape to the surface.

There came to her ears a mighty splashing, then she heard Rafael's voice, felt his harsh touch on her shoulders as he dragged her upright. "My God, I thought you were drowning. What on earth were you doing lying beneath the water?" he asked, anger ablaze on his face, his eyes dark with horror.

"I only lay on the bottom for a moment, just long enough to rinse off entirely," she said, trying ineffectively to conceal herself from him as he held her upright. Her hands flailed the air, seeking to cover her breasts, then the brush of curls at the base of her belly. And in both endeavors she was pitifully unsuccessful.

With a groan of frustration, he took her to the bank and wrapped her in his clean shirt, holding her against himself for a moment, as though he would protect her from some unknown danger. "I didn't mean to frighten you," he began, his explanation obviously not one he relished, for the man seemed not to explain his actions to anyone, so far as she could tell, merely doing as he wished.

This time he had not allowed for her pride and dignity, and she felt that both had been badly ignored. She twisted from his grip and glared at him. "You said I could bathe in privacy. Why did you turn around and look at me? You would not have thought I was drowning if you'd kept your back to me, minding your own business."

"You *are* my business," he told her. "Everything you do is a concern of mine. I've apologized already, Isabella. Enough of this."

"*That* was an apology? You need a lesson in manners, I'd say." She stood before him, shivering as the night winds began to blow, clutching the shirt around her body, feeling naked and vulnerable. The sun was at the horizon and the day would soon become twilight, yet there was not enough darkness surrounding her to hide the long legs that were exposed to his view, nor the shivering body that had thoroughly dampened the fine fabric of his shirt. Her form was clearly visible to him, and she was desperately aware of the state of her nudity before the man.

His eyes met hers, his gaze determinedly averted from the view she presented. "We need to move along. We've taken long enough here to satisfy a woman's pride. Now, put your dress on and ready yourself for the rest of our journey."

"A woman's pride? What foolishness. I merely wanted to be clean. If that is a matter of pride, then most women must suffer from that fault."

"Many women are slovenly, at least the ones I've met in my limited lifetime. Cleanliness is far down the list of priorities they hold dear. I am happy that you have a desire for a clean body. I'm sure I'll appreciate it even more after we are married." He grinned at her suddenly, his mind reverting back to the thoughts he'd harbored during their long ride.

"It was one thing I noticed about you right away, Isabella. You smell clean, your hair is well cared for and you have a womanly way about you. I like all that I've come to know about you. You please me."

"Well, I'm sure that will add to my happiness, señor. Knowing that you approve of my personal habits is a mark in your favor. And those marks are few and far between."

"You wound me, sweetheart," Rafael said, grinning with delight. The woman was spunky, abrasive and ready for an argument. A refreshing change from the usual females who had managed to haunt his footsteps since he'd become of an age to marry. Women, in his short history with the breed, seemed inclined to be agreeable, humble and eager to please him. He needn't fear any such reactions from Isabella, for she was obviously dead set on putting him in his place with regularity. Her presence in his life would be a challenge, one he looked forward to facing on a daily basis.

Now she looked at him with sparks flying from her eyes, her chin tilted upward, her jaw set as she shot a query in his direction. "How long will it be until we arrive at this place you call the Diamond Ranch?" Her voice slurred across the name of his inheritance as though it were not fit to mention and he felt his own temper flare.

"If you hurry along, it will be less than an hour." As though she had caused a great delay in his schedule, he led her through the brush to where the other men waited for them. He rued the trembling in his hands, undoing the knots in the package where her new dresses were packed, and his voice was harsh as he hauled one of them forth.

"Put this on." With no attempt at civility, he tossed the dress in her direction and waited.

Again her chin lifted and though pride was apparent in her stance, she hesitated, wavering as she clutched the dress to her breasts. "I have no underthings to wear," she whispered, and then watched in silence as he reached beneath the second dress to locate a chemise he'd instructed the storekeeper to include in the purchase. It was sheer, a filmy bit of froth, and she blushed anew.

But she need not have feared, for he went to the others and as one, they turned and walked into the edge of the forest, leaving her alone to dress…a feat she accomplished in less than a minute. The chemise was soft, forming to her body, and over it the dress fit her, once she had adjusted the belt that came with it. Indeed it might have been made to her specifications.

"I'm ready," she said quietly, aware that the men were growing impatient with her dithering. Rafael turned to look at her, his glance sweeping from her head to the bare toes that peeped out from beneath her hem.

"We'll ride then." Without another word, he gathered her discarded clothing, stuffing it into a saddlebag, then found his horse and mounted with an easy movement. She watched him, only too conscious of her bare feet, yet unwilling to ask him to locate her slippers. The thought occurred to her that she might consider being thankful for the dresses he had purchased for her benefit, but she was still too offended by his behavior to offer her cooperation. The man was arrogant, there was no other word for it.

As if he would not cause her to be further upset, Manuel came to her as he had before and lifted her up with circumspect pressure on her waist, placing her within Rafael's reach. With an easy motion, he gripped her firmly and she was placed in her usual position on his lap.

"All right?" he asked quietly, and at her nod, Rafael set off down the trail, the others following apace.

"Your heart is pounding as if you've had a great fright," he murmured, holding her close to himself as was his wont. The flat of his hand was against her middle, above her waist, and his fingers spread wide, his thumb resting against the curve of her breast. "Are you fearful of meeting my people?"

"I'm fearful of what will happen to me." She knew no other way to describe her apprehension, for though the man—Rafael—did not bring fright to her heart, or dread to her mind, she felt a deep fear of the unknown, of those she would encounter, their thoughts of her as an outsider.

"I will take care of you," he said simply. And with that she had to be content, for the other men were speaking of what would come to pass during the next days, of work left undone, of their wives and children who awaited them.

They had barely gone another quarter mile when fencing suggested a property boundary beside the road they traveled, white boards that kept great herds of cattle from the road. The white-faced steers stood watching them, one of them occasionally bellowing his welcome, all of them sturdy and heavy with the weight of lush grasses and good feed.

"Closer to the barns you will see some of the horses we raise here at Diamond Ranch," Rafael said. "And beyond the barns you will see the main house and another dozen or so smaller homes where the men live with their families. There is a bunkhouse out back for the men who are unmarried, and assorted coops and sheds."

"Do you have dogs?" The vision of her father's huge wolfhounds remained in her memory, a frightening reminder of her vulnerability.

"There are shepherd mixtures, dogs to help in herding the cattle. I have one in the house, a mixed breed who showed up one day and decided to make his home with us."

"Does he bite? Are the children on your ranch frightened of him?"

His glance swept over her face, as if he searched for a motive for her query. "I suspect he'd bite if someone tried to break into the hacienda, or if a stranger approached one of the children who live on the place with evil intent. But he's not a vicious dog."

"My father had huge animals that listened only to his commands. He delighted in frightening me with them."

"He was a cruel man, Isabella. No decent father would do such a thing to his child. Especially not a little girl who would not have the defenses necessary to protect herself."

"My being a girl was the problem, Rafael. He wanted a son, but had to make do with me. I don't think he ever forgave my mother for birthing a girl child."

He laughed, as though her words amused him greatly. "Didn't he know that he had as much responsibility for that as she? It's surprising your mother did not resent him for his feeling that way."

"I'm sure she did, but she knew better than to accuse him of being unfair."

"She feared him?"

A quick, sidelong glance was his answer, her mouth tightening as if the reply were none of his business.

"And did you fear him, Isabella? Was he cruel to you? Did he strike you? Or was his cruelty directed at your mother?"

"Oh, he was a man who delighted in being in control of his household, most especially my mother. Tell me, what would you call a man who made arrangements for his fourteen-year-old daughter to be betrothed to a man almost thirty years older than she? I feared Juan Garcia, for his eyes were cruel and he looked at me in a manner that made me shiver with dread. Yet I feared my father even more and thought his hatred of me was the reason for my betrothal. That and the fact that Juan Garcia was willing to give him a large amount of money for my hand in marriage. Apparently he knew that my father had willed me his property and he's a greedy man."

"Is that what your father's will said? That you were to inherit? Surely it was read as soon as he died, and the convent would have been notified. Unless he left money for your keep there until you were of age."

She shrugged her shoulders. "There was money for that purpose, and Mother Superior agreed that I should wait to be married. But she hadn't heard any more until Señor Garcia wrote and told the Mother Superior that he would be coming to get me as soon as I reached eighteen years of age, according to the betrothal agreement, and would arrive very soon."

She shuddered in his arms and he tightened his grip. "I wasn't looking forward to his arrival," she said, her voice calm, but underlaid with a desperation he could not have missed.

His voice deepened as if anger had made it harsh. "It seems I arrived just in time, then. For I'd have had to seek you out if his arrival had been any sooner. If he had taken you away, I fear I wouldn't have been a patient man. I don't know why I was so set on having you, Isabella, but I'd have followed wherever the trail took me to find you, so strong was my need to possess you. And all for a woman I hadn't even seen, who lived in my mind only as others had described her."

He laughed, almost as if he mocked his own words, and yet his eyes were intent, his face almost grim as he spoke his mind, and in so doing, revealed the strength of his determination. "I was resolved to have you, Isabella, most especially after I'd caught sight of you. No matter the circumstances, Juan Garcia never stood a chance at marriage with you. I'd have killed him first had he tried to thwart my intentions."

"You sound like a cruel man, Rafael," she said, speaking his name quietly, as though it tasted strangely on her tongue.

"Not cruel, just determined. A man like Garcia does not deserve you. For many reasons, he wouldn't be a good husband."

"And you, Rafael? Do you deserve me?"

He was silent, and then his hand moved to touch her chin and he turned her head to one side, the better to speak more directly to her. "Whether I deserve you or not is of little matter to me right now. Just know that I will not be cruel to you, nor will I cause you pain in any way, not by word or deed, Isabella. We may not always agree, but you will find that my position as your husband, though one of authority, will not be overly binding. You will make your own choices in our marriage, unless they are markedly opposed to my rules."

She shot him a look of challenge. "Rules? I'm to be subjected to a set of rules?"

"Everyone is obliged to obey certain rules in marriage, sweetheart. Have you heard the term 'love, honor and obey'?"

She nodded. "I've never been able to understand how speaking those words can possibly force a woman to feel love for a man. I'd think such a feeling must grow with time and be nurtured by his behavior.

"Tell me, Rafael McKenzie, what rules will govern your behavior?" she asked. "Or as a man, are you not obliged to answer to anyone but yourself?"

"I will pledge myself to protect you against any harm, to tend to your needs, to fulfill your desires to the best of my capabilities and above all else to give you a home and family that will provide for you a shelter from the world around us."

She heard his words, wondering if they were spontaneous, or if he had thought long and hard about what his attitudes toward marriage should be when the time came for him to take a wife. Almost as if he had pledged to himself his responsibilities, he spoke them aloud to her now and his voice rang with heartfelt assurance.

"You really mean that, don't you?" Not a question but a recognition of his promises to her, she spoke quietly, softly, and her mind felt an easing of the troubled waters she had found herself wading through during the past days.

"I really mean it. Believe that I do not make promises lightly, but only after much thought and with due consideration as to my ability to perform as I have said."

She found herself nestling back against him, forming herself to his powerful body, as though he offered a sanctuary for her, a resting place where she would be safe and secure.

A barking dog roused her from the depths of her contemplation, and she sat upright, looking ahead eagerly, yet with a reticence that was reflected in the shivers that swept her frame. Ahead of them rose the lines of a hacienda such as she had never seen. Built of sandstone, blending into its surroundings as though it had grown there over a period of time, it was large, with wings both right and left of the main portion of the house. A wall kept it separate from the rest of the homestead, with several gates that led off into gardens and toward the barns and stables. Flowers bloomed in wide beds beneath the windows and a mellow glow gleamed from the wide windows at the front of the house.

"This is the home of Simon McKenzie, my father," Rafael said quietly, a sense of pride covering his words, his tone almost reverent. That he loved his home and the man who waited inside was apparent to any who might listen.

Ahead of them, a woman stood in the doorway, her hands buried in a glistening white apron, her smile wide as she moved forward, opening the screen door and stepping out onto a veranda. Behind her came three other women, two of them but girls, probably not yet twenty, the third a young woman who seemed to bear an arrogant image, and who looked at Isabella with a disdainful glance.

Rafael mentioned her first with simple words. "The taller one is Lucia, the woman of whom I spoke earlier," he whispered in her ear. "The others are maids, and—"

He ceased his explanations abruptly as the white-aproned woman smiled broadly.

"Maria." His simple speaking of her name brought life to the older woman's face and she stepped onto the path toward the group of men whose horses milled just beyond the gate. Rafael's voice was tender, his eyes shimmering with emotion as he dismounted from his horse and lifted Isabella to his side, then walked quickly forward to where the woman awaited them.

"Maria." He spoke her name again, and bent his head to press his lips against one cheek, then the other, the gesture obviously pleasing to its recipient.

"Señor. Rafael." She spoke his title, then his name, the latter in a soft, revealing fashion. There was obviously much caring between these two, Isabella decided, and that bode well for Rafael's ability to care for his wife in the same manner.

"This is my bride, Maria. My Isabella." His voice was quiet, filled with dignity, as if he were proud of his acquisition, as though Isabella were a prize package he valued highly. His arm drew her to stand before him, where she was the focal point of all the females gathered before her. "We will be married as soon as possible."

"Ah, yes." Maria's gaze swept over Isabella, almost as if she recognized her, as though her appearance was not a surprise. "This is the one, Rafael. I knew you would not give up until you found her."

Pleasure filled the words as Maria gazed her fill, her eyes intent on Isabella's face and form.

"I tend to be a stubborn man, Maria. You know that."

"Your persistence paid off, my son. She will be a proud mistress for your home."

Isabella felt as though she were on display, and indeed, she was, for the four women before her had taken note of every inch of her, their eyes touching on her hair, her face, the length of her body, and then to her bare feet. She wished she might sink to the ground and pull her dress down over the indignity of being without shoes, but Rafael's pride in her would not allow her to falter. She stiffened her shoulders and smiled, a small but sincere movement of her lips that gave notice of her appreciation for the welcome allotted her.

The woman Rafael had designated as Lucia was silent, although Isabella had thought she would greet Rafael with affection. She was a distant cousin, true, her looks more refined than the two maids beside her. Yet she stood back and observed, for there was no other word for the woman's dark glances as she ignored Rafael and turned a dismissive look in Isabella's direction. Her proud head lifted, her dark hair swung behind her shoulders and she tilted her chin in an arrogant gesture.

"So this is to be the favored one, Rafael? This child you have brought to Diamond Ranch will be fit to do the work of a woman here? And is this what you took so long to find? She is nothing but a ragged child, certainly not a woman to fill the role as mistress of this house."

With a sniff of disdain and a look of dismissal, she turned and retreated into the house, and Rafael uttered a sound that sounded like a curse word to Isabella. "She has chosen her path, Maria. I will not have her here," he said, his voice a low tone that reverberated with anger.

Isabella touched his hand, drawing his attention to her, and smiled at him, begging him silently to ignore the woman's behavior. Being usurped as temporary mistress of the hacienda apparently did not sit well with Lucia, and Isabella feared that Rafael's anger would further cause problems.

Beside her, he took her hand, squeezing it gently as if he wanted to gain her full attention and then he spoke, casting an appreciative look her way. "Enough of Lucia and her childish ways. I fear that Isabella is very weary, Maria. Perhaps Elena or Delores will take her to a room where she might wash and refresh herself. We haven't had access to such things as a basin and towels for two days.

Isabella has been uncomplaining, but I know she would like to freshen up a bit."

The two younger girls might have been sisters, Isabella thought, so similar were they. Small in stature, with dark hair and flashing eyes, their appearance was pleasing and their smiles welcoming. Giggling a bit, they approached her and one took her arm in a loose grip as, together, they led her into the house. She looked back at Rafael, taken aback by the quick assumption of her care by the maids, but he only smiled and lifted a hand to her, as if releasing her to their able hands.

The room she was shown to was large, with a cool breeze blowing past the white curtains at the window. A wide bed was made up with a colorful quilt atop it, a colorful tapestry hung on one wall and a dressing table sat against another, a mirror over it. The warmth of color and comfort welcomed her within its walls as one of the girls ran from the room and the other turned Isabella toward a chair near the bed.

"Let me help you take off your clothing, and Delores and I will make you a small bath. Do you have fresh clothing with you?"

"Rafael…" An ineffectual motion of her hand toward the door turned Elena in that direction, and with a smile, she left the room. Within a minute, the other girl, Delores, as Elena had called her, came back in with a large pitcher of steaming water. She went to the dry sink across the room, pulling a screen in place before it, and then proceeded to ready the hot water in a basin, with towels and cloths for bathing set upon a low stool.

"I'll help you undress," she said, her speech a bit of Spanish and English combined, more than understandable to Isabella, who had been raised in a mixed culture. Delores towed the weary traveler behind the screen and in moments had shed her of the dress she wore and settled her on a stool. "Let me wash you."

It was not an offer but an announcement of intent, and Isabella found herself the subject of a bathing such as she'd not enjoyed in her life. To have some other person wield a warm cloth over her face, to have that same woman add soap to the soft fabric and soothe it over her arms, neck and shoulders was a luxury she basked in.

Her chemise was on the floor, and Isabella was not quite certain how it had been shed so easily, but did not quibble, for the sensation of being pampered and catered to was one she found most enjoyable.

The dust of the road was removed quickly and within minutes, Elena was back in the room, the paper-wrapped bundle that held Isabella's other new dress in one hand, a voluminous white garment in the other.

"The señor wishes you to be dressed in the sleeping gown. He says that tomorrow is soon enough to wear your own clothing, and sent this in for you to put on." With giggles and whispers she did not understand, the two girls dressed Isabella in the gown, a confection of muslin and lace, with smocking and tiny flowers decorating the bodice and a full-length skirt that fell to the floor in yards of fabric. She was well-covered, she decided, the material soft against her aching body.

But it seemed the best was yet to come, for a knock at the door and the opening of the portal revealed Maria, her full face wearing a broad smile, bearing a tray with steaming dishes displayed thereupon.

"Señor Rafael will join you for your supper in a few minutes," the older woman said, her tone implying that Señor Rafael was not complying to the dictates of good behavior. Her words echoed that as she placed the tray on a table near the bed and turned back to Isabella.

"He will leave the door open while he is in this room with you, and he will sit on a chair across the table from you. I have told him his behavior is incorrect, but he *laughed* at me." Her emphasis on his reaction said much for Maria's opinion of the doings Rafael had set into place.

Isabella sat on the edge of the bed, wondering if it would be terribly impolite to forego the meal and just lie down on the sparkling linens. But she was given no choice, for Rafael came in the door, nodded briefly at the two girls, who scampered between screen and doorway, gathering up towels and basin and the ewer, now empty of hot water. They made their departure silently, but Isabella could hear their whispering as they went down the hallway.

Maria looked at Rafael with obvious disapproval and pushed a straight chair for his use next to the table. "I will leave the door open," she said shortly, and turned to leave the room.

"Please, Maria," Isabella said. "Wait for just a moment. I wanted to thank you and the girls for helping me and for bringing me this meal. I'll try not to be so much trouble once I'm rested."

Maria's face lit for a moment with a smug grin. "We are honored to serve you, for you are Rafael's choice and will be the mistress of his house." With a tiny nod of her head, she turned and left the room, leaving the door standing wide.

Rafael looked after her, his mouth twitching in a smile that softened his face, made him seem younger, more approachable. And then he turned and pulled his chair next to the bed, so that he was but inches from Isabella, instead of across the table, as Maria had planned.

He stood beside the seat and looked down at her, his eyes taking in the length of her hair, hair that Elena had brushed for long minutes and then left to hang down her back, waving as it fell against her gown. His gaze touched the white garment she wore, as though he could see beneath the fabric that covered her and kept the sight of her skin from him.

"The gown is heavier than I'd thought," he said, looking just a bit displeased, but Isabella was too tired to care about his moods tonight.

"Sit if you're going to," she said, lifting her gaze to his, all of her strength concentrated now on staying upright, as she picked up a fork and offered another to Rafael, then looked down at the food before her.

"I'm not very hungry, but I won't hurt Maria's feeling by not eating. I'm sure she went to a great deal of trouble to prepare this for us."

Rafael did not move, but stood, his trousers touching her gown, the warmth from his body reaching out to hers through the layers of fabric between their legs. Then, in a movement she had not expected, he knelt beside her, taking her hand in his and placing the forks she'd held onto the tray.

His mouth touched her hand, his lips brushing over her fingers and across the narrow expanse of her wrist. "We will eat our first meal together tonight in my house," he said, as if it were a ceremony of sorts and he would make her aware of its importance. "Maria wanted it to take place in the dining room, but I knew you were too weary for a formal meal...so, this." He waved his hand at the tray, telling her that the supper they would share was at his bidding.

"I'm not dressed to be in your presence, and we're in a bedroom together. This isn't proper." She had to make a protest, small as it was, but as if he understood her need to make noises about propriety, he only smiled and dipped his head, then brushed his lips across her forehead.

"You're not listening to me," she said more forcefully, gritting her teeth at his familiar behavior.

He only smiled and settled in the chair beside her. "We've spent two full days and nights on a horse and in a very small tent together," he said. "I think we have traveled far beyond the boundaries of proper behavior. I will treat you with respect and honor, as my bride, but I will not let you forget who held you in his arms over the last two days and whose warmth kept you safe during the night hours."

"I would not like Maria to think that you had become…too familiar with me, Rafael. She would look at me with eyes that did not give me respect if she thought you had not treated me as you should."

He laughed, a sound that denied her words. "Maria knows that I am a man of honor, Isabella. She does not suppose for a moment that we have been as husband and wife on this journey. And now, since I have acted the gentleman with you until this day, I will tell you that I am in my own home and will do as I please."

There was no reasoning with the man, Isabella realized. He was arrogant and determined, a combination she was ill-equipped to deal with tonight. Bearing that in mind, she brushed the skirt of her gown down smoothly and picked up the cover that hid her meal from view.

A blend of vegetables and meat sat in the earthenware bowl, steaming and giving forth an aroma that pleased her. Another container, made of heavy pottery, revealed the presence of warmed tortillas and a third contained tomato salsa. Cheese had been coarsely shredded and filled a bowl almost to overflowing, completing the appetizing meal. Tall glasses of water lured her and she lifted one to her mouth, savoring the simple, clean taste of water.

"Would you like wine?" Rafael watched her, leaning back in his chair, his gaze on her hands, the movement of her throat as she swallowed. He picked up a tortilla and covered it generously with the mixture provided, then ladled cheese on before he rolled it over on itself and lifted it to his mouth.

"Water will do well," she said, and indeed, she could not have asked for more than the cool water provided, for she felt refreshed and more able to put forth the effort to serve herself and eat the food before her.

The tortillas were hearty, the beef and vegetables tasty, peppers and onions blended in a savory mixture. She found she could not eat as much as was usual for her, for her eyes were heavy and would not cooperate with her need to be wakeful. She feared falling asleep with food in her mouth, for the day had been wearying and the full effect of her travels weighed heavily on her, now that she had settled in one place and begun to relax.

"You look as though you're doing your best to stay awake and not quite able to manage it," Rafael said, smiling at her. Then at her look of confusion, he laughed and took the remaining bit of tortilla from her hand and put it on her plate. "I think you've had enough, sweetheart. I've never had a woman fall asleep on me before when I was trying to woo her over supper, but I suppose there are mitigating circumstances tonight. Let me help you into bed."

She stood, watching him as he pulled back the quilt and sheet and then fluffed the pillows before turning back to her, one hand outstretched. "Maria won't like this," she said defensively. "She'll think I'm trying to—"

"Nothing of the sort," he said bluntly, breaking into her murmuring. "I'm not seducing you, nor are you enticing me, though you could perform that deed with just the twitch of an eyebrow." His grin was easy, as if he feared giving her reason to doubt his integrity. "If I could withstand temptation in that tiny tent with you in my arms, this should prove to be no great feat."

He lifted the table and set it aside, then lifted her glass and offered it to her once more. She took it gratefully and drank deeply before she handed it back. "Thank you." Her voice was muffled by a yawn as she turned and knelt on the mattress and then eased herself to lie on the soft bed, pulling the gown down circumspectly to cover her legs. She heard him then, the sound he emitted almost a groan, and she turned quickly to search his face.

His lips were taut, thinned as if he held back words he thought better of, and his eyes roamed over her with a heated interest that she recognized from several occasions on their journey. He lifted the sheet and pulled it up to cover her and she tugged it up above her breasts, holding it there like a shield, much to his apparent amusement, for he laughed again, bending to touch his lips to her forehead.

"You are thinking as would a child, Isabella, holding that sheet tightly, lest I peek beneath it. And so I shall give you the kiss I would give to a young sister, not the touch of my mouth against yours that I would prefer.

"One word of warning, sweetheart, and this is not meant as a threat, but a promise. Should I want to touch your body, that bit of cotton would not keep me away. Know that the day will come when I do not allow a mere sheet to come between us. And on that day, you will give me your body and accept mine."

She looked up at him, at the ruddy line that delineated his cheekbone and jaw, the simmering fire in his gaze, the taut line of his lips, and felt a pang of fear strike her, deep within her, where she had never known such feelings.

"Please, Rafael." What she asked for, what her pleading whisper demanded, she did not know, but apparently he did. For he straightened and brushed a speck of dust from her pillow, then touched her shoulder with his fingertips as his lips formed the words she'd thought he might say aloud.

"Good night."

Her eyes drifted shut as he lifted the tray, blew out the bedside candle and then turned toward the threshold of her room. His body filled the doorway, his head reaching almost to the top of the frame as he stepped out into the hallway. From beneath her eyelids, she watched as he turned back and leveled those dark eyes on her once more—seeming to take on the persona once again of a man on the prowl, the consummate hunter.

For his head lifted, his eyes focused intently on her with a look of possession she could not mistake. He singled her out, then inhaled deeply, as if he scented prey nearby.

CHAPTER EIGHT

THE DOOR WAS OPENED QUIETLY, yet the sound caught Isabella's ear and she turned to face the woman who stood within the portal of her room. Maria was smiling, her arms holding a tray upon which covered dishes were arrayed.

"Are you ready for breakfast?" she asked, approaching the bed.

Isabella swung her legs over the side of the mattress and nodded. "It must be late, Maria. The sun is already high. I should have risen earlier and saved you the trouble of carrying my meal to me."

"Señor Rafael asked us to let you sleep as late as you could," Maria said, depositing the tray on the table by the bed. "He said you've had a long journey and would be feeling the effects for a few days."

Isabella laughed, brushing the hair from her face and peering at the covered dishes displayed before her. "Not true," she said, lifting an earthenware lid, exposing a plate of scrambled eggs. "I'm young enough, and certainly strong enough, to recuperate quickly, I think."

Maria nodded her approval, pouring coffee into a cup and unfolding the napkin for Isabella's use. "The elder Señor McKenzie is awake and has been told of your arrival. Rafael asked that you prepare to meet his father. He will come to fetch you in an hour."

Isabella nodded slowly. "If I may bathe first and ready myself…"

"Of course. I'll send Elena in with hot water. Your dresses are clean. I'll have Delores bring them to you."

The breakfast was hot, the food flavorful, and Isabella ate heartily. A natural reticence held her from questioning the two maids about her circumstances, but she was bursting with curiosity about her where-abouts. The knowledge that Rafael would soon appear filled her with a mixture of dread and a surprising sense of anticipation. She should be angry at him, for her natural inclination was to seek escape from his home…yet she felt safe here, and for just a short while, she wanted to soak up the security of this place.

And yet, it was not to be a peaceful time, this breakfast she anticipated. For Lucia entered the room without warning, closing the door behind her and leaning back against the solid wood.

"So you think to marry Rafael, do you?" she asked, her eyes sparking fire in Isabella's direction.

Silence followed her query as Isabella sought out a reply that would pacify the other woman, yet make her own position clear.

And then she spoke, the words the truth as she saw it. "I had no intention of marrying anyone, señorita, but Rafael chose me to be his wife. I came here with him at his request." *Request?* She bit her tongue at her own choice of words, and then continued.

"If his decision is not to your liking, I fear it will not make a difference to him, for I have found that Rafael McKenzie is a man determined to have his way. He is strong and arrogant and his choice is apparently made. He tells me we will be wed in less than a week."

· "And you think you are a fit woman to be his bride? That you have the knowledge to run his home and make him happy? That you can give him children and the pleasure of begetting them?"

Isabella felt confusion encompass her and she was quiet, thinking for a moment. And then she spoke again, not willing to argue with the other woman, but unable to be silent about her own abilities.

"I am capable of running a house, of cooking and cleaning and raising a garden. I hope I will make Rafael happy in doing all of that. As to what he finds in our marriage bed, and I assume that is what you are speaking of with your talk of *pleasure,* I think that will be up to him. He will find whatever he pleases, and if this marriage takes place, I will be a good wife to him."

"If? You haven't decided whether or not you will marry him? What a fool you are, little nun. He has been the object of women's attention and affection for a long time, for years, and you speak as though he is but a common man, one you can take or leave, as it suits you."

"I think you are interfering in something that is

none of your business," Isabella said softly, wishing fervently that she could somehow cause Lucia to vanish from her sight.

"You speak bravely for a child," Lucia said bitterly. "And we shall see what the outcome of your plan will be."

"I have no plan, only what Rafael has told me would come to pass."

Lucia shot her another look of hatred and opened the door, slipping from the room silently.

Isabella walked to the window, fearful suddenly of the ill feeling of the woman who had spoken so harshly. If it were not for the knowledge that she was safe from Juan Garcia, she might feel more inclined to be angry with Rafael, for as she'd said, he was arrogant and determined to have his own way.

And foremost in her mind was the knowledge that it was not her own choice to have been brought to this place. A confusion such as she had never known reigned in her thoughts, and only the words spoken by Maria, and the promised arrival of Rafael within the hour, gave her the impetus to bathe and dress for the day.

He had left her last night while she was abed, dressed in the lacy white gown, and her natural sense of modesty rebelled at that memory. He'd made himself at home in her room, her bedroom, and such was not the act of a gentleman. It took little to work up a surge of anger, directed at him as he entered the room.

She was once more at the window, garbed in the second of her new dresses, her fingers busy with the business of braiding her hair, when she heard him behind her. His footsteps across the floor announced his arrival, and she turned to face him. At first glance, he appeared worried and she wondered if his father had become more ill. But then his eyes met hers and she noted instead a hesitation about him as he drew closer.

He spoke without hesitation. "You are trembling, Isabella. Who has upset you?"

She shook her head. "I only spoke for a few minutes with Lucia. She makes it plain that I don't belong here. I think she would like to take my place in this wedding you have planned." Never had she been so blunt, so ready to speak poorly of another, but her memory of Lucia's words and the woman's opinion of Isabella's worthiness had cut deep, leaving an open sore upon her spirit.

"She has no business coming in this room. I will speak to her."

Isabella turned from him. "You cannot erase the words she has already spoken, Rafael. And perhaps she is right, for I don't pretend to be the perfect candidate for the position of your wife."

Authority resounded in his words. "I will be the judge of that. I'll hear no more of this talk. If Lucia has any more to say, she will be seeking an escort to her father's house."

His voice was dark with anger, and yet, Isabella heard a note of some other concern as he spoke and she turned back to look at him. He was frowning, and his face seemed strained as though he had a worry, apart from Lucia and her troublemaking.

Isabella reached for his hand and held his fingers against her palm. "What is it, Rafael? Is there something wrong?" And such a foolish question, she thought, from a woman who was in the midst of a situation where nothing seemed to be right.

He hesitated as if loath to speak, and then nodded. "You have been a lady through all that has come to pass. I cannot fault you in any way, and I should be trying to smooth your path. Yet I am here to ask a boon of you, Isabella." He halted, only a small distance between them, and his mouth was taut.

She only watched him, stunned for a moment at the thought that he should feel she owed him anything, let alone a favor of sorts. She had been captured, kidnapped and held hostage in his home. Now he had the unmitigated gall to ask a boon of her.

Her lips tightened in a pout, and she tilted her chin defiantly. "I owe you nothing," she told him, tossing the braid over her shoulder to hang down her back.

His own mouth thinned as his gaze passed over her form, and his tone was angry and arrogant as he taunted her. "Nothing? Hah! Perhaps your life? Or would you consider it a pleasing existence to be married to Juan Garcia? Would he be your choice?"

"I was given no choice, and it seems that it is too late to make such an offer."

"You came with me, Isabella. Don't deny that you

wanted to flee the convent and the man who would soon be claiming you as his bride."

She felt a surge of anger overtake her and stepped closer, her chin tilting upward, their bodies almost touching. "Don't place any fault on me for being here. Perhaps I would have been allowed to take vows as a Sister of Charity had I stayed at the convent. That might have been a better choice for me than either you or Señor Garcia. And there is no promise that he would have found me there and taken me to be his wife."

His laughter was harsh and she felt its sting. "You have inherited your father's land, Isabella. That alone is enough to bring Garcia to your side. I'll warrant he is even now in pursuit of you. If not in the next few days, then by next week he will have heard of your disappearance and will be on your trail."

She felt a pang of fear at the thought of the older man's plans for her life. "Perhaps I should return to the convent and continue on with my plans to become one of the sisters there. It is a divine calling, one I can seek out and devote my life to."

But it seemed that Rafael had other ideas, for he laughed and denied her claim. "There are other things in life for a woman than to pray and work for the poor. As my wife you will be permitted to give of my wealth to the church and do all the good works you please. Our parish has many needs, and if your hands are willing, you will be welcomed there."

He reached for her, his hands at her shoulders,

gripping her, pulling her close, and she stiffened, becoming rigid in his embrace. "You expect too much of me, Rafael. I am not your wife, nor have I promised to marry you. You have no right to touch me, no right to expect favors of me."

His eyes were kind now as she chanced a glance upward, his mouth softer as if it prepared to touch her own. "Only the rights that I assume as mine," he said. "You tempt me, Isabella, with your spark, your temper, your sharp words and the knowledge that beneath that dress is the form of the woman I will own as my wife."

She jerked in his grasp, but to no avail, for his strength was the greater and he would not relent. "You would bruise me, Rafael? Leave your marks upon my skin?"

His laugh was mocking. "I would leave marks you know nothing of, my innocent virgin wife. But I would not cause you pain willingly, lest you turn your face from me in fright."

"I will not be innocent for long if you have your way," she said sharply.

He smiled, and she felt a shiver of apprehension slide the length of her spine. His words gave her reason for her fear, for he leaned close and whispered against her ear, speaking of that which was foreign to her. "If I take you to my bed, or turn you and lie with you on your own mattress, you will find your innocence to be an encumbrance, a thing easily shed, Isabella. For your journey from bride to wife is one that will bring you pleasure. Trust me, sweetheart."

His breath against her ear, the warmth of his body pressing against hers, the strength of his arms as he held her—it was more than she could fight, for she found herself yearning to lean into him, to allow her weight to be upheld by his body. It would be simpler to accede to his urging for a favor, she decided, than to fight with her own inclination to bend to his physical appeal.

"What favor did you need of me, Rafael?"

He eyed her with surprise apparent in his demeanor. "You amaze me, Isabella. One minute you are arguing with me and denying your debt to me, the next you capitulate readily to my begging a boon of you. I don't understand your dithering with me. Is it so difficult to make yourself agreeable? Or is it your desire to spend our days in conflict?"

She felt a blush climb her cheeks as he so easily punctured her attempt at an argument, as his reasonable query struck home, making her rue her words of strife. "I am out of sorts, Rafael," she confessed. "I'm in a strange place, with a man who is making demands of me, and my heart is yearning for the calm and peace of the convent. The sisters were kind to me, and demanded little of me, only that I do my share of the tasks assigned to me." She inhaled as she halted in her listing of the dilemma she faced.

"Now, I've acceded to your request for a favor. I am truly trying to be agreeable. What is it you want of me?"

"Only that you go with me this morning to meet my father. He is in his room, unable to walk to the table for breakfast. He asks that we join him in breaking his fast. Will you do this for me, and try to be kind to him?"

"I am not a mean person, Rafael. I have no reason to be hateful to your father. I am sure he has nothing to do with my being here in your house."

His smile was quick, his eyes seemed to light with a secret knowledge she could not read, and yet he was all that was agreeable as he nodded, whether in agreement with her words or merely a gesture of courtesy.

"Will you go with me now? He awaits us."

She gathered herself, smoothing the lines of anger she knew still remained on her face, brushing back her hair and straightening her skirts as she followed him to the door. "I am not hungry, I fear, Rafael. I have already eaten. If you had warned me, I would have waited, but Maria brought me a tray over an hour ago."

"Merely drink a cup of coffee with my father, and speak with him while he sips his tea. He is not a demanding man, and will give you the courtesy due a lady in his home."

She followed him through the doorway, down the corridor and across a bisecting hallway to where a large set of double doors announced the presence of the master's suite. Rafael rapped twice on the door, and then opened it quietly, stepping inside and reaching to draw her behind himself. His fingers were firm on hers, and she did not resist his strength, but walked beside him now, toward the white-haired man who sat in a chair by the window. Before him was a small table on which a tray rested, food dishes and a small teapot at his fingertips. He glanced up, his eyes sharp and piercing, his gaze black, yet seeming to soften as he caught sight of Isabella. Raising one hand, he beckoned to her.

"Come, girl. Sit with me. I would know about you." He looked at Rafael quickly. "If you have business elsewhere, you needn't stay." Even seated, he exuded strength that seemed to add to his stature. Thus would Rafael look in another thirty or forty years, Isabella thought, admiring the older man's harsh, yet somehow beautiful features.

Rafael spoke quietly then. "I'm here to introduce you to Isabella Montgomery, father. She is to be my bride." Turning to Isabella, he bowed his head in a gesture of respect. "This is my father, Simon McKenzie."

"The servants have already told me of your return, and the woman who accompanied you here. She is not what I expected."

Isabella inhaled sharply. She had not thought to be rejected out of hand in such a way, and her tender pride ached from his words. Not that she was hoping for an all-inclusive welcome, but at least a warm word or two would not have gone amiss.

"Don't look so hurt, child," the elderly man said quietly. "There is no insult intended. I thought my son was bringing me yet another woman more like those he has dallied with in the past, perhaps a female whose only worth is measured by her beauty and the pleasure she offers to a man.

"Blame yourself, Rafael, if you don't like my words. I only meant that she is altogether different than your usual choice of female. Indeed, she seems more of a lady than any woman you have escorted up until now. I am pleased with her." His eyes shifted to Isabella and he asked his question without apology.

"Are you a lady, Isabella? Do you come from a good background, and are you prepared to marry my son?"

She was stunned, her mouth opening and then closing as if she thought better of the reply that had formed on her lips. Rafael was silent, his father intent now on pouring tea from the teapot into his cup. He glanced up at Isabella. "Will you have tea with me?"

She nodded. The coffee was stronger than any she'd tasted, and tea would be welcome. "Thank you, señor," she whispered, finding her voice to have vanished. She cleared her throat.

"I am a lady, sir. My family is of good stock, and I have been living in a convent for several years, learning the ways of a woman, cleaning, sewing and working as a fledgling nun, for I had hoped of late to make it my life's calling." She looked at Rafael and her mouth tightened.

"Until your son came and took me from the convent, I had hoped to live there for the rest of my life if it were at all possible."

"You wanted to be one of the sisters?" His tone was incredulous, and his smile mocked her calling.

"I would make a most suitable nun, sir. The Sisters of Charity is a fine group of women, all of them living a good life, tending to the poor of the surrounding countryside and helping wherever they can."

"And that is a suitable calling for a woman such as yourself?" He smiled at her, his lips softening as he swept his gaze over her length, lingering on the fine lines of her face, the slender form of her body.

"I would be a good nun," she said quietly. "I have no desire to be a wife to any man. My father promised me to a man who is far too old for me. I have heard that man—Juan Garcia—is cruel and that women fear him. Why my father pledged me to him remains a mystery to me."

Simon's eyes darkened with a hint of anger as he spoke. "Money. Land. The two most important things to be gained from such a contract," he said bluntly. "Garcia would gain your inheritance, your father would gain a substantial amount of money for your hand. Such things are done every day."

She wilted, her shoulders slumping as she stood before him. "I have often wished I were a man, señor. But never as much as I do now. As a woman I have little choice in my future, and I resent the fact that I must forever do as a man tells me."

"Even if that man is my son?" He watched her closely. "He would make you a good husband, and his temperament is not cruel. He would provide you with a home to be proud of, give you children, and he would be faithful to you. What more can a woman ask of life?"

She lifted her chin and met his gaze forthrightly.

"A choice, señor. A choice of which man she will marry. A choice of where she will live and who will father her children. Thus far, I have not been allowed to choose even the color of my clothing. Your son picked this out for me in a general store two days ago. I prefer a dress made in the fashion of a habit such as the nuns wore, but I was not given a choice."

He smiled, this time with a look of utmost satisfaction. "I think you will be a fine addition to my home, Isabella. I sent my son to find a wife. I believe my words were to find a bonnie wee lassie, and he has done that."

Isabella heard the rough burr in his speech and was charmed by the words he spoke.

"How is it you came to be here?" she asked. "Your speech tells me your background was not in this area."

"Aye, I'm an immigrant, born in Scotland, and blessed by my marriage to my bride, whose parents left her Diamond Ranch. Our circumstances were much as yours, for she was claimed as my bride, as you were by Rafael. Blessedly, we were happy together."

"I have already told her that, Father." Rafael spoke quietly, but with authority as he set his gaze on the woman he had chosen to marry. "I ask now that you approve my choice and allow me to make the arrangements for our wedding."

The white head nodded slowly, and a smile swept over the elderly man's face. "You have chosen well, my son. She is beautiful, and has a quick tongue. I think she will not allow you to run roughshod over her, and that is good. I like a woman with spirit." He smiled kindly at Isabella.

"I have not agreed to marry your son, señor. He has captured me and brought me here unwillingly. This isn't a good beginning for a marriage, to my way of thinking."

"Ah, but it is a common enough thing, done many times in the past," Rafael's father said with a smile. "My own bride came here as a captive, from a family who would have sold her against her will. A very similar arrangement to the one Rafael has brought into being."

"And was she happy with you, sir?" Isabella asked quickly.

His eyes closed for a moment, and then fixed on her warmly. "We had almost forty years together, and our happiness was complete. Only her death separated us, for we spent our days and nights here in this house, until the morning she was carried up the hill to the graveyard just two years ago."

"I am sorry for your loss, señor," Isabella said, her words sincere, for she felt the pain he projected. The man had loved and lost, and grieved yet.

"It will not be long before I join her. For my days are numbered, and my only wish is that I see my son settled in a good marriage, and my hacienda in good hands." He caught his breath, and she recognized that he seemed to have difficulty in speaking, for he faltered, his words becoming faint.

"You are tiring, sir," she said quietly. "I will not

cause you to be weary. Let me drink my tea and then be excused from your presence." She sipped from the cup she held and met his gaze again. "I am pleased to have met you, Señor McKenzie. I have been well treated in your home."

He nodded, words obviously too hard to come by, for he gasped once as he would have spoken. Rafael stepped to his father's side and laid a hand on his shoulder. "You must rest now, sir. We will come another time."

With a movement of his head, he called Isabella to his side and she obeyed, placing her cup on the tray and touching the withered hand that reached for hers. It was thin, chilled as if the blood did not run well through his veins, and she found a smile for him, even though her tears were not far from being shed. Her head dipped and she touched her lips to the shriveled flesh, obeying her instinct to give him her allegiance.

Then, turning away, she grasped Rafael's hand as if it were a lifeline and she a drowning sailor. He took it in his other palm and wrapped his left arm around her waist, holding her fast, her fingers tight within his own, her waist encircled by his warmth. Leading her to the door, he opened it, and they stepped into the corridor beyond, where she halted, hearing the click of the latch behind her.

Her tears would not be denied any longer and they fell, hot and thick, down her cheeks. Without speaking, Rafael turned her into his arms and held her head against his chest. She did not think to argue or dispute his right to do such a thing, for her heart was rent with pain as she thought of the man who suffered within the walls of the room they had just left.

"He will not live long, will he?" she asked, holding back the sobs that had fought for release.

"No. He has but a few weeks left, days perhaps," Rafael said softly. "He knows he will not be long with us, Isabella, and he has accepted it. He told you what he wants, if you remember."

"Yes. I know. He wants a marriage for you."

"Do you begin to understand why I have pushed you so hard for your cooperation?"

She nodded, tilting her chin up, holding her head high, even as the tears began to dry on her face. "I am so sorry, Rafael. Losing a father is cruel, and when he is such a good man, and so well loved, it is even more harsh.

"I did not grieve when my father died, but I can grieve for your sake, Rafael," she said. "I would not wish your father to die and leave you alone, and when he is gone, I will share your tears."

CHAPTER NINE

THE DAY WAS SPENT within the walls of the hacienda, for the courtyard was almost a part of the house itself, and Isabella found herself there for most of the morning. A wooden bench sat beside a fountain, and she caught a breeze there, the cooling of the water making the warmth of the sun a pleasant thing. Flowers bloomed around the fountain and for a while she knelt barefoot in their midst, pulling errant weeds from the soil, then removing the withered blossoms and gathering the pile of refuse near the bench.

"You've been busy," Rafael said quietly, approaching her as the sun began to slide beyond the earthen walls on the west side of the hacienda. He bent and gathered up the litter she'd accumulated, a handy basket which had been tucked behind the wall holding it easily.

"I looked for a container to use, but didn't find one," she told him. "I enjoy working in the flowers. I spent many hours in the garden at the convent."

"I think you spent more time with a hoe or a shovel, sweet," he said, lifting her hands and turning them to his view. For not only did she wear the calluses earned by scrubbing floors and heavy pots and pans, but her palms were hardened by the work she had done on a daily basis in the gardens.

She curled her fingers, hiding the condition of her hands, and her cheeks felt hot as she suffered the embarrassment of her skin being exposed in such a way. "I am sorry I don't have the hands of a lady," she whispered.

"You have the hands of a woman," he said, lifting them to his lips and kissing her palms, as if he would honor her in this way.

"I know how to work. I can scrub and scour in the kitchen, and I'm not a stranger to the soil in a garden."

"You will be pampered in this house," Rafael said firmly. "We have those who earn their living by scouring and scrubbing in the kitchen, those who work in the gardens and grow calluses on their palms. You will not be one of them."

She looked up at him proudly, her head lifted high. "I am not ashamed of the marks of work I wear. I am strong and have earned my way, Rafael."

"You need only be the lady of the house here, Isabella. I don't expect you to do the work of a servant."

"I value being in the garden, caring for the flowers and picking the vegetables," she said. "Don't keep me from doing those things I have enjoyed in the past."

His smile was quick and bright, as if the sun shone on her suddenly. "All right. You may do as you wish," he said, modifying his stance, as if he would bend to her. "I want you to be happy here, but I don't want you to overwork as you did at the convent. If caring for flowers and picking beans makes you happy, then so be it. Just don't think you must do these things in order to earn your way."

"And how will I earn my way while I am here?" she asked.

"By smiling at me and pleasing me in all things."

"That may be more difficult for me than digging potatoes," she told him. "I can smile, but I must have a reason, and I'm not sure I know how to please you."

"When the priest asks you to repeat your vows in the chapel, it will please me if you do as he says," Rafael said simply. "If you promise to honor and obey me and be a good wife, I will be happy."

"I fear I've never been very good at obeying, Rafael," she said with a grin. "I even had a hard time at the convent sometimes, when the tasks were harsh and I was weary. *If* I marry you, I will do as you ask. But you must give me time to decide if I will wed you."

"Time is one thing we have little of, my sweet. My father must see me married before he dies. I have promised it." He looked down at her feet and humor tugged at his lips. "We will take you to town for a pair of decent shoes, Isabella. You need something to cover your feet."

"My slippers are worn through," she whispered, lifting her feet, hiding them beneath the hem of her skirt.

"It is my responsibility to provide you with the necessities now. We'll make the trip into the general store and find shoes for you as soon as it is possible."

She nodded, rising from the bench where she sat, and turned from him, recognizing that the window she faced was that of his father's room. Beyond the opening, she saw a faint shadow, knew it to be the elderly man who had greeted her earlier in the day and forced a smile to her lips. She would not frown in his presence, but show her respect to the man.

"My father watches you from his room," Rafael said. "He told me he had been keeping an eye on you while you worked out here by yourself."

"I was safe, wasn't I?" she asked.

"Yes, but he found pleasure in keeping an eye on you. He told me you were a beautiful woman and fit to grace this house. He watched you pulling weeds, and said you seemed familiar with the posture of being on your knees."

She lifted her brows high. "I should be. I spent hours on end in prayers in the convent."

"And this is the life you thought you would prefer to marriage?" he asked.

"Preferable to being the wife of Juan Garcia," she said swiftly. "Beyond that, I cannot say."

He grasped her hand and pulled her closer to himself, holding her only by her fingers, not embracing her, but keeping her near him. His head bent and he set his lips to hers, a soft kiss of promise, with no demands upon her but that she submit to his caress.

She stood quietly, unwilling to return the pressure of his mouth, but acquiescent to his touch.

"Do you know how to kiss a man, Isabella?" he asked, his breath sweet against her lips.

She shook her head. "I have never touched another man but you, Rafael. And then only because you forced me to sit on your lap on the horse, and lie beside you in your tent. And now because you kiss me on my lips as if you had the right."

"I have the right," he announced firmly. "You will marry me in three days' time, in the chapel in the village."

She twisted in his grasp and ducked her head, resting it against his chest. Rafael held her close, inhaling the sweet scent wafting up from her hair, the aroma of woman that seemed so much a part of her. With a smile, he recalled sleeping beside her in the tent, and then corrected himself silently. *She* had slept and he had held her, his arms encircling her through the night, promising himself that he would soon claim her as his wife and thereby have the right to possess her body.

Now he felt impatience rule him, the promise of her in his bed riding him with spurs of lust, and he closed his eyes against the throbbing desire that filled him. His hands swept the length of her back, holding her fast, his chest warmed by the soft curves of her breasts, his thighs taut as they measured the length of hers. She was woman, soft and giving, tender and sweet, and he was filled with an urge so great he felt himself racked with the pain of denial.

"Rafael?" She struggled against his hold and he hushed her, his arms loosening but a little, his head bending low to brush his lips against her throat, pushing the neckline of her dress aside, as he caught a scent of her skin beneath the fabric.

"Hush, hush, my sweet." His voice was guttural, the tones harsh, and he rued his impatience, but his male needs were strong and she was within his grasp. He slid long fingers to her waistline, then lifted his hands until his thumbs rested beneath the heavy weight of her breasts. Her flesh was firm, her breasts full and rounded, and he wondered at the womanly size and shape of her. She was small and slender, all but the curves that designated her as woman, the lines of her bosom that promised sustenance for his sons and daughters, the soft swell of her hips that promised a cradle for their resting place before their time of birth.

His palms slipped farther upward, and he held the weight of her breasts in his palms, feeling the shiver she tried to hide, hearing the gasp of inhaled breath, the jerk of her body as she would have moved apart from him. But he was far stronger than she, and though her muscles were firm, and her strength was more than that of most young women, he outweighed her by a hundred pounds or more, and his own muscular frame had been formed by the hours of riding, throwing his lasso and throwing half-grown steers to the ground.

His back was roped with muscle, his thighs were hard and sinewed, and his strength was well-known to him. But now he battled himself, gauging his touch, mindful that he not use his greater power against her. He must only hold her against his body, his hands careful to cherish the flesh he cradled.

"Please, Rafael..." As though she could not ask for release, but only beg for his sufferance, she spoke his name, and he felt a sense of shame he had not thought to possess wash over him. His hands released her, sliding to her back, where he soothed the long lines of her spine, his fingers firm, brushing with gentle touches. It was not what he wanted, for his masculine urge was to take her to his bedroom and strip from her the clothing she wore. The image that flashed into his mind of soft, tender flesh, of curves and hollows, of slim arms and legs and rounded breasts, made his breath catch in his throat.

"I am sorry, Isabella." His hands fell from her and she swayed against him, offering him the opportunity to once more touch her, this time only to hold her upright, to keep her from settling to the ground.

"Let me sit on the bench," she begged, trembling in his grasp, and he lowered her to the wooden seat and knelt before her there. His hands touched hers, held them gently and securely within his grasp, lifting them to his lips.

"Forgive me, Isabella. I forgot my good intentions. What I want and what I will cause to happen are two different things today. For my wish is to take you to my bed and keep you there until I am sated with your warmth, until my body is emptied into you and I have claimed you as my bride."

He heard the choked sound of denial she uttered, and his only thought was to soothe, to comfort and assure her.

"Hush, sweetheart, and listen to me. I must respect you and recognize you for the virgin bride you will be, and so the cry of my heart will not be answered today." His laugh was low and bittersweet. "Even now, I will guarantee my father is watching and wondering just how low his son will descend into the jaws of lust. And I will not give him the opportunity to berate me for my use of you."

She turned her head, as if she would seek out the sight of the window behind which the elderly Señor McKenzie sat, but Rafael touched her chin and held her before him. "No, don't look. He will know that you are aware of him being there, and I would not have you shamed by his knowledge of my use of your body. He would be angry with me if he thought I had insulted you in these moments together. I have been careful not to expose my hands touching you to his sight, but he is a man who knows me well, and his opinion of me is important."

"Rafael, I am… I think I am afraid of what you will do to me." Marriage to this man loomed as a given, and though she dreaded it, remembering the stories the nuns had told her, she felt a natural curiosity as to his treatment of her. Would he be kind? Would his caresses be welcome and sweet? Or would he change in the darkness and become a man bent on pleasure and the use of her body.

And that seemed to be a foolish thought, for surely he would use her as he wished, and her concerns would not be his. If she could trust in the knowledge of the women who had been her mentors over the past years, there should be no doubt in her mind but that his lust would be poured out upon her youthful self. The sisters had said it would be an initiation, the entrance to her life as a wife, a part of her journey from innocence to knowledge.

"You need not fear me," he said firmly, his hands gentle as they touched her, his fingers spreading over her arm, the other arm circling her waist. "I am not a cruel man, Isabella. I have promised you that I will be kind to you. I want you to be happy here with me, and I would be foolish to cause you pain or sorrow. You must learn this for yourself, for I can talk the whole livelong day and not convince you of my intentions. You will have to marry me with no promise for the future but what I tell you now."

She felt very young, very innocent, and with good reason to fear what lay ahead for her as a bride. Beholding her future was indeed a lesson in trust, as Rafael had said. For surely the sisters' knowledge came from the tales of women who sought refuge at the convent from cruel husbands, wives who bore the scars gained in the marriage bed.

And yet, Rafael held her with arms that offered a promise of pleasure and happiness at his hand.

Doubt filled her mind, for she was hard put to know what was true.

She had never felt so alone in her life. The women of this household could not be expected to offer her any succor, for they were servants—all but the cousin who had cast her looks of disdain, a woman she could certainly not rely upon for aid.

She thought of the day to come when she would dress for her wedding, thought of the chapel, of the vows he would insist she speak, and knew in that moment that she was committed to the future he had deemed proper for her. She would become his wife, bear his children, and she would be there when he buried his father and became the owner of Diamond Ranch.

The knowledge that she had no choice, that she must accept his plan for her, swept over her and she bowed her head in defeat. He was the lesser of two evils, and yet that was an exaggeration, for the future he offered her was far more inviting than the alternative.

She lifted her head, and her eyes met those dark orbs that watched her with a look of almost pity, she thought. A look that might even promise his forbearance, one she must claim as her only refuge. "I will marry you, Rafael. I will no longer fight you or cause you trouble. If you will vow now to be patient with me, I will speak the words in the chapel and become your bride."

He smiled, and she watched for the look of triumph that would surely twist his lips now, the flare of excitement that would surely light his gaze as he bent it upon her. But there was only a gleam of anticipation that lit his eyes, a quick flickering appraisal of her face and form that showed his approval of her.

"Thank you, Isabella. My father will rejoice that there is to be a bride in this house, that his family will continue on in the marriage between us. He is most anxious for me to have sons and daughters to carry on his name, children to take their place here on Diamond Ranch."

She heard the sound of joy in his words, saw the quick triumphant look he cast at the window behind her where surely his father, even now, watched. And she turned herself to the window, lifting her hand in a small wave of acknowledgment to the man who had helped to bring about this marriage.

"Come, we'll go inside now," Rafael said. "It is too hot for you to stay out here for so long a time. I want you in good health for the wedding."

She cast one last look at the window where the elderly man sat in the shadowed room. "I hope your father will find me a good mistress for your home," she said, and heard Rafael's whispered affirmation as they headed for the doorway into the parlor.

Maria stood in the opening and smiled as she welcomed them into the house. "Your father would like to spend some time with Isabella," she told Rafael. "I'll take her to him now."

FROM HIS CHAIR, Rafael's father beckoned Isabella closer. Upon hearing Maria's words, she had responded to the summons. And, trained to obey, she had done as Simon had asked, walking down the hallway to where his door stood open. He awaited her by the window and she looked past him to where she had been, just moments ago, with Rafael, where she had stood, held in his arms, in full sight of the man who faced her now.

"Have you and my son come to an understanding?" Though his voice was frail, his hair white, and his body showed distinct signs of his aging and the illness that wracked his frame, the eyes that gazed at her were sharp and keen, and Isabella felt his strength vibrate between them. Though a tragic sickness had claimed his body, his mind was alive, alert and aware of the doings of his household.

"Yes, señor, we have. I have agreed to be his bride. We are to be married in the chapel soon."

"He tells me it will be in three days, Isabella. Have you agreed to this? Has he notified the priest to meet you there in the village to perform the ceremony then?"

She looked at him, confused by his queries. "He hasn't told me anything but that the marriage will take place. I have only to prepare myself for it."

"And how will you do that, my child?" His mouth curved into a smile, an indulgent look that told her of his pleasure in her words. "Do you have a gown to wear? Have you spoken to Rafael about moving your clothing into his room or perhaps buying more items for you to wear? You'll need a veil and flowers, but I suppose Maria will see to that." His gaze traveled to her feet. "I think you will also need covering for your feet, my dear. Rafael has been negligent, not to provide you with the things you need."

She only nodded, for she was confused by his listing of the requirements she must consider. "Rafael hasn't spoken of where I will be staying, whether in his room or whether I will remain in my own. I have no wedding dress, but I do have two new dresses he bought for me while we traveled here.

"Perhaps Maria will tend to flowers for me or I may be able to find a suitable assortment in the garden. There are many planted around the fountain that would make up a pleasing arrangement."

He smiled at her, and she was struck by the acceptance in his gaze, as if he already considered her a part of his household, that the wedding would be only a formality, that she was already a permanent part of his son's life. His words verified her thoughts for he spoke warmly, his face alight with pleasure.

"You will be a beautiful bride, Isabella, one any man would treasure. It is my son's privilege to be the man to win your hand in marriage. This house has long needed a woman to make it come alive again, as it once was when my own bride was here. You will take her place, and yet make it a place of your own. You will have free rein, for it will be your home, and you will be mistress of all you survey."

"Lucia has been efficient in the running of your household, sir," Isabella said quietly. "All seems to be in place under her control."

"Ah, yes. Lucia. The one who casts long looks at my son, and would marry him herself if she could. It was a smart move on the part of her father to send her here, to offer us her service after my wife died, but all has not gone as she and her family wished it to. Rafael did not look to her for comfort, and though she tried to entice him, he was not interested in her, other than as a cousin, and a distant relative sent to help fill the place of a woman in this household."

His lips thinned as if he disliked speaking such words, and then his head rose in a majestic pose and he seemed to take on the persona of a man who would set out the rules by which his house must be run.

"Lucia will be going back to her family before the wedding, Isabella. She will only cause trouble here if she remains, and you must have a free hand to do as you please."

"I will feel guilty if she is banished because of me." And would feel the hatred of Lucia in either case, Isabella thought ruefully. The woman did not like her, and it would be wise to keep a watchful eye on her for however long she remained in the hacienda.

"You must not feel guilty for any reason," Rafael's father said firmly. "You will be Señora McKenzie in three days' time. There is not room in any house for two women to be in charge. As my son's wife, those duties will be yours. And though I am thankful that Lucia came to help for a time, that time is now at an end. She must leave."

A pang of apprehension touched Isabella, sending

a chill up her spine and drawing the warmth from her. Yet she could not argue with the elder Señor McKenzie, for he was the man in charge, and his words were law in this household.

From the hallway beyond his room voices were raised, and Isabella turned to the door just as it opened. Without ceremony, Lucia burst into the room, Maria hot on her heels.

The housekeeper's words were quick and agitated, her glance at Lucia one of aggravation. "Señor, Lucia has refused to leave before the wedding. I have told her it is not her place to set the schedule, but she is determined to stay—even though we've summoned her brother to meet her in town."

"I only want to stay for the ceremony and the grand party to follow," Lucia said quickly. Tears filled her eyes as she knelt before Simon. "Surely you would not deny me this pleasure."

"I cannot understand why you want to witness the marriage, Lucia. You have your heart set against it, and there will be no pleasure for you in watching Isabella become Rafael's bride."

Lucia blinked furiously and allowed tears to fall down her cheeks, her look pitiful. Yet beneath the display, Isabella doubted that her true emotions were exposed. Lucia's dark eyes were hard and angry, the look she cut in Isabella's direction one of rage and disdain.

It seemed that Rafael's father was not fooled by the tears or the cry for pity, for he touched Lucia's arm and bade her rise. "You will go now, Lucia. I will consider your words, and if Rafael is agreeable, you may stay for the ceremony and the party and then take your leave. But do not attempt to convince me that you have any great love for any of us in this household. Your actions have given me reason to think otherwise, for you have not welcomed Isabella here, or given her the respect due Rafael's bride."

"I beg your pardon, uncle, for the slights you imagine. But I have not had the opportunity to spend time with Isabella. Indeed I have barely spoken to her, for she has been busy with Rafael, and I have been caught up in dealing with household duties. Running your hacienda has not been an easy task, but I have done my best to make things go smoothly in your home."

"I will decide tomorrow when you should leave, Lucia. Go now and make ready your clothing for the journey." Dismissing the girl from his presence, the elderly man leaned back in his chair and closed his eyes. Without speaking, Lucia arose from the floor and sailed past Maria, out the door and down the hallway.

Isabella followed, albeit at a slower pace, and when Maria caught her eye, she hesitated. "Do you need me, Maria? Did you want to talk to me?"

The housekeeper nodded and took Isabella's arm, leading her from the room and closing the door behind them.

"We must speak of your wedding, and do it quickly, for the plans are already in motion. Rafael has sent for the village priest and he is to set up the chapel for the ceremony to take place. We must arrange for your dress and veil and then plan the food we will serve."

Isabella felt overwhelmed. "All of that in three days' time?"

Maria smiled confidently. "We can cook ahead of time, and Delores and Elena are already making cakes and pies. There are meat pastries to be made, but we will do that tomorrow. The men have been told to butcher a pig and a steer to be cooked over open fires out by the barn."

"I'll help, if I can. I know something about cooking, but I fear the food I helped prepare at the convent did not include such things as pork and beef and pastries. We ate a lot of porridge for breakfast and greens for dinner, with an occasional chicken when one could be spared from the henhouse."

Maria clicked her tongue and angled her head, the better to examine Isabella's slender form. "It is no wonder you are so skinny with such food to eat. You will be round and healthy after you have lived in this household for a while. We'll put roses in your cheeks and some meat on your bones." Nodding vehemently, as if she had made a pronouncement of great worth, she towed Isabella to the kitchen.

"Now sit down there and I will make you a good meal." Bustling to the stove, she lifted the lid of a large kettle and peered within. "Ah, as I thought, the soup is ready to eat. You shall have the first of it, Isabella, and tell me if it is to your liking. I shall be cooking for your tastes from now on and I will want to serve you well. If you'll let me know your favorites, I'll try to please your palate, and perhaps we can add some curves to those bones of yours."

"Those bones of hers are curvy enough to please me." From the kitchen doorway, Rafael's voice spoke quietly, his tone teasing and yet the meaning clear. He would not take kindly to any criticism of his bride. His steps were long as he made his way to Isabella's side. "Are you hungry, sweetheart?" he asked, crouching on one knee beside her chair, his head on a level with hers.

She blinked, catching the scent of him, the fresh smell of a man who wore clean clothing and a flavor of the outdoors. It appealed to her, this male aroma that defied description, for she had not been so near to another man before Rafael's entry into her life.

"I didn't know you were here, Rafael." Her heartbeat increased as she inhaled again, this time recognizing the essence of the man himself. She would not send him away, not when she felt the need of his presence, and so she invited him to join her. "I'm going to have a bowl of soup. Will you join me?"

"How could I resist so gracious an invitation?" he asked, his voice teasing, yet his eyes filled with pleasure at seeing her here in his kitchen, speaking with Maria as might the lady of the manor.

"We were discussing her favorite foods, señor," Maria said quickly, "and deciding what I should cook for the wedding feast."

"And what have you decided?" he asked Isabella, pulling out a chair to seat himself beside his bride-to-be. "I noticed the steer has been butchered and the men are even now digging a pit for the coals."

"I've decided that Maria is much better equipped to handle such a menu than I could pretend to be. I can tell her that I like roasted corn and baked potatoes, but I'm willing to agree to whatever is easiest for her to prepare."

Rafael smiled and his arm slid over the back of her chair. "Well, you're what will make this wedding day one of perfection for me, Isabella. Anything else is but an additional blessing. Knowing that my life will be complete once we speak our vows is enough pleasure for me to look forward to."

He eyed her bowl of soup with a look of hunger then, and laughed aloud. "All of this talk of weddings and food has reminded me that I was offered a meal just a few moments ago. Does that offer still stand, Maria? Am I to share the noontime soup with my bride?"

"I think we can arrange such a thing, especially since the señorita has offered you a place next to her." Maria found a bowl and ladled it full of the hearty soup, then placed it before Rafael.

"Whatever you decide to prepare will be perfect, Maria," he said, viewing the meal she'd offered. "So long as you have baked bread to go along with the feast, my father will be pleased. He enjoys tortillas, but your light bread is his favorite."

Maria's face sobered as she heard his words, and

she spoke softly, as if she would not want to be over-heard. "I will do whatever it takes to make Señor McKenzie sit up and eat, for he has not the appetite of a flea these days. I'd thought that having the señorita here and planning for the wedding would give him more appetite and a desire to join more with the family meals. But I fear he has secluded himself in his room in preparation for the end of his life."

"Don't say so, Maria." Isabella placed her spoon on the table and pushed away from the meal. "He must remain a vital part of the family, for if he loses his will to live, it will leave a huge, empty place in this house-hold. We must do all we can to bring him into the plans we make, for he must realize that his place cannot be filled, that to lose him would leave us bereft."

In silence, Rafael lifted her from her chair and carried her to her bedroom. He stood with her inside the door and his arms circled her and drew her close.

CHAPTER TEN

ISABELLA TURNED HER HEAD, resting it against his heart, hearing his voice surrounding her as it vibrated within his chest and sounded warmly in her ear. His murmur was soft, his tone touching her with its tenderness.

"Dear heart," he whispered. "You make me proud to be your husband, with the acceptance you have given my father, and the concern you show for him."

Tears filled her eyes as she tilted her face upward, pressing her lips against his. "I have no father to fill my thoughts, Rafael. If he still lived, he would not have wanted my regard. Be aware of how blessed you are to know that father is still with you, even though he is not well. You must cherish each day he yet lives."

"Consider him also as your father, Isabella, for I am more than willing to share my house and family with you. When you are my wife, you will be the mistress of this house, and all within it will be under your control. We men, my father and I, are but poor males who will depend on you for the care you give us." He smiled as he spoke and she recognized that his tone was teasing, as if he would lift her mood with humor.

"Maria is better equipped than I to tend the men of the household, for she will remain in charge of the kitchen, and if my memory serves me right, the menfolk are more interested in their stomachs and what is available to put into them than in being pampered."

Rafael's chuckle was quiet, his breath warm against her throat as he bent his head to taste of the soft skin there. "This is one man who is looking forward to the pampering due a husband," he told her quietly, as his arms curved her against his needy body. "I crave the sweet words of my wife and the soft touch of her hands when I am weary from my labors. I appreciate having clean clothes and good food on the table, but there are more important things for a wife to be concerned with than those everyday chores."

Isabella stilled, her hands finding a place in her lap, her breathing almost halting as she considered what he spoke of, for they had not talked before of her duties to him as a wife, only that he wanted to touch her and kiss her, that he enjoyed holding her in his arms. That there was more to the relationship of husband and wife than that was a fact of life, but the details of it were mostly unknown to her.

"Isabella? Have I upset you speaking of this? Are you still frightened of me?"

She lifted her head and her gaze touched his. "Not of you, Rafael, for I have learned to trust that you will do as you say. You know what my fears are for I have already spoken of them to you."

From outside her bedroom, a foot shuffled against the tile floor and a woman cleared her throat. "Lucia." Rafael's voice was almost silent as he murmured the woman's name, and then he released Isabella and opened the bedroom door, revealing Lucia just outside.

She smiled at Rafael, ignoring the presence of Isabella behind him, and her words were of the wedding to come. "No matter what you think of me, Rafael, I am pleased that you are to be married. I'm pleased that Señor Simon has said I may stay to help with the cooking and preparation of the food. I would not be happy to miss the family gathering and the friends from the village who will be here, even though I must leave for my father's house soon afterward."

Her voice held a hint of humility, but as she stood before Rafael, the look she cast in Isabella's direction held only anger, and she spoke more to the point. "I have worked hard for this household for two years, and now because of this woman, I am to be banished without cause. The unfairness of this pains me deeply."

"Your place here is one that will be taken by the woman of the house, Lucia," Rafael told her. "Now that I've brought home a bride, there will be a new mistress of the Diamond Ranch, and there is never room for two women to be in charge in the same household. You knew when you came here that it was a temporary thing. You have no reason to be angry that your time here is at an end. It is more than time enough for you to go to your father's house and seek out a life of your own."

Rafael spoke quickly, as if he would impress on Lucia his decision, placing his support behind Isabella without a trace of uncertainty. "You need a home of your own and a husband to give you children, Lucia. Your father has already been considering the young men of your village, seeking out a husband for you."

Her skirts almost tangled around her legs, so quickly did Lucia turn to walk down the corridor toward her own room. "I will pack now then, and leave the two of you to make your plans. I only hope that Isabella is well aware of the work awaiting her here and the expectations you have for her, Rafael."

Isabella watched her, cognizant of the anger in each step the other woman took. "Now what did she mean by all of that?" she asked aloud, even as Rafael shook his head at the harsh words Lucia spoke.

"I'm not certain just what her problem is, sweetheart. but I know that it is well beyond time for her to leave. She has become a troublesome woman and would like nothing better than to create problems for you. I won't have it, and it is better to have her gone than to attempt to keep track of the tricks she is capable of."

"I think she feels that she has been used by the men here at the Diamond Ranch," Isabella said quietly.

"She earned a good wage while she lived here," Rafael said, and Isabella looked at him in surprise.

"She was a hired servant in this household?"

"Not a servant, but a woman paid for her worth. She has been a boon to us, but the time for her to leave has come. According to what Lucia has just said, my father has said she will leave here right after the wedding. I'm sure he will send her into town to meet her brother then."

An unwelcome pity for the woman filled Isabella. She stepped past Rafael and returned to the kitchen, where Maria tended to the dishes and readied a tray for the elderly man. "Thank you for the meal, Maria. The soup was good. Perhaps I can carry that tray to Rafael's father for you."

"I will prepare it and you can take it while I finish up here in the kitchen," Maria said. "And then you and I must spend some time deciding what you will wear for your wedding, and perhaps we should go to the village and see what the general store has to offer."

"I will take her, Maria," Rafael said quickly. "After you do your work here, it will be time for your siesta. I will have Manuel harness the mare to the buggy." He turned to Isabella. "We have already spoken of shoes, no doubt more than one pair. Will that please you, my bride?"

She nodded. "I will do as you ask, Rafael. But you should not see my dress for the wedding ahead of time."

"Then I will wait outside the store while you make a choice from what is available," he said agreeably.

"Until I let my father's lawyer know where I am and receive funds from him, I will have no funds for a gown or shoes," she said, feeling like a beggar at his table, as she awaited the words that would surely come.

He did not surprise her with his edict, and even though it was delivered with a smile, she knew there would be no sense in protesting his decision. "I will pay for your clothing from now on," he told her, "including your wedding dress. The storekeeper will put it on our account and it will be paid for in due time."

Knowing that it was useless to argue the point, Isabella left the kitchen, going back to her room, her steps heavy as she considered the upset that filled the household. It was not a good omen for the happiness of her marriage that Lucia was being banished, that Rafael felt such animosity for the woman and that her own presence here seemed to be the cause of Lucia's unhappiness.

She readied herself for the trip to town, almost ashamed at the feeling of excitement that gripped her at her first venture from the ranch. It seemed almost sinful to be happy at Lucia's expense, but there was nothing to be done, for the girl had forfeited her right to be at the Diamond Ranch, with her actions so against the elder Señor McKenzie's feelings.

She opened the back door, not surprised that the buggy was readied for the trip. As she walked down the steps toward him, Rafael joined her, taking her arm and then, as they neared the buggy, lifting her to the seat. He tucked her skirts inside the frame and then walked quickly around to the other side, climbing up on the seat with a smooth movement. Lifting the reins, he snapped them sharply over the mare's back, setting her into motion. She trotted smartly down the lane and then onto the road to town, Rafael's competent hands light on the reins, his face wreathed in a smile as he turned his head to watch her.

The outskirts of the village were reached in short order, and Isabella gazed about at the scattered houses with a good number of smaller huts here and there. Children played in the dirt, several with tools or sticks with which they were digging, others tossing a ball back and forth, all of them seeming cheerful, waving with delight at the buggy as it passed them by. Rafael was the recipient of many shouts of welcome, the children appearing to know him well, for he called several by name.

Isabella was quiet as the buggy rolled on into the small business area, consisting of a hotel, several saloons and the general store. An adobe building sat apart from the rest of the establishments, a hitching post in front, several men standing before the door, deeply involved in a conversation of sorts.

One of them wore a silver badge that caught the sunlight and glittered against the dark fabric of his shirt. He nodded at Rafael, took a second look that involved Isabella, and then, as the buggy came to a halt in front of the store, he strolled across the road to approach the buggy.

"Rafael. I'd heard you had a pretty lady at your hacienda," he said boldly, his gaze openly appreciative of the woman before him. "One of your men told the men in the saloon that you were going to be married, and soon. This week, I believe he said."

Rafael laughed, shaking his head, as if in disbelief. "It certainly took no time at all for the news to travel, my friend. It was no doubt Manuel who spread the word. He came into town last night for a while, and I suspected the first place he would stop would be the tavern. Probably the last place, too, from the looks of him when he rode into the barn."

"When does the big event take place?" The lawman's grin was wide, his hands on his hips as he quizzed his friend.

"In three days. I've sent word to the padre to be prepared for the wedding. We'll come into the village and have the service at the small chapel by the cemetery."

"And a party afterward, I suspect?"

"Everyone is invited. In fact, I'm going into the general store right now to leave an invitation on the board for everyone in the village to attend." He turned his attention to Isabella and took her hand. "This is the local lawman, Paulo Cameron. And this is my Isabella, Paulo." He spoke more quietly now, as if his words were of great importance. "Don't ever be fearful of asking for his assistance. If you're ever in need of any support of any kind, you can depend on him for help."

She nodded, smiling at the handsome man who watched her. "Thank you, señor. I hope I'll never need your services, but it's good to know that there is someone here representing law and order."

He tipped his hat, his eyes intent on her. "I'm pleased that Rafael found such a lovely lady for his bride. And I'm sure his papa is more than pleased. He told me the last time I visited with him that he was worried about Rafael not finding a woman of his own. Not that he would have any problem finding one in the area. There are several young ladies who will be unhappy that he has brought home someone from afar to wed."

"She is exactly the one I have been looking for," Rafael said quietly. "I had heard of her, and so sought her out."

A knowing look spread over Paulo's face and he stepped closer to the buggy. "Is this the woman who was spoken of when the older man came through a few months ago with a herd of horses for sale? The man who said he knew of a beautiful woman who was living in a convent, and he intended to marry her?"

Rafael nodded soberly and proceeded to tell Paulo about Isabella's arranged marriage to Garcia and how he had taken her from the convent to become his bride.

"And are you pleased to be the new mistress at Diamond Ranch?" Paulo asked her, his smile warm, his eyes approving as he turned his attention back to her.

Rafael spoke quickly, not waiting for Isabella's reply, as though he were unsure of what she would say. His own opinion was what mattered here, it was obvious. "She will be happy with me and my father. He is pleased with her and welcomes her to our home."

With a lithe movement, he climbed down from the

buggy and reached for Isabella, his hand open, the meaning obvious as he waited for her to grasp his fingers. "Come, we'll go in and buy your things now," he said, offering her no option but to slide across the seat and accept his help. He smiled then and grasped her waist, swinging her to the ground easily. "Are you ready?"

She nodded, wondering what the sheriff would say if she turned to him and asked him to take her to her father's ranch, or perhaps find someone to go with her. As if he read her mind, Rafael turned her toward the double doors of the store and with a strong arm around her waist, he led her up onto the sidewalk, turning his head to nod a quick goodbye to the sheriff.

"It is time to choose the dress you will wear for your wedding, Isabella. Come with me." He led her to the man behind the counter and introduced her, telling the storekeeper than she was to purchase whatever she wanted and it would be paid for as was usual when he settled their bill at the end of the month. And then, with a last look in her eyes and a smile of anticipation that pleased her, he left the store. And for the first time in her life, Isabella was free to spend whatever she pleased.

She was the center of attention as she looked at the variety of clothing offered, from simple white blouses and flowered skirts to flowing petticoats and soft batiste chemises. It was more than she had imagined she would see in such a small town, but the storekeeper apparently carried a wide variety of merchandise.

Two skirts with blouses that would look well with them were chosen, a layer of frothy petticoats met her fingers and she was charmed by the soft fabric, so used to the homespun she had worn at the convent, she could barely resist the opportunity now to choose otherwise.

A chemise with layers of lace lay in a glass box and Isabella lifted it, holding it up the better to see it, and then with a sigh, she replaced it. "Do you have any plain vests?" she asked, mourning the loss of such a bit of froth, but determined to buy only what was necessary.

"I believe the señor would like you to choose from the best of my line of ladies' wear," the storekeeper said quietly. "And this is the finest of the undergarments we offer."

With a fleeting thought for Rafael's purse, she lifted the chemise again, and with a sigh, placed it atop the items she had already chosen.

"I need something to wear for my wedding now," she said, looking over the gentleman's shoulder at the glass bins from which dresses and other bits of apparel spilled. The shopkeeper climbed his ladder and lifted down a bin from the top shelf and placed it before her.

"This is the sort of clothing usually worn for such special occasions," he said, lifting several dresses from the container. He held one up for Isabella to view and she inhaled sharply as she watched the layers of fine fabric unfold before her. Her hand touched the bodice where lace was tucked in long rows, emphasizing the fullness that would outline a lady's bosom.

"It's lovely," she breathed, and watched again as he took another dress from the bin and offered it to her, as if he understood her fascination with the soft, silken material of his wares. She shook it from its folds and held it before her, measuring it against her own form, noting the white ruffles that formed the hem. It was more than she had considered wearing, more costly, more elegant, and she looked down at herself, imagining the sight she would present in such a garment.

"I think Rafael will like this one," she said and then wondered at her daring, for certainly the dress would be costly, and in addition to the pile already before her, she would likely strain the boundaries he had set for this shopping trip.

But there was yet more to come as the storekeeper waved toward the display of footwear across the store from where they stood. Isabella walked where he designated she should go and surveyed the wealth of items there.

From the leather house shoes to tooled leather boots, a vast array of choices awaited her. Both shoes and boots appealed to her feminine side, for riding a horse was a fond memory of her past and the boots she had worn as a child, though hand-me-downs, had been cherished.

Now she looked with interest at the display on the counters, ruing the penury that had reduced her to this state of need, and determined that she should own shoes to be worn for any occasion, primarily that of her wedding. And to that end, she picked up a pair of black leather slippers that looked close to the size she would need. A nearby bench provided a seating place and she sat to slip them on her feet, even now clad in someone else's discards.

Maria had located a pair of black half boots in the attic, a reminder of days long past, when Rafael's mother had been alive and had worn this footwear. To Isabella's mind, they would have been sufficient for her use, but Maria had hushed her, telling her that stylish leather on her feet was one sign of a lady, and she owed it to Rafael to look the part she would be called upon to play in his house.

The storekeeper neared and watched her as she turned her foot before her, admiring the black leather of the slipper she'd donned. And then he knelt in front of the bench she sat upon and touched her foot with long fingers.

"This shoe is too large for you, señorita. Let me find a pair that better fit your small size." And so saying, he slipped the rejected specimen from Isabella's foot and lifted another pair from the counter at his side. Simple, yet elegant, they fit as though made for her foot and she blushed as she offered her thanks to the man for his help.

"Do you wish more than one pair?" he asked.

"Señor McKenzie has said I should have two pair," she told the storekeeper. "I think boots would be a good choice for the second."

He nodded his agreement and in moments she stood in a pair of riding boots, the tops covered by the hem of her skirt. She walked to a small mirror near the wall and lifted her skirt a bit, the better to admire the sleek leather that some craftsman had worked with his tools.

"They're beautiful," she said softly, turning to one side, holding one foot before her.

"As is the lady who wears them." The voice could only belong to Rafael, she decided, recognizing the deep tones, and her thought was realized as she turned her head to see him just inside the door of the general store, watching her with a half smile that made his eyes sparkle.

"Do you like the boots?" she asked and was rewarded by the look of admiration he wore.

"You can wear them one day when we ride the boundaries of my ranch," he told her, coming closer and glancing toward the clothing piled on the counter.

"Do you have enough there? Did you choose a dress for the wedding?" he asked, walking to where the storekeeper had placed her choices.

"Don't look at them, Rafael. My wedding dress is there and I don't want you to see it until I wear it to the church."

"Is there a good choice here for the señorita?" he asked the storekeeper, who appeared to be adding up the wealth of purchases as he spoke.

"I think you will find she is well-dressed, Señor McKenzie. I would have suggested more undergarments, but she is a conservative lady, I fear."

Rafael tossed her a look that admired her qualities, both those seen and unseen, and made a request of the man who stood before him. "Add whatever else you think she should have. My bride does not ask for much, and I fear I must teach her the ways of a woman who requires a more extensive wardrobe than what she is used to."

With awe, Isabella watched as the storekeeper added more of the filmy garments in the bin to the pile. Surely she could not use more than two of the soft chemises, and more than one petticoat at a time was an excess. But she would not argue with Rafael, for it was his place as her husband-to-be to make such decisions for her.

And her place as his wife to wear what he chose for her. A task she would not find wearisome, she was certain, for he pointed to another bin and from it the storekeeper chose an assortment of stockings, and from another two soft robes to be worn over her nightgowns.

"But I have no gowns to wear to bed, Rafael," she whispered as she approached him, out of hearing of the man who handled her clothing and began wrapping it as he wrote down the prices on a bit of paper.

He bent closer to her and his words were warm against her ear. "You will wear the robes until bedtime, Isabella, and after that, I will keep you warm."

She thought a flush dwelt high on his cheekbones as he spoke and his eyes darkened as if he saw beyond her clothing to the woman beneath. "Are you satisfied with your purchases?" he asked and she could only nod, knowing that she had been indulged beyond her wildest dreams today.

CHAPTER ELEVEN

THE WHOLE VILLAGE was involved in the wedding, from the eldest gentleman, who claimed the right to escort the bride since she had no father to do so, to the youngest child, who offered flowers as she entered the church. A bouquet of cheerful blossoms, it was an armful she could barely hold, and indeed, the child had breathed a sigh of relief when she accepted it, for he seemed fearful of dropping it himself.

She lifted it to her face, inhaling deeply of the sweet scent, and offered him a smile of thanks. He flushed and ducked his head, then turned his face into his mother's apron, the woman who stood behind him, her eyes alight with pride in the behavior of her small son.

The priest stood behind the altar, a prayer book open in his hand, and the benevolent smile on his face welcomed her. Beside him Rafael stood straight and tall, his eyes warm, his smile an invitation to her to join him. The elderly man who walked with her down the aisle bowed to Rafael and at the designated time offered Isabella's hand to her groom in the accepted manner.

His fingers were warm against hers, his palm dry, and her smaller bones were held captive by the possessive grip he took upon her. As if he took her fully into his keeping with this symbol of his ownership, he drew her close to his side, looking down on her with a primitive knowledge in his gaze. As if he could peer within her very soul, he vanquished her with but a look, and she was brought to a state of trembling in moments.

His head bent to her and his words were warm against her ear, a whisper she strained to hear. "Don't be afraid, my love. I'll take care of you."

I don't want to be cared for as a child, but given the right to be a strong woman.

She felt the wave of anger surge through her, the implacable will of Rafael McKenzie again becoming the foremost reason for her presence here. A bride should be in control, she thought, looking up at him with defiance. And the total lack of control she felt at this moment was frightening.

She'd thought to approach her wedding with joy, with a sense of facing a future that promised happiness. She looked deeply into the dark eyes of the man she was to wed, seeking perhaps that promise, only to find triumph and a scalding desire directed at her.

The priest was speaking, words she had heard but one other time in her life, when a couple were married while she herself was but a child. One of the men on her father's ranch had wed a girl from town, and the ceremony had taken place in the chapel there, with the whole town in attendance.

She had almost envied the bride her happiness that day, thinking ahead to the wedding her father would have her undertake with Juan Garcia, for it had been just weeks before her own trip to the convent. Now those words were being applied to herself and Rafael McKenzie, the man who had chosen her.

She felt the heat of his gaze upon her as she repeated the vows the priest spoke. *To love, honor and obey.* They vibrated in the air as she spoke the syllables softly and slowly, her promise binding her to this man. Love for a man had not seemed a likely thing for her to consider before. Certainly not for Juan Garcia, for his would have been a lonely household for her, and his will would certainly have been law. Perhaps love might enter into this marriage to Rafael, she thought, listening as he spoke words of promise in her hearing.

The priest prayed, and she knelt before him, her hand in Rafael's, her heart in her throat. An undercurrent ran through the chapel as she gained her feet, Rafael holding her arm as she caught her breath and got her balance. He turned her to face the people of his village and she was welcomed into their midst with smiles and embraces that warmed her. The women seemed ready to take her under their collective wings, wanting to mother the girl who had no mother of her own on this, her wedding day.

The men viewed her in a different manner, and even to her innocent mind, she felt their eyes taking her measure, viewing her figure and finding it to be worth their attention.

Rafael must have sensed their regard, too, for his arm went around her waist and he led her down the aisle quickly, as if he would remove her from watching eyes. They walked into the sunlight and into the village street, followed by the crowd, who were ready to celebrate the wedding.

A carriage was ready for them, two black horses drawing it with majestic beauty, their tails and manes braided with flowers entwined in the ribbons, their harnesses shiny from hours of polish by willing hands. The carriage gleamed, its surface shining, each nook and cranny filled with flowers, until Isabella wondered if there would be room for her and Rafael to sit on the seat.

He opened the door with a flourish, then lifted her onto the seat and joined her there. The carriage was open, exposed to the elements and the good wishes of the crowd that surrounded them. With a crack of his whip, Manuel set the black horses in motion and the vehicle turned in the direction of the ranch, moving slowly so that the gathering crowd could follow on foot.

It was only a short distance, less than a mile, and the air was filled with song as the people lifted their voices in the melodies that were associated with weddings, singing in harmony that fell on Isabella's ears with music such as she had never heard.

"They are welcoming you as my bride," Rafael said softly, bending to her with a possessive look. His arm was around her waist, his other hand holding hers, his smile warm and expectant. She willed her lips to form a smile of her own, looking up at him, her trembling mouth giving away her fears.

"Don't be worried, Isabella. Everything will be well for us. Just a few hours to spend with the friends who wish us well, then a moment alone with my father before I make you mine." He looked back at the buggy that followed them, his father having been assisted onto the seat, Matthew holding the reins. "My father is smiling, Isabella. Will you look back at him and assure him that you are all right?"

It was little enough to ask, she thought as she turned in the seat to catch sight of the man who rode in their wake, upon the seat of the black buggy, with Manuel holding the reins. She lifted a hand in greeting and a frail hand responded, the elderly Señor McKenzie smiling, even though he looked to be weary and more than ready for his bed.

"Will he be all right?" she asked quietly. "He seems so fragile, so weary."

"He was determined to attend our wedding today, and I think he is stronger than we realize," Rafael told her. "You've given him a new lease on life today, sweetheart. His heart is rapidly failing, for the doctor has increased his medicine once again, but he needed to do this and I would not have denied him the privilege. His spirit is lifted by this marriage. He will die happy, knowing that his grandchildren will fill his house."

Isabella felt herself shrink within the curve of his

arm. "I don't think I'm ready for a child so soon. I'm not sure I'm fit to be a mother yet."

"It takes almost a year to gain the title," Rafael said with a grin. "By the time you spend nine months carrying my child, you will be ready for motherhood. I promise you." His arm tightened around her waist and he pulled her closer, lifting his other hand to wave at a familiar face in the crowd surrounding the carriage.

"At this rate, we'll be half the day just getting back to your father's hacienda," Isabella said softly.

"This is tradition, the long walk to the party. It gives the people a good appetite, readies them for the meal that is waiting," Rafael told her. "I have been one of those walking, surrounding the carriage, more than once. A wedding is an occasion for celebration, and my people are very good at it."

"Will we stay at Diamond Ranch after the wedding?" she asked, knowing that it was commonplace for a newlywed couple to travel after the wedding, taking time to learn each other's ways.

"With my father not well, it would be best for us to move into our own rooms right away," Rafael said, his tone coaxing, as if he would not disappoint her if her heart was set on a trip. "When there is opportunity, later on, we'll perhaps visit one of the big cities and enjoy ourselves shopping, perhaps seeing some of the stage presentations that occasionally come this far west."

"I will be happy to stay at home, Rafael. I'm not a very adventuresome woman."

"There is one adventure I'm going to take you on, Isabella. I hope it will be enjoyable for you."

She looked up at him, her mind not grasping his thoughts for a moment, and then she blushed as the meaning of his words sank in. "Can we talk about it first?"

"Talking will not postpone it. It is a part of marriage, Isabella, one I look forward to."

"I know." She felt a flush climb her cheeks and she bowed her head, unwilling to meet his gaze. "But I'm not sure I'm ready yet for it to happen."

"You will be." As though he could foresee her future, he spoke with authority, and she cringed away from him, only too aware of the crowd that watched them, unwilling to defy him in this, yet not willing to comply with his wishes without speaking her mind.

As if he sensed her thoughts, he sighed softly. "We'll speak of it later, after the party, when the guests have gone."

THE FOOD WAS in abundant supply, the dancing was fast and furious, the music loud and inviting to the ear, and yet, there was a part of her that seemed to stand aside and watch and listen, fearful of joining into the general merriment. Isabella was tense, standing stiffly beside her groom, receiving congratulations from the crowd, smiling pleasantly and saying all the appropriate words in reply to their greetings. She tried, and realized that she was failing miserably, to be a happy bride. Her smile was forced, her hands trembled and her eyes felt unexplainably teary as she watched the dancers glide around the floor of the barn.

The men had cleaned it with brooms and mops, had made benches from long planks of wood and tables from sawhorses and more planks for the food to be displayed upon. The scent of meat being roasted in the pit had filled the air for the past day and a half and Isabella knew that the people from the village were pleased at the variety of foods provided for their meal.

Maria had outdone herself, the girls helping her until they were weary, and then continuing as if this were a meal of a lifetime. And indeed it was, for Rafael would only be married once, and it was a celebration to be remembered by all. The elder Señor McKenzie sat on an overstuffed chair in the barn, listening and watching as the dancers swayed before him, speaking to those who stopped in front of him to offer their best wishes.

"My father will wish to see us dance together," Rafael said in a low whisper, speaking softly to Isabella as they watched from their seats of honor near the food-laden tables. His words teased her, their message making her recognize her duty to Rafael. "Can you smile for me and for my father's benefit? He wants you to be happy tonight, as do I. You are a beautiful bride, Isabella. Now, make the picture complete by looking at me as if I were your fondest dream come true."

As he must have known she would, her lips curved and she smiled with a radiance that made her glow.

"I don't know about that, Rafael, but certainly you were not my worst nightmare. I'll leave that honor to another. And I don't know if I can manage to dance with you. I've never been taught how, only watched when I was a child. There wasn't an opportunity to dance at the convent, you know."

He laughed, looking down at her with a tender smile. "I'll hold you close and show you how, love. All you have to do is follow my lead. We won't be doing any of the fancy footwork, just a simple swaying back and forth to the music. And so long as I'm not your worst nightmare, I'll accept that you're not entirely unhappy to be with me here tonight."

She nodded her acquiescence and he rose, taking her hand and leading her to the center of the crowded floor. The others formed a circle around them as they took up their position, and Isabella found herself held in his arms, her head tucked neatly under his chin as he held her closely, one strong hand on her back, the other holding her palm in his. He led her in time with the music, a waltz in a slow tempo that did not challenge her skills, and she found her feet following his as if she had been born for such a thing.

"You see? It is not so difficult as you thought, is it?" His eyes were warm as he looked down into hers, his mouth forming a smile that soothed her.

"Dance with me closer to your father, Rafael. I want him to know that his fears can be put to rest and that we are happy together."

He looked down at her, his eyes darkening, his

mouth unsmiling. "And are we happy, Isabella? Are you content to be here with me tonight?"

"I am determined to be happy, for this is my destiny. And I would not have your father leave here tonight, returning to his bed without the knowledge of our wedding being one of joy."

He whirled her about, her dress whipping around them both as they danced closer to where his father sat. "You are the woman of my heart," he said quietly. And then he smiled. "See how he watches us, as if we are the two most important people in the world." Simon's mouth moved in a smile of joy, his hand lifted in a salute that might have been a blessing, Isabella thought. She brought Rafael to a halt as they reached the spot on the barn floor right in front of his father's chair.

Leading Rafael to where the elderly man sat, Isabella found herself on her knees before him, looking up into the wise, dark eyes of the man who would be her father from this day on. "Will you give us your blessing?" she asked, and was pleased by the look of pure delight that possessed his features.

Rafael knelt beside her, his arm holding her tightly as if he were telegraphing his pleasure at her words in this way. His attention was on his father, and he placed one hand on the older man's knee. "Isabella and I would have you bless our marriage, father."

With a smile of benevolence and a countenance that seemed to glow with happiness, Simon Mc-Kenzie leaned forward and placed their hands between his palms, forming a bond that included all three of them in its boundaries, then lifted his palms from theirs to rest atop their heads, speaking words of blessing that seemed to come directly from his heart. It was not a rehearsed speech, but a simple phrasing that expressed his joy at their union.

Isabella allowed the tears to fall that had threatened to be expressed all day long and Rafael bent to her. "Don't be sad, my love. Father is wishing us the same happiness he shared with my mother. He would not want to cause your tears to flow."

"I'm not unhappy, only touched by his love for you, Rafael." Her whisper was low, intended only for his ears, and indeed, her smile negated the message of tears, for an onlooker could not have mistaken her expression as anything but joyous.

Rafael lifted her to her feet and offered his hand to his father, then watched with pride as Isabella leaned forward to kiss the elderly man's cheek. "Thank you, father of my husband. For you are now, and forevermore will be, my father, too, and I will do my best to make you proud of me."

The crowd leaned closer as she spoke and, as one, they burst into applause, her words apparently striking a collective chord in their hearts. She could not have chosen a better way to solidify her position in the household had she tried, and so, unknowingly, she pleased the people of the village and made a smile bloom upon the face of the man who was so large a part of this community.

And who had recognized that he would not live to be a part of his family for very long.

As though an unseen voice had spoken, the people of the village prepared to leave, as a group finding their children and setting off on the journey back to town.

Rafael and Isabella stood in the doorway of the barn and watched the exodus, waving and calling out their farewells to those who had joined in the celebration of their wedding. In mere moments, the crowd had dispersed and in the silence, they made their way to the house. Behind them, the men brought the elder Señor McKenzie to the house, carrying his chair, bearing him with loving care to the room where he was living out the last days of his life.

Isabella watched from the doorway of her bedroom as they passed by, lifting a hand to wave a last good-night to her father-in-law. Behind her, Rafael stood as a dark presence, his form close by, his breath warm against her nape.

"We will sleep in my room, Isabella. Take what you need for tonight with you. Maria will have your things moved tomorrow. For tonight, your brush and the clothing you will need for the morning is enough."

She nodded, crossing to the bureau where her underclothes lay in deep drawers. Drawing forth a robe, one of those items purchased from the general store, and clean underwear, she turned to him. "I'll just get a dress from the closet, Rafael."

He looked with disdain on the long white garment

she had chosen to wear to bed. "You won't need that, Isabella. I prefer to see you without covering tonight."

Her heart seemed to flip over in her chest, and she felt faint for a moment. "I always wear a gown to bed," she managed to whisper.

"You've never been married before, sweetheart. As I told you before, there is no need of a garment while you sleep. I'll keep you warm." His promise was accompanied by a smile that guaranteed her well-being, and she only shook her head.

"Perhaps I should just stay here tonight, and we can begin this marriage tomorrow."

His mouth tightened and his eyes narrowed, his expression allowing no room for discussion. "And perhaps you will come with me to my room now." He would not play this game any longer, for as he took her hand and led her back into the deserted hallway and down the corridor to where his bedroom lay, his fingers were firm on hers, his grip leaving her no choice but to follow where he led.

ISABELLA CHANGED FROM the bridal gown she had chosen just days ago, and rued the excitement she had felt on that day. No longer did her heart beat hopefully as she thought of her wedding day. For it was upon her now—in fact, it was almost over—and she knew that tomorrow would find her changed from the innocent girl who had given herself in marriage to Rafael McKenzie.

To love, to honor and to obey. Those words nudged

at her, reminding her, as if she needed their prodding, to remember the service in the small chapel. Of her own free will, she had given her life into his keeping. Now she would pay the cost for her safe haven here in this house.

Her gown lay across a chair, and she looked down at the chemise and petticoat she wore, then gasped, Rafael's long fingers touching the buttons of her bodice. As if he were an old hand at this, he slid each tiny pearl fastener from its hold and her chemise fell open, exposing the pale breasts beneath.

She heard his harsh intake of air, the breath he held for long moments before his hands returned to her clothing. The tapes of her petticoat were unknotted quickly, and he released them, allowing the heavy garment to fall to the floor. Clad only in the undergarment she wore, a soft cotton pair of underpants such as those she'd been allotted at the convent, she felt a hot blush sweep up from the naked rounding of her breasts, covering her throat and cheeks with a fiery hue that brought quick tears to her eyes.

"I swore to myself that you wouldn't make me cry, but I've lost the battle already, haven't I?"

Rafael breathed an oath under his breath and picked up the quilt from the bed, wrapping it around her trembling body. "I never meant to make you cry or be unhappy. Especially, I would not embarrass you, Isabella. I was so intent on taking your clothes from you, I didn't stop to think how you would feel about it. I should have known. I'm sorry, sweetheart."

He pulled her into his arms and she found herself resting there as might a fledgling nestle beneath its mother's wing. "Sister Agnes Mary said our bodies were shameful and cursed, ever since the days of the Garden."

"Shameful?" Rafael shook his head. "There is nothing shameful about the beauty that God created in that garden. The shameful part was when the man and woman realized they were naked and covered up the beauty God had made. Sister Agnes Mary was wrong. I will never believe that God meant for the human body to be covered and hidden from each other by those who live together in a state of marriage."

"I was taught by the nuns to keep myself modest and covered from sight at all times, Rafael. I can't just change my ways in the blink of an eye."

"I know that, but I also know that in the privacy of our rooms you will not hide yourself from me, Bella."

She cast a look of pleading in his direction, and he was tempted to give in to her appeal tonight. But the knowledge that he must begin as he meant to go on was uppermost in his mind, and so he shook his head, tempering the motion with a smile that was admiring of the picture she presented before him.

The quilt had slipped a bit, exposing the uppermost curves of her breasts, and he would not allow her to pull it back in place, but held her arms at her sides, not forcefully, but with a tender grip that nonetheless was an unspoken message.

"Please, Rafael. I need to wear my robe. I would

prefer a nightgown to cover me, but if this is what you have chosen for me, it will do." She could not hold back the whispered plea, much as she wanted to toss her head and defy him more strongly.

"Put it on, Bella. But when I tell you it is time to remove it and drop it on the floor, you will obey."

She refused to meet his gaze, but turned away and pulled the fullness of many yards of white fabric over herself, allowing it to fall about her body, covering the quilt. Rafael scooped the patchwork quilt from the floor and tossed it at the foot of the wide bed they would share, then turned back to her.

"Get into bed, Bella. I will join you shortly."

She did as he had ordered her and turned on her side, facing the windows and the wide door that opened onto the courtyard. She pulled the sheet up until only her head was exposed, and curled her body beneath the all-concealing robe.

The candle on Rafael's side of the bed was still glowing when he turned back the sheet and lay beside her moments later. His arm slid around her waist and he pulled her gently back to rest against his body. She felt the heat of his flesh behind her, knew the warmth of his desire as his arousal pressed against her bottom, and shivered at the knowledge that his body had already prepared itself to consummate this marriage.

He held himself still, only his hands moving as he encircled her with his arms, allowing his fingers and palms to press gently against the soft parts of her body. Her breasts responded to his touch, seeming to swell within his palms, the tender crests firming against his skin, only the single layer of fabric keeping him from the silken skin beneath.

"I would have you remove your covering now, Bella mine."

The words she had expected nonetheless came as an almost physical shock to her, for opening the front of the robe and exposing herself to him again was almost beyond her ability to accomplish.

"I can't, Rafael. Don't make me do this, I beg you."

He stilled, his hands unmoving against her body, his breath almost seeming to cease as he became once more the man she had feared during the long journey to this place. "You are my wife, sweetheart. I have the right to your body, according to the laws of the church and the land, and I would hold you in my arms now without this bit of fabric between us."

She shivered, feeling as though the cold winds of a desert night were chilling her skin, as if she were exposed to the winds atop the highest mountain peak. This was what it meant to be alone, without a shelter, only the forbearance of a husband intent on having his word obeyed between her and the terror to come.

"I can't." She uttered the words in a hopeless whisper and spoke her fears aloud. "I was meant to be a nun, a Sister of Charity, not a wife, Rafael. The life of the mistress of your household is not for me. Rather I would sleep alone in my cell at the convent. I did not ask for this, and I know I told you I would be your wife, but I find I can't do as you ask now. If you take my body now, if you take me to wife, it will be without my consent, without my cooperation."

"That would be rape, Isabella. And a man with any honor at all would not force his wife to be covered in that way."

"You're an honorable man, Rafael." She spoke the words that decided her fate for this day, that gave her a reprieve for this night.

"I want you to be my wife for the rest of our lives, Bella. I cannot begin our life together with an act worthy of a beast. You will sleep tonight as a virgin. Until you are ready to feel my hands on you, my body upon yours in the act of marriage, I will hold you in my arms and allow you the freedom of choice."

She lay very still beside him, hope growing within her heart that he might be not only honorable, but honest with her. That his words were just what they seemed, a promise for mercy, a vow that she would sleep in this bed with him, as a virgin.

"I would give much to have your fine mentor at the convent before me for five minutes. I would give her a great deal to think about," he said, anger alive in each word. "She had no right to speak to you of marriage and fill your ears with such lies. She had nothing by which to judge me."

"When I heard of the marriage bed, the nuns didn't know who my husband would be, Rafael. They only spoke of men in general."

"Even more reason why they should not have filled you with fear at the thought of being a bride.

None of them have had anything solid to base their opinions upon."

"Sister Ruth Marie was a refugee from an unhappy marriage," Isabella said softly. "She came to the convent, fleeing from a cruel man, and was given shelter there. She knew of what she spoke."

"She knew of the acts of one man, Bella, not of all men."

Silently, she absorbed his words. Could she be so wrong? Could the sisters have been doing Rafael, or any man for that matter, an injustice? "I will think about this. It may be that by tomorrow, I will be willing to trust you in this, Rafael."

He drew her closer, his hands circumspect now as he held her close, warming her trembling body with the heat of his flesh, the banked fire of his desire.

"Sleep now, Bella mine. I'll be here with you and no harm will come to you."

Her eyes closed as he spoke, her fears soothed by the assurances of the man she had married. And in moments she was asleep.

CHAPTER TWELVE

"IF YOU WANT TO GO BACK to the convent, it is possible to do so." Lucia spoke the words in an undertone as Isabella sat at the kitchen table drinking her morning coffee. The girl had been watching for her, waiting for this opportunity to speak, it seemed, and Isabella wondered for a moment just what her reasons were for such a statement.

That it would place Lucia back in control here at the Diamond Ranch was almost a certainty, for with Isabella gone, the majority of the decisions in this house would be put back on Lucia's shoulders. Surely Rafael and his father wouldn't send the girl back to her family if Isabella were not here.

"Why do you say such a thing?" Isabella's words were low, not intended for Maria's ears. The housekeeper stood at the stove, cutting up vegetables into a huge pot, preparing a thick stew for the noontime meal, and it would not be wise to make her privy to this conversation, Isabella decided.

"Have you had enough of married life yet?" Lucia asked quietly, her tone almost sympathetic. "Surely a woman such as you, who has devoted her life to a convent, is not prepared to spend her years with a man. Especially not with the demands men are prone to make upon their womenfolk."

The thought of what lay ahead for her in Rafael's bed had been uppermost in Isabella's mind all morning. That she had escaped the feared initiation last night was a fact. That she would no doubt be forced to face that same duty tonight or perhaps tomorrow night was also a fact. And she shivered as she thought of the times to come when she would lie beneath Rafael and perform the duties of a wife.

She rose and went out to the porch, Lucia hot on her heels. Isabella turned to face the woman who seemed set on taunting her, offering a challenge of her own. "How would I get back to the convent?" And if Lucia had a plan devised that would make it a possibility, perhaps she would consider it, would think well on the life she would be permitted to live there, the solitary life of a novitiate.

The thought that she had vowed to obey Rafael entered her head. She had promised before the priest and the Almighty that she would be his wife, so it was a stumbling block to do such a thing as escape to the convent, but the thought was alluring.

Rafael was a good man, but the memory of long days working in the gardens, hours of privacy in her cell, the solemn masses that fed her soul with the peace she gained from her hours of kneeling in prayer—all these were parts of the whole. She had considered taking the veil. Indeed, if not for Rafael's appearance at the convent, she would likely be even now preparing for the initial vows.

"I've promised Señor McKenzie that I would be his daughter from now on," she said musingly. "I would be making that vow a lie if I left here now and walked away from the commitments I have made."

Lucia shrugged nonchalantly. "Rafael would find another bride, and the church would no doubt annul your marriage. Unless it has been consummated already." Her eager eyes fed on Isabella's reluctance to speak. "Has he bedded you, Isabella?"

Isabella felt a flush climb her cheeks, and her refusal to look at Lucia seemed answer enough for the other girl.

"I thought not. He probably thought you too tired last night to make your marriage a reality. Or did you refuse him?"

"I don't think it's proper to speak of this with you," Isabella said cuttingly. "I'm sure my life with Rafael is none of your business."

"I'm trying to do you a favor," Lucia said quietly.

Isabella considered the idea. If she could leave here and return to the convent… The idea was appealing. She had become fond of the people at the Diamond Ranch, had become more than fond of Rafael's father, and had come close to accepting her place as Rafael's wife. But the lure of the convent was great. It was a safe place, her home over the past five years, a place where she was secure, where her future was not in question. And certainly the life of a nun was one she could accept and enjoy.

"Well?" Lucia prodded her, her eyes bright with expectation. "I only want to help you to escape this trap Rafael has set for you."

"Let me think on this. I'll speak to you again this afternoon."

"Matthew is willing to take you," Lucia told her. "He said he would do as you wished and return you to the sisters. I think he feels guilty that he was a part of taking you from the convent. He said it was the wrong thing to do, that you'd had no choice and Rafael should not have taken you captive."

"Matthew is a good man. He was kind to me," Isabella said, remembering the respectful way she had been treated by the red-haired man. He was different from the other men on the ranch…a gringo, as they called him. Here, in the territory of New Mexico, where most of the hands on farms and ranches were men from below the border, he stood out, red haired, fair skinned and taller than most others who worked at Diamond Ranch.

Lucia seemed almost to stalk her, Isabella thought, ushering her slowly, her words persuasive as she coaxed Isabella toward the barn, where horses could be seen, saddled and waiting. "Then go with him and he will help you return to the convent. After all, that's where you belong. Rafael had no right to abduct you, and surely God will not bless a marriage that results from such an act."

From the stable, a man walked with a measured pace to the horses, his eyes intent on the house, his manner stealthy. A wide-brimmed hat shadowed his face and hid the color of his hair, but Isabella recognized him. Matthew was waiting for her, and she felt a chill of foreboding as she wondered at the deed she was about to take part in. Surely, her return to the convent would be according to God's will. Certainly Rafael would find a woman more suited to be his bride were she gone from his life.

But her feet were heavy, dragging on the dusty yard as she went toward the barn and approached the man who waited there. Her soft shoes seemed unfit for the day ahead of her, yet should she return to her room to find her new boots, something more suited to travel, she might not escape.

Even though her conscience nudged her and she regretted the hurt she would deal to both Rafael and Simon she made a quick decision. "I will go with him. The sisters will know what to do, and Father Joseph will pray for my life to be as God wills it." She went across the porch and Matthew saw her, lifting her swiftly to sit atop the smaller of the two horses. He mounted his own gelding and lifted the reins.

"Are you ready to leave?" he asked Isabella, his eyes watchful as he scanned the yard and outbuildings.

She gripped the saddlehorn with both hands. "Matthew, I am not used to riding. I have not been in a saddle since I was much younger, and have not ridden alone since."

Matthew's horse was beside her and he leaned forward so that she could see his face. His nod was firm and his smile promised safety.

"Then we'll not be in a hurry until you are accustomed to the mare. I don't want you to fall or be harmed in any way, señora."

There were no other men about, Rafael having long since left his bed and eaten his breakfast before he set out for the day's work. The hands had apparently gone with him and there were no witnesses to see the furtive movements of the man and woman who rode from the hacienda and disappeared quickly, a cloud of dust rising behind them the only evidence of their departure.

"Will Rafael be terribly angry with you, Matthew?" Isabella thought of the man who was helping her, aware that he had no doubt lost his position on Diamond Ranch through his actions.

"I won't be returning here," Matthew told her. His jaw was set, his eyes watchful as he rode, quartering the countryside around them, intent on leaving the area quickly. They rode into a flat area, beyond the borders of Diamond Ranch, their mounts fresh and willing to travel at a good pace. But Matthew kept them to a walk for a bit, then allowed his gelding to break into a slow lope that covered ground much more quickly. Around them the earth was arid, the grass sparse, and only the promise of a wooded area ahead made the heat bearable.

Matthew set his pace to accommodate her slower

mare, seemingly aware that Isabella rode in a distracted manner, unsure of her actions, unused to the activity she had taken on this morning. She was silent as though she bore second thoughts in her heart, and he slowed his horse's pace, allowing her to catch up to him, then leaned close to speak to her.

"Are you certain this is what you want to do, Isabella? Lucia was determined to help you leave the ranch, but if returning to the convent isn't your desire, there's still time to take you back. Rafael will never know that you have gone unless you tell him yourself. And there is a long journey ahead if you choose this. We will be on the road for over two long days." He paused, as if uncertain of his actions. "Be sure that you don't let Lucia set your path, Isabella. She may not have your good in her heart."

"I've made my choice, Matthew. Rafael is better off without me there. My heart is not set on a marriage with him, and I only fear that his father will be upset over my leaving. I doubt Rafael will be heartbroken." Her words sounded bitter and held a remnant of sorrow, she thought, then brushed the mood of darkness from herself and touched the sides of her horse with her heels, nudging the mare into a faster pace.

"The quicker we leave this part of the territory, the quicker we will achieve my destiny, Matthew. My place is in the convent. I'll tell Father Joseph I have chosen to become one of the sisters. It was meant to be, I think."

Matthew looked uncertain, but he loosened his reins and his gelding kept apace as Isabella rode more quickly now, her mind made up, her confidence in her ability to sit well atop the mare seeming to grow as they traveled.

"I WOULD LIKE TO SEND a message to the ranch of Juan Garcia. It is a long way to travel, but time is of the essence, and he must be reached by tomorrow. The directions are drawn on a map, and the way is written plainly on a note I will give you." Lucia's words were almost a whisper as she approached the newest of the ranch hands, a man who had been hired on only days before.

"I have been told to work on the fencing on the pasture here by the stable," the young man said, his look dubious as he listened to the lovely young woman. "I don't think the señor will be pleased if I leave to deliver a message for you."

Lucia pressed a small bag of coins into the youth's hand, then handed him two pieces of paper. "The sealed note is for Juan Garcia. The other is the map I promised that will guide you easily to his holdings. I am paying you well for this," she said with a teasing smile. "And, when you return, there will be a much more valuable reward for you to claim."

"And if I fear returning here once I have done such a thing as you ask? My position at the Diamond Ranch will be a thing of the past, and I will have to answer to Rafael if he knows what I have done. And whatever reward you offer me will be impossible for me to claim."

"I'll take care of Rafael, and when you return, your reward will be waiting. You'll have only to come to me at night and let me know that all is well." Lucia tossed the bag in the air, listening to the jingle of coins as she teased the young man with the generous bribe she had accumulated over the years of her work. "Just go and deliver this note to Juan Garcia. No one else, only the man himself. He will probably also reward you. Just know that the way is long, for he lives over fifty miles from here, to the northwest. But the directions will get you there in time if you ride quickly. Take another horse with you to trade off on, for your mount will be weary."

The lure of easy money seemed to be strong, for the youth quickly mounted his horse, and with a quick salute, rode toward the barn, from which he appeared in a few minutes, leading another gelding by a lead rope. As he rode down the lane, Lucia watched as he slid the money he was earning into his pocket.

She walked quickly to the hacienda, letting herself in the door and busying herself in the kitchen, her smile triumphant.

THEIR HORSES WERE FRESH, and when Isabella seemed to be growing more confident of her ability, Matthew set a rapid pace as they headed north toward the convent. They stopped for food in the afternoon, Isabella weary from the hard riding, and Matthew seemingly unwilling to force her to a state of collapse. In a small grove of trees, they rested on the grass, food from Maria's kitchen in one of the saddlebags providing them nourishment. Food left from the wedding feast filled the bag, and it was with a sense of sorrow that Isabella ate the meat and bread rolls she had only sampled the day before.

She thought of Rafael, of his kindness to her during the night just past, and for a moment she rued the actions she had taken, leaving him after only a day of marriage. He would be angry, she knew, and perhaps even sad to believe she had thought so little of him as to ride off without a word of farewell. And yet, she knew he would not have allowed her to ride away, would have halted her return to the convent, had he been able.

"WE NEED TO RIDE ON, señora," Matthew said, hours later, as she felt sleep begin to overtake her. They had continued on after a short rest, her stomach satisfied with the food she'd eaten, but her head was heavy as she leaned forward over the saddle. "You can sleep tonight when we find shelter, but for now we must ride."

Matthew had gathered together the saddlebags from the ground, put them on his gelding's back and led the way as they set out.

Silently, they rode to the north, to where the convent was sheltered between two low mountain peaks. It was full nightfall before they halted. Matthew tethered the horses in a grassy area, then returned to

Isabella and laid out a bedroll for her before he took his place nearby, watching her as she slept.

They ate sparingly the next morning, then approached the small village where they'd purchased food on the trip from the convent mere days before. Matthew instructed Isabella to wait for him beneath a tree just outside of the village, lest she be seen and her presence noted. He rode to the small general store and purchased a glass canning jar filled with milk and filled his canteen with water from the pump at the horse trough.

Returning in half an hour, he offered her the milk to drink, and a small loaf of fresh bread from the general store, waiting patiently till she ate and drank quickly. They rode north, skirting the village then, and settled in for the long ride ahead. Familiar landmarks were apparent to Isabella as they rode, and she realized that they were traveling faster than they had on the earlier trip.

"When will we be at the convent?" she asked Matthew, their horses walking as they rested them a bit during the late afternoon.

"Tomorrow, early in the day," he said. "We've made good time."

But his words were not to be fulfilled, for when daybreak came, Isabella awoke to find a man standing over her, his hands on his hips, his eyes flaring with triumph as he watched her awaken.

"Good morning, my dear bride." His words were harsh, as if he mocked her, and though she hadn't seen him in many years, Juan Garcia's face was familiar to her, his small, dark eyes gleaming, his black hair long and in disarray. She sat up quickly, dizzy from her sudden movement, and then was pulled to her feet, her arms grasped roughly by the man before her.

"You kept me waiting," he said, his voice a snarl. "I thought to find you last night. But you did not travel as rapidly as did the man who brought me news of your whereabouts."

"Who would do such a thing? How did you find us?" She whispered the queries, feeling faint as he held her firmly before himself. Surely it was not mere fate that had brought him here. Somehow, he must have had news of their travel, of their seeking out the convent for her return.

"The woman, Lucia, sent me a message that you were on your way, and I left immediately to hunt you down. I lost no time in seeking you out." His words answered Isabella's questions and she sagged in his grasp. At her right, Matthew stepped closer, earning himself a murderous look from Garcia. Undeterred, he stood by her side.

"Don't harm her. Whoever you are, you have no right to touch the señora. She's the wife of Rafael McKenzie, and he would kill the man who causes her pain or grief."

Garcia laughed, a harsh sound that sent a chill of fear down Isabella's spine. "I fear no man, and especially not Rafael McKenzie. He stole my bride from the convent and when he is dead, I will marry her myself. It was meant to be, for her father gave her to me many years ago. Even when she was but a child, he promised her as my bride."

Matthew seemed to be thinking, halting his advance, then he spoke to Isabella. "Is this true? Is this man being honest with us? Was he to have been your husband, before Señor McKenzie took you from the convent?"

She closed her eyes, nodding in silence, admitting to Matthew the circumstances her father had set in motion when she was but a child. But her words when she spoke were those of a woman who has been a victim of the men surrounding her all of her life.

Matthew stood silently beside her for long moments before he replied. "I will help Señor Garcia in his mission to take you with him to his home. If Rafael cares enough to follow us, he will be walking into a trap, and no more than he deserves, for he should not have taken you captive."

Isabella slumped, and Garcia lowered her to the ground. Matthew's words seemed to be the final blow to her spirit, for she had not thought him a traitor to Rafael. She had hoped he would help her to escape the hands that held her. Garcia knelt before her as she hid her face in her hands, her tears flowing.

"You will be mine, Isabella," he muttered, his hands more gentle now, as if he would comfort her and halt her tears. "I'll take you to my home and marry you, once Rafael McKenzie is out of the way.

He had no right to take you from the sanctuary of the convent and then marry you."

He stood then and looked down at her. "Are you truly his wife? Has he taken you to his bed?" He watched her closely and she thought quickly, aware that what she said might influence his actions. Should he find that she was still a virgin, she might be treated as a more treasured captive now. For his pride would not be damaged by a bride who had not been sullied by another man.

"I slept in his bed, but he did not—" Her words ceased as Matthew and Garcia both jerked to attention as she spoke. She looked into the dark eyes that seemed to be feeding on her, for Garcia bent closer and his gaze was hot and his body was taut and tensed for action as he reached for her again.

His hands were harsh against her flesh, and though she wore long sleeves, his fingers would leave bruises on her skin, she knew. He lifted her to her feet and his mouth was hard and cruel as he bent to her, kissing her lips with a force she thought she could not bear. Her mouth felt bruised, the taste of blood making her gag as she jerked her face from his.

"You've hurt her." Matthew's voice was a snarl and she turned to him as he lifted a hand to her mouth, wiping a drop of blood from her lip.

"Don't touch her." Garcia's words were a warning. "No man will ever touch her again but me, as her husband."

Isabella felt the blood drip from her lip, and it fell

to the bodice of her dress, where it lay like a crimson tear against her breast. "You are a cruel man, Juan Garcia." Her words were quiet, but her heart was beating heavily, her fear making her voice tremble. The kisses Rafael had bestowed upon her lips were but a memory now, wiped away from her conscious mind by the cruel fact of Juan Garcia's brutality. And with much more of the same to come, she was certain.

I was a fool to leave. Lucia planned for this, and I fell right into her plans. I knew she wasn't to be trusted, but I allowed her to bend me in this direction. Her thoughts spun in her mind as she watched Garcia as if from a great distance, her body shrinking in upon itself as she slumped again to the ground.

"She's fainted." Matthew's voice penetrated the dimness in her mind and she knew a moment of relief as she was placed to lie prone upon the ground, and then the darkness took her and she knew no more.

"Lucia sent word to Juan Garcia that Isabella had left here and was returning to the convent." Maria's words were accusing as she faced Rafael, Lucia sitting in a chair, with the print of Maria's hand vivid upon her face. "She admitted it to me, Rafael, told me she helped Isabella get away, and persuaded Matthew to take her."

"My own man took Isabella from me?" Rafael was white with anger, his eyes flashing as he glanced at the slumped figure of his cousin. "And you helped him? Why would you do such a thing?" he asked in a strident tone.

Lucia looked up at him, drawing herself into a ball of frustrated womanhood. "You should have married me, Rafael. I would have made you a good wife and run your home for you and borne your children, as my father planned when he sent me here.

"Instead you brought back this creature who knows nothing of being a woman, a girl child who is no more ready for marriage than a youngster from the village. I'll warrant you didn't even consummate your marriage to her when you had the chance on your wedding night, for she looked as innocent yesterday morning as she did the day before the wedding." Her laugh rang out then, mocking him, and Rafael was sorely tempted to leave his own mark upon her face, so angry was he with her taunts.

Even more so because they were true. He had allowed Isabella's fears to keep him from her, and his wedding night remained in his mind now as a farce, a promise unfulfilled.

"I'll find them, and God help you, Lucia, if Isabella has been harmed. Matthew is a dead man already, for his breaths are numbered, and once I find them, he will learn to fear the name of McKenzie."

"I MEANT WHAT I SAID YESTERDAY. I'll help you get her to safety, Garcia." Matthew's offer was made in an offhand manner, but Isabella watched his face as he glanced in her direction. He was playing a game with

Garcia, she was certain of it, and she would go along with it, for it seemed to be her only chance of escape.

Matthew approached her and lifted her easily to her feet, holding her shoulders lest she collapse onto the ground.

"I'll take her," Garcia thundered. "I told you not to touch her again, gringo. If you would ride with me, you'll have to obey my orders. No one touches the girl but me, no hands but mine will bring her food and drink and no eyes but mine will be upon her as she rides."

Behind him, his assortment of men looked at each other warningly, apparently used to the man's threats and temper. Matthew nodded in agreement with the edicts and stepped away from Isabella, shooting her a look that penetrated her fear, her hopes rising as she recognized that she had an ally.

"I can't return to Diamond Ranch anyway, so I might as well throw in my lot with you, Señor Garcia," he said with lazy candor. "I'm a good man with a gun and no one can dispute my riding and roping ability. If you want me to work for you, I'm available."

Juan Garcia cast him a look of disgust. "We will see. If you so easily leave one man to work for another, I'll have to watch you. I must be able to trust those who work on my ranch."

He had Isabella's horse brought to him and with hot, hungry hands, he lifted her into the saddle, his fingers squeezing her rib cage, bringing a gasp to her lips.

"Do you enjoy causing pain to those weaker than you, señor?" she asked, reaching for her reins and settling herself in the saddle.

"There are different kinds of pain, my love. Some of which you might find most enjoyable at my hand. We shall see. At any rate, I'm pleased that you recognize my strength as being far beyond yours. That knowledge will better keep you in line. I will not allow you freedom. You will be obedient and do as you are told, or pay the price. And now we must ride, for with you to consider, it will take longer to reach my hacienda than it would were you not along with us. We will not be home until tomorrow."

Isabella shivered at his words. The man was beyond cruel, she had decided, aware of the bruises that were forming on her ribs from his rough treatment. Matthew was a puzzle, but she was certain that he would offer his help if the chance arose. For now she could only do as she was told and obey Garcia, as frustrated as the idea made her feel.

They set out, Garcia's men, four in number, surrounding them, two in front, two bringing up the rear. Garcia, Matthew and Isabella rode in their midst, her smaller mare between the two men, who both rode tall geldings. They set a pace that did not cause her to tire easily, but didn't stop for food or water until after the sun was high in the sky.

"We'll stop for a short while," Garcia decided, drawing his mount to a halt. Beside him, Isabella did the same and cast him a beseeching look.

"I must get down, Señor Garcia. I need a few moments' privacy."

He eyed her with a gaze that made her shiver, then dismounted and lifted her from her saddle. "I'll follow you, so don't try to escape me."

She went into a patch of tall brush, looking back over her shoulder, aware that he watched her. When she was out of sight of the rest of the men, he cast her a warning glance, then turned his back. "You have one minute of privacy."

She inhaled sharply, for she'd feared him watching her as she tended to her needs. He apparently had decided she could not go far while he stood so near, so she took advantage of his leniency and relieved herself on the ground, pulling her clothing into place with haste, lest he turn back before the minute had expired.

She walked back to where he stood and offered appreciation for his actions. "Thank you, señor. I feared you might not allow me to have a moment alone without being watched."

He smiled, and though he was not an unhandsome man, there was about him a sense of evil that did not allow his features to appear anything but harsh and unbecoming to her eyes. "You will find me a lenient husband, Isabella. If you obey and do as you are told, I will be kind to you."

Somehow, she doubted his ability to express that particular virtue, for kindness seemed to be beyond him, but she forced a wan smile to her lips and nodded at his words. Together, they walked back to where the men had torn open a pack of supplies and were passing around the food they'd carried with them. A small fire had been lit and, already, a coffeepot was hanging from a tripod over the blaze.

Garcia led her to a place apart from the others and motioned to a blanket that had been placed on the ground, apparently at his command, by one of his men. "You may sit here, and I'll bring you something to eat and drink." She did as he ordered, drawing up her legs and lowering her forehead to rest against her knees. Her eyes closed as she sat there in the quiet of the shadowed clearing. She was weary, yet the morning's ride had not been hard on her physically. But the thought of what was to come, the hope of rescue at Rafael's hand and the knowledge that Matthew would not abandon her without a fight, wore on her emotions, and she fought the tears that threatened to fall.

I won't let him see me cry. The words that vibrated in her mind gave her strength and she forced the hot, salty drops back, knowing he would rejoice in her weakness should he see them. From beneath her lashes she saw his booted feet before her and she swallowed hard, then looked in his direction.

"I have brought you food, Isabella. Eat some bread and meat. There is water for you to drink, unless you want coffee." Leaning forward, he offered her a towel that held the food he'd brought for her meal and she took it from his hand, knowing that she must eat in order to keep her strength up. For should an opportunity to escape come her way, she must be ready, and it would not help to starve herself.

The food was tasteless in her mouth, but she chewed and swallowed until it was gone, then realized that she did not even know what sort of meat she had eaten, for it was but ammunition for her body to use in its struggle for survival.

She drank from the canteen Garcia gave her and then put it into his waiting hands. "You have ten minutes to rest," he told her, turning away and returning to the men who sat around the campfire waiting for the coffee to finish boiling.

She decided she needed the rest, and lay on her side, her arm bent beneath her head. A scarf she'd carried with her for protection against the weather was in her pocket and she drew it forth, then covered her face with it, hoping to seek out some bit of privacy in this way.

"She is sleeping." The voice from overhead woke her, and she sat erect, grasping the scarf that fell to her lap and folding it to replace in her pocket before she looked up at the men who stood over her. Garcia was watchful, his dark eyes flaring as he looked beyond her to where the trail they had traveled stretched southward. "I expect Rafael McKenzie will try for a rescue by nightfall, unless we hasten on," he said. "What is your opinion?" he asked Matthew, who stood next to him.

Matthew shrugged. "He's a determined man, but not foolish. He will not expose himself to harm for the sake of a mere woman. If the opportunity comes for him to be successful in seeking her return to the Diamond Ranch, he will take it, but the man isn't a fool. Unless he brings a small army with him, he cannot succeed in foiling your takeover of the girl. And he doesn't have a small army at his disposal, for his ranch is widespread and the men are scattered to the four corners, repairing fences and rounding up horses for a sale."

It was a lie. Isabella lowered her gaze to her feet as she heard Matthew's words, knew his lie was an attempt to set Garcia's mind at ease. And if Garcia was half as smart as she thought he might be, he probably wouldn't fall for the ruse.

But he seemed not to argue with Matthew's words, for he only offered Isabella his hand. When she ignored it, he bent to her and snatched at her, his bigger fist grinding her fingers into his palm as he lifted her to her feet.

"Don't ignore me when I would put my hands on you, Isabella. You will find the consequences not to your liking if you make me angry."

She turned from him, careful not to jerk from his touch, even though her anger was rising and she detested his hands upon her skin. A quick glance at Matthew showed his lips taut, his jaw knotted and his hands clenched at his sides. The man was having a hard time hiding his feelings, she thought, but she would not call attention to him, lest Juan Garcia saw him as she did.

She walked before the two men back to where the fire had been smothered by sand and the men were mounting their horses in preparation for the ride to the Garcia ranch. Her own mare stood nearby and she approached the animal, her hand lifting to rub tenderly at the mare's long face, speaking soft words against the animal's jaw as she prepared to mount.

Again, Garcia lifted her, his hands not so harsh as before. But she still felt each fingertip as they touched the area where her ribs already bore bruises. She winced as she settled in the saddle and he smiled, an evil look that frightened her.

"You have found that my touch is not always easy, my love," he said snidely, his hand lying against her thigh, his skin hot through the layers of her dress. "If you behave yourself, you will save yourself from pain. Try to remember."

She nodded silently, aware that she must appear to give him his due, lest he grow angry with her again. They set off and Matthew rode on her left, Garcia on her right, the other men taking up their positions as guards.

CHAPTER THIRTEEN

THE ROAD LED ACROSS meadows now, the altitude higher, the grass more lush here, and ahead of them lay a patch of woods, the trail seeming to pass through it. She did not recognize the path they took, for they had taken a westward direction this morning, instead of traveling due north to the area where the convent was situated.

Ahead of them, she saw a flash of brown that caught her eye, and thought perhaps it was a deer, or a mountain lion. Perhaps it was a lion and it would jump on Juan Garcia as he rode past, she thought gleefully. If something should befall him, there was a chance that she and Matthew could escape.

But it seemed that her wishes were futile, for they passed through the edge of the patch of woods uneventfully, their horses being forced now to go single file due to the overhanging boughs and the undergrowth that lined their path. The air was still, no hint of a breeze blew through the trees, and the wild animals that inhabited this area were silent around them, perhaps disturbed by the humans who had invaded their territory, she thought.

Ahead of them was a rise, where to one side a huge rock pile had come to rest at the foot of the hill. The trail curved around it and off to the right, and Garcia sent two men ahead to be sure the path was clear. They rode ahead, the rest of the party halting, awaiting their return, the horses seeming to be pleased at the chance to rest.

Isabella sat with her head bowed, listening intently, for her inner voice told her that things were not as they seemed. Ahead of them, she heard the men's voices, heard one of them calling out for the rest of the group to come ahead. It was a muffled call, but Garcia did not seem to doubt its veracity, for he nudged his horse into a walk, signaling for the rest of the men to follow him. Isabella waited until he was ahead of her, then moved into place behind him, aware that Matthew was close to her, his horse nudging her mare's flank.

She allowed several more feet of space between her mare and the horse that Garcia was riding, slowing down her progress as much as she could without arousing the suspicion of the men who followed Matthew. If only she could find a place, a break in the trail perhaps, where she might ride off through the woods and escape.

Her eyes darted around the area as her horse took the curve in the trail past the rock slide and within sight of Garcia's horse. From overhead, a man jumped down atop the horse and rider in front of her, knocking Garcia to the ground. She looked beyond him, certain that the two men who had ridden ahead would turn and see his peril, but there was no one there.

Until suddenly, four horsemen rode into view, and she recognized them as hands from the Diamond Ranch, employees of Rafael and his father. She drew her mare to a halt and turned to see Matthew's back as he turned his gelding, allowing him to face the men behind him. He had drawn his gun and he was holding them at bay, shouting out words of warning to the man who fought a vicious battle on the ground ahead.

Garcia's men turned tail and rode away, apparently unwilling to enter into a gun battle with odds that were against them, and Matthew let them go, riding up to reach for Isabella's reins, holding her mare steady, lest the animal bolt.

Ahead of them, Rafael stood, leaving Garcia prone. And then he turned to where she sat, watching him.

"Are you ready to go home, Bella mine?" he asked, his jaw firm, his eyes casting her a look without pity. Behind him, several of his men waited on his words and she tried to see beyond them to where Garcia's men should have been waiting for their employer. The path ahead was empty, and Rafael's words told her of their doomed foray to scout out the trail.

"The men you look for are around the corner, tied and awaiting their fate," he said harshly. "We were waiting for them and surprised them before they could call out an alarm. Did you think my voice sounded like one of them when I called out to

Garcia?" His laughter rang false as he looked at the
woman who had escaped from his ranch.

"Did you think I would not follow you, Bella?
Were you so anxious to go with Garcia? Or did he foil
your chances to finally enter the convent and devote
yourself to being a nun?"

"She was not going willingly with Garcia," Matthew said from his place almost beside her. "I hoped
to be able to get away with her and head back, but
hadn't had the opportunity when all this happened."

"You will answer to me later, Matthew." Rafael's
eyes were hard, his scowl murderous as he faced the
man he had trusted. "Why did you take her? What did
Lucia promise you?"

Matthew appeared to think quickly. "I knew if I
didn't take her as Lucia asked, she would find another
and my own life would be forfeit, for she couldn't
take a chance on my telling tales if I refused the job."
He shrugged and put his gun back in the holster on
his hip. "Believe me or not, as you like, McKenzie.
It doesn't seem to matter, for I'm at your mercy now.
I intended to return your bride to you unharmed, but
Garcia had other plans."

"It doesn't matter now," Rafael said bluntly. "We'll
settle it after we get back to the ranch. For now, let
the man lie where he is. We'll make tracks and hopefully ride through the night. I want to be well on our
way home by tomorrow morning."

Without further words, they set out, leaving
Garcia's two men tied just a few yards from where

Garcia lay on the trail, unconscious but alive. Their horses were scattered, but if luck was with them, Garcia's other men would catch them up and return to their aid.

LUCIA WAS GONE, her clothing with her, when they returned to Diamond Ranch. Maria was angry at having been so taken in by the woman, and told Rafael that she had fled during the night. A horse was missing from the herd in the corral, and Lucia was a competent rider, so it was assumed that she had ridden in the direction of her father's home. Rafael secluded himself in his office and wrote a note, which he sent by way of one of his men to be delivered to that distant relative.

His anger was still more than apparent to Isabella, but he seemed to have softened his stand regarding Matthew, for he allowed him to go back to work without raising the issue of his perfidy. She was relieved, for she recognized that the man had not wanted her to suffer harm, and for that she was grateful.

But for Isabella, Rafael had no sufferance, for he was harsh, sending her, with but a direct order, to go to her room. She did not argue, but did as he commanded, sitting on the edge of her bed, fighting tears of discouragement. When a bath was brought for her by Delores and Elena she quickly stripped from her clothing and climbed into the tub, drawing up her knees in order to fit. She soaped and washed her hair quickly, then used the fragrant suds to clean her body, uncertain as to her own fate at Rafael's hand, fearful that he might come into her room while she was in such a state.

That her escape attempt had met with total failure was not her main worry. The anger she'd felt surging from Rafael on the return trip made her fear for her physical well-being now. He was a proud man, a man determined to rule his private kingdom with an iron hand, and though he had given her an enormous amount of leeway in their marriage thus far, she feared his retaliation for her insulting actions.

Maria sent clothing in for her, Elena explaining that her own things were in the laundry and would be washed tomorrow and hung to dry. For now she would wear a simple heavy cotton dress that had been in Rafael's mother's closet, out-of-date but still wearable. She was able to tie it at her waist, making it fit reasonably well, then slid her feet into the pair of soft house shoes purchased at the general store days earlier, and donned a pair of drawers. She wore nothing beneath the top of the dress, and felt exposed, even though the fabric was heavy enough to conceal her breasts adequately.

Sitting before the dressing table, she picked up a hairbrush and bent her head, working at the length of hair that had required two sudsings to clean it properly. It was snarled and she fought for a few minutes with the heavy, wet tresses before she heard the latch on the door and saw in the mirror that, behind her, Rafael had entered the room.

"I let you stay here for your bath, Isabella, but after you have rested you will return to my room. If you think to have escaped your role as my wife, you are in for a huge surprise, for I will not let you foil my plans for my house."

"For your house?" She turned to look at him, puzzled as to his meaning.

"The house of McKenzie. An honorable name, with no taint of dishonor upon it for over two centuries. You accepted the name when you spoke your vows in the chapel, and along with that the responsibility for continuing the line. I will not relieve you of that task, for when you married me you made promises I intend to hold you to."

"And wouldn't any woman have done as well for a brood mare for your grand *house?*" she asked disdainfully.

"You are the woman I have chosen, whether for good or ill, and when I look at you right now, I wonder why I paid the price to bring you here. My father is lying in his bed, his heart reminding him that he has little time left, and the knowledge that you rode away as a thief in the night from his home has brought him pain. He asked a promise of you and you gave him your word, Isabella. And then you forgot your promise and ran off on a fool's mission."

"I didn't forget. I felt great shame that I had gone without speaking to your father, but when the opportunity arose, I snatched at it."

"And if another such opportunity arises, will you

again snatch at it? Or will you take your place here and be a wife to me and a daughter to my father? Can I ever depend on you to do the right thing, standing by the word you have given of your own free will, or will you always be selfish, thinking only of what you want?"

She stood, her hair in disarray, falling over her shoulders, still snarled from her bath. She brushed it from her face, distractedly, looking around the room as though she sought an escape route from his words. Her heart was beating at twice its usual tempo, and she found herself gasping for a breath, unable to speak, her hands trembling until the brush fell from her grasp. The events of the past three days seemed an insurmountable barrier to her future and she fought silently for the strength to reach the bed where she might sit and allow her body to rest. And still she felt the beat of her heart, increasing with each breath, taking her vision and replacing it with a gray cloud.

Rafael stepped closer, his eyes intent on her, his mouth moving as though he were speaking, but she heard nothing, only the harsh sound of a million bees in her ears, and she put her hands up to muffle the drone that would not cease. She stretched out her hands to hold him away, for she feared he would grasp her in those wide palms, that his male scent would overwhelm her and she would find herself leaning on his strength. And then her hands went once more to rest against her ears as it seemed he would speak to her again.

Just inches away, he halted and peered into her

face. Again he spoke, and again she heard nothing, until he reached to remove her hands from either side of her head.

"I want to speak with you, Isabella. Don't try to block your hearing."

"Please, Rafael. Not now. Let me rest, for just a bit." She turned, stumbling as she headed for the bed. It was only a few feet across the floor, but she saw it as if it were a great distance and she was doomed to fall weakly to the floor before she reached it. Her feet tangled in a brightly colored rug at the bedside and she fell forward, the upper half of her body on the mattress, her feet dangling just above the floor.

Rafael was there in an instant, turning her to her back, lifting her legs to the mattress and sitting beside her. His head bent low and he touched her throat with his lips, inhaling as he did so, then exhaling again, the warmth of his breath sending a trembling quiver down her spine. His whisper was low, but she heard each word as a promise he would be bound to keep.

"Tonight you will be mine, Isabella. I have been too patient with you, and given you reason to think you owe me nothing. Now, you've set yourself up for your own seduction, for I can wait no longer, given your penchant for flight. You will learn to be the mistress of my household and take your place here, where you belong."

She twisted away from him, turning her face into the pillow and pushing at his body as it levered over her. "You have no right to say where I belong, or who

I must be or where I will sleep, Rafael. You have taken my freedom from me, and I will never forgive you for claiming me as yours when it was not my wish."

His hands turned her easily back to face him, but she fought him off, her nails clawing at his arms, her hands trying with desperate strength to reach his face with harsh intent. She would have dug her nails into his jaw, slapped at his face, punched him if she'd been able, but all to no avail; for he held her down, capturing her smaller hands in his large palms and bending over her as silent tears slid from her eyes to form damp trails down her face.

"When will you learn not to fight me, Bella? How long will it take for you to accept your place here? I have not taken your freedom from you, only given you new areas in which to express yourself. Be a wife to me, run my home as you please, bear my children and make a name for yourself in this territory as the matriarch of an esteemed household."

He pulled her up from the mattress, drawing her into his arms and across his lap, his hands soothing against her back, his greater strength holding her against himself as he spoke.

"I would have you go to my father and speak with him. He is waiting to hear from your own lips that you are safe and sound, that you did not suffer any harm from Garcia."

"How do you know that Garcia did not possess me?" she asked, her chin tilting as she tossed him a scornful look. "How do you know that I am still a virgin, that he did not claim my body as reparation for your stealing me away from him?"

Rafael smiled, a dark, taunting expression she could not read, for she was not accustomed to men. Feeling young and inadequate to spar with him on this level, she retreated, turning her face from him again, this time burying it against his shirt.

"Aside from the fact that I would have known when I looked into your eyes, Matthew has told me that Garcia did not touch you in such a way. That's not to say that he wouldn't have, very soon in fact, but when we caught up to you he had not had the opportunity to rape you, not without exposing your body to his men, for you were never really alone with him."

"And what would my eyes have told you?" she asked, her words muffled against the fine fabric of his shirt.

His hand grasped her chin and he forced her to turn toward him. "Open your eyes to me, Isabella." His grip tightened and she jerked in his grasp, but he would not release her, only held her even more firmly. His fingers pressed into her soft skin and she bore the pain only a moment longer before she opened her eyes and met his gaze. His own was almost black, his expression harsh, yet there dwelt in the depths of those ebony eyes a look of yearning she could not mistake.

"I can see your innocence shining forth like a beacon, Isabella. You have the look of a fawn, a female who has not known the overpowering needs of a male. Your face is that of a girl child, not a woman who knows a man's body. For when you have become mine, you will wear the look of a woman, your eyes will be filled with the knowledge of what it means to be possessed by your mate. There will not be a man alive who will be able to look into your face and miss the look you wear."

"I don't believe you," she cried, her voice breaking as she considered what he'd said. That she would be so transparent, that her emotions would be so easily read by others, was not to be tolerated, and she vowed silently not to give him the satisfaction he would surely crave, knowing that she wore the stamp of his possession.

"Believe me or not, it is the truth, Bella mine. When you look into the mirror tomorrow morning, you will see the face of a woman, your eyes will be filled with the knowledge of my power over you, the strength that will woo you to my side."

"You speak like a madman," she said, spitting the words at him in anger. "You may take my body, tarnish me with your lust, but you cannot take away the spirit within me, for I will not submit to you easily, Rafael. Bear in mind that you may force me to your will, but you cannot make me love you. And the act of marriage cannot be one blessed by God without some sort of mutual liking between husband and wife. You don't love me, and I don't even like you. There are no soft, loving feelings between us. Don't pretend otherwise."

"I will argue with you on that angle, Isabella." He

held her upright in his arms now, his face before her, his jaw clenched with some emotion she could not gauge. "I have feelings for you. I can't pretend to any great love between us, for we don't have common knowledge of each other to that extent. I only know that I admire you for your strength and independence, and I don't want to stifle that quality in you, for it makes you the woman I want in my life.

"You are capable of much, Isabella. You are intelligent and I hope you have the knowledge of what is involved in running a house, for I assume the nuns taught you well over the years."

She spoke then, proud of her background at the convent, knowing that it did not lack in knowledge. "They taught me all I know."

"Can you direct the cooking and cleaning of my home? Do you know what must be grown in the garden and how to preserve it for our use? Have you done the physical labor required to keep a house in order?"

She heard his questions, rattled off in rapid succession, nodding her head in reply to each query, and when he paused and looked at her inquiringly, she spoke, her voice haughty, her expression that of a woman who feels her talents have been questioned.

"I have already told you of what I was taught at the convent, Rafael. You know that I worked in the garden and preserved the food we harvested there. I washed clothing on a scrub board and hung it to dry, then heated the sad irons on the stove to use in ironing the nuns' clothing and that of the women who lived there but were not a part of the convent."

She held out her hands, and as if he had never seen them before, as if her calluses and the rough skin that proved her words were unknown to him, he held them in his own and rubbed his thumbs over her palms, lifting them to his mouth to place soft kisses upon the surface of those hands. "Your hands show the hard work you have done, Isabella. I cannot doubt the words you speak, and I have faith in your word that you can do as you have told me. I will gladly turn over the running of my home to you, and the women who work for you will do as you ask without argument. You may choose what you want done and they will do it."

"I cannot ask Maria to be merely a servant, Rafael. She is like a member of the family. It wouldn't be fair to her to take the reins from her hands. I would rather be silent and let her do as she will in your house. I will not argue with her or question her in any way."

His lips formed a smile and he bent on her a look of approval as he spoke. "You can work out with Maria any changes you want made, Isabella. My hands will release you to do as you will. You will answer to me at the end of each day, but only so that I may be certain you are happy in what you do and that no one gives you problems. For I will not stand for you to be without power in your own home."

He held her apart from himself, his eyes looking deeply into hers, as if he would send a message of his support in that way. And then he bent forward and touched his lips to her forehead. "Can we at least be friends, Isabella? Can you forego your thoughts of escape from me long enough to see if there is a life here that will be pleasing to you?"

"Will you be able to trust me if I answer as you wish, Rafael? Or will you always look at me with eyes of distrust, wondering when I will snatch the opportunity to leave you again? How can you know that I will do as you ask, when I don't even know myself what the future holds for me?"

"If you will go with me now and speak with my father and renew your vow to him, I will believe you, Isabella. You have learned in the convent to honor your vows and fear God's wrath should you not do as you have said. I will learn to trust you if you give your word to my father that you will stay here and act as you should, as the wife of the house of McKenzie."

"Tell me one thing, Rafael. How did a man by the name of McKenzie come to own such a place as this? It seems strange that a man from across the ocean, in the place called Scotland, should be the owner of Diamond Ranch, here in a land where the Spanish have ruled for so long."

"He fell in love with my mother, Isabella, and her father owned this place before she was born. An only child, she inherited it upon the death of her parents, and my father married her in order to provide for himself and his descendants a heritage for the future."

"And this is why you felt it only right to take the wife you chose, even without her consent? Because your father used his wiles to get a wife for himself, by claiming her and her possessions?"

"My father was happy with her for many years. She took his name as her own without hesitation, for she knew he was strong and would shield her from harm and care for her and her possessions for the rest of her life. My mother trusted him with all that she owned as the child of a Spanish aristocrat."

"And this is where you get your great arrogance," she said, as if satisfied by her deductions. And then she nodded dutifully, aware that her choices were limited to following his word or being held prisoner in this room and given no freedom in any area. "I will do as you ask and see your father now, Rafael. For I fear that life will not be easy for me if I do not obey you in all things."

He lifted her from his lap, stood beside the bed and drew her to her feet. His arms circled her body and he held her for a moment, his manner kindly, his silence speaking of his forbearance with her. She stirred in his embrace and stepped away from him.

"Let me comb my hair and put it into some sort of order, Rafael. I am not fit to see anyone as I am. My clothing is not tidy, nor my appearance fit for company."

He smiled, and she thought he was amused at her words for he spoke softly, yet with a touch of humor. "You are ideal as you are for the surroundings you stand in, Bella. I like to see you tousled and unkempt in our bedroom, but I agree that you should tame your hair for a visit to my father."

His hands lifted to spear through the long, dark locks that fell to her waist, and his eyes darkened with an emotion she could only wonder at, for his lips parted a bit and he uttered a sound she could only interpret as a growl as he drew her nearer with just the tugging of his hands in her hair.

"I would see you this way tonight, Isabella. In my room, in my bed." And then, as if it caused him an enormous effort, he released her and turned her to the dressing table where her brush and comb waited. She sat before the mirror and lifted the brush to her hair, working at the quickly drying locks that defied her taming touch. Dragging the brush the length of each strand, she unsnarled it and then twisted the length into a knot, lifting it to her crown and placing bone hairpins in place, anchoring it there.

Wisps of black hair hung about her face and she brushed them back impatiently. "My hair is difficult to control, Rafael. This is the best I can do for now."

"You will be more than presentable if you but straighten your dress and put on your slippers." He bent to retrieve the soft shoes she had worn inside the house, and with ease, he lowered her to sit on the edge of the mattress once more, then knelt to slide the shoes on her feet.

"There. You are ready," he said, lifting her again with a strong hand wrapped about hers. "Come, Isabella."

They left the room and as they did, Delores and Elena entered the room behind them, Delores nodding at Rafael as if to assure him that she would do as he had asked.

"Are they going to move my things?" Isabella asked him quietly, glancing back at the closed door behind her.

"You will find your clothing and personal belongings in my bedroom within the hour," he said. "And I expect them to remain there." His final words were harsh in her ears, a warning she knew she would do well to heed.

The door to the senior member of the household was closed and Rafael rapped on it once, then opened the latch, standing back to allow Isabella to walk through ahead of him. She entered slowly, fearful of the displeasure she would find on Rafael's father's face. But it was not to be, for the elderly man merely held out his hands to her from where he sat by the window.

"Come to me, Isabella," he said softly. "Let me look at you and see that you have not been harmed by your adventure." She walked close to him and when he took her hands in his, she fell to her knees by his chair.

"You need not kneel to me, my child," he said, attempting to pull her once again to her feet, but she would not allow it, only bent her head to rest upon his knee.

"I am sorry to have caused you worry. I did not even think about that when I left here to return to the convent. It was a quick decision on my part, and I left without considering the effect it might have on your well-being. I am sorry," she whispered, her heart aching as she considered what might have happened to the man while she was traveling from his hacienda.

"I don't want your tears, Isabella. Only your promise that you will not do such a thing again," he said, his hand reaching to touch her hair. "I want you to be happy here and unless you accept your place as Rafael's wife that will not happen. I want you to be my daughter, and learn to care for me as you would your own father."

She lifted her head and her gaze met his. Her words were low and filled with grief, for she could not help but feel sorrow for the lack of feeling she bore toward the man who had been her sire. "I already feel more affection for you than I did for my own father, señor. He was thoughtless of my needs and affianced me to a man old enough to be my father, a man his own age. And when I disputed his choice for me, he finally agreed to send me to the convent north of here where the Sisters of Charity work. He allowed me to live there to learn the skills I would need to run a household, and when he died before my time there was up, I was given the opportunity to remain there until my eighteenth birthday.

"But his choices for my future were not with my happiness in mind, only the thought of combining our house with that of Juan Garcia, a blending that would provide Señor Garcia with an enormous holding and would, while he was yet alive, give my father the necessary funds to run his ranch."

She looked up at the man who sat before her. "I would have been dreadfully unhappy with Señor Garcia, for he is a cruel man, not given to kindness to those he deals with. I fear him and his hands upon me, and I know that Rafael will be by far the better husband. Had it not been for Lucia sending a message to Juan Garcia, I might even now be back at the convent, where I had planned on asking Father Joseph to allow me to take my vows and become one of the sisters.

"Perhaps it was meant to be that I be returned here. I don't know the answers to all the questions that have arisen in my mind, but I know that I am better off here, with Rafael, than I ever would have been in the hands of Juan Garcia."

She bent her head again and felt his hand, warm against the crown of her head. His voice was low, as if the man were weary and ready for sleep. "You will be a fine addition to my home, Isabella. I understand your yearning for the convent and the life you led there, for it was a place of safety to you. But know that your years here will be serene if you so wish it, for Rafael will care for you gently and tend to your wants and needs as a husband should."

He inhaled deeply then and his hand rose and fell once more, the caress soft against her hair. "I will sleep now," he said. Isabella rose to her feet, Rafael by her side, lifting her carefully lest she lose her balance.

"Come, Bella," he whispered. "My father needs to rest, and his nurse will help him to bed."

Isabella nodded, turning with Rafael to the door, aware that her husband offered his hand to his father, saw from the corner of her eye that the older man grasped it for a moment and murmured several words she could not decipher.

The door closed behind them and she was led straightaway to Rafael's room, to the bed where she had slept several nights before. He lifted her easily, placing her atop the brightly colored quilt and adjusting the pillow beneath her head.

"I would have you sleep now, Isabella. You need to rest, and when you awaken we will eat together in the dining room. But for now," he said, his hands busy with slipping her shoes from her feet, then drawing up another quilt to cover her lightly, "for now, just close your eyes and rest."

She felt his body next to her, the mattress sagging a bit as he sat down next to her hip, and she knew the weight of his hand on her arm, felt the warmth of his skin against her own. It was comforting, and she thought dreamily of the difference between his contact with her flesh and that of Juan Garcia, who had bruised her ribs and brought pain with his touch.

"I will sleep," she whispered, turning her hand to place her palm against his, feeling his grasp as a comfort. Her eyes were heavy and she did not even attempt to open them to see his face, but breathed in the clean scent of the pillowcase beneath her head and allowed her senses to shut down, allowed her mind to stop spinning.

CHAPTER FOURTEEN

AND SO HE SAT WITH HER as she slept, removing himself
after an hour from the bed to pull a chair nearby and
settle there, his feet on a footstool while he kept watch
over her. After the sun had slipped from the courtyard
outside to hover on the edge of the garden wall, he
heard the sound of Maria at the door, her knock soft,
her words but a whisper.

"Señor. Rafael, are you there? Your meal is ready
and already on the table. Will you bring the señora to
eat now?"

"Come in, Maria," he said in a low voice, and
watched as the door opened and the housekeeper
stuck her head in the door, smiling as she caught
sight of the sleeping woman on the bed. "I'll wake
Isabella and we'll be there in just a few moments. She
will want to wash her face and repair her hair before
we eat, I'm sure."

"*Sí*, señor." Maria smiled and returned to the
hallway, closing the door behind her.

Rafael stood, flexing his muscles as he felt the
ache from his hours of hard riding earlier in the day.

Isabella lay quietly and he considered leaving her there to rest, but he knew that she would feel better if she ate and walked around a bit before nightfall came. The hours she would spend in his bed tonight would not be easy for her, and he vowed as he looked down at her that his touch would not be hurtful, that his need would not be more than she could meet and accept.

His hands were gentle as he roused her from slumber, his words soft as he spoke to her of the meal awaiting them, and he lifted her from the bed, then knelt and put her slippers back on the narrow feet he admired. She rose and stifled a yawn, one hand lifting to her mouth to cover it, stretching a bit, as if her muscles were protesting the movements of her body.

"I must wash up a bit, Rafael," she said, her voice still holding the shards of sleep in its even tenor. "My hair is mussed and it will take a few moments to put myself in order."

"I can wait, Isabella, and in the meantime I will watch you, and enjoy seeing the way you put yourself in order." His words were soft, his look admiring, and she glanced at him with suspicion.

"Do you try to soothe my feelings with your kind words, Rafael?"

"I only try to let you know that I am willing to do whatever it takes to make you agreeable to be mine tonight, Bella. I want you to be happy in my bed, not fearful of what we will do together."

She met his gaze, and he saw the fear she could not

hide. "I will try," she said, her voice firmer now, as if she had made a decision and would abide by it.

"I know you will." He followed her to the mirror on the wall over his dresser where her brush lay atop the surface, next to his own. She lifted it and smoothed back the sides of her hair where the pillow had mussed the orderly strands into disarray.

"I fear I won't look the part of your bride tonight, Rafael," she said lightly, bending closer to the mirror to inspect her face. "I have sleep marks on my cheek, and my pins have slipped out of place."

"I think you look lovely," he said, wondering at his own ability to remain apart from her, for she tempted him mightily, her hands lifting over her head, pulling the fabric of her borrowed dress against the curves of her breasts. His eyes feasted there as she worked quickly to ready herself, then watched as she went to his washstand where a bowl and pitcher of water awaited her.

Tipping the pitcher, she poured water into the basin, then bent her head and splashed water on her face, rinsing her hands and using the handy towel to blot the liquid from her skin.

"I'm as ready as I can be," she told him, standing erect once more and waiting for his instructions.

He took her by the hand and led her to the door, and from there down the corridor to where the dining room emitted the scents of food, where the table held a display of dishes meant to tempt her palate.

She settled in her chair, placed next to his at the

head of the table, and watched as he ladled food from the various dishes onto her plate.

"I don't know if I can eat all of this," she said, looking at the varicolored vegetables that filled her dish.

"Eat what you will. Just know that it is a long time until breakfast, and you need your strength. You haven't eaten well for a couple of days, and I don't want you to be ill because I haven't taken care of you properly."

She nodded, listening as he made the sign of the cross and then spoke a brief blessing on the meal, then lifted her fork and ate the food before her.

Rafael watched her closely, not wanting her to be aware of his scrutiny, but needing to know that all was well with her. She ate sparingly but steadily, her fork filling and lifting to her mouth as she made inroads on the food he had given her.

"I don't think I can do much better," she said after ten minutes or so, placing her fork back on the table covering and sitting back in her chair.

"Will you eat dessert?" he asked, looking up as Maria came in the door from the kitchen with a bowl of pudding in her hands. "Maria's sweets are tempting, Bella. You should try a few mouthfuls."

She looked dubious to his watchful eye, but nodded in agreement, drawing a smile from Maria, who bustled forward and placed a small bowl before Isabella. She ladled pudding into it, only a small amount, to be sure, but enough to give the girl a generous taste of the sweet offered.

"Thank you, Maria," Isabella said politely, her smile offered freely. "I appreciate all your kindness to me."

"You are the señor's wife. I will do anything I can to see to your happiness here." Maria's words brought joy to Rafael's heart as he heard her earnest wishes expressed aloud.

Isabella lifted her spoon and as Rafael was served, she began to eat the pudding, her eyes lighting with pleasure as she scraped the bowl clean. Her smile was acknowledgment of the flavor and her tongue touched the corner of her lip where a stray speck of the pudding had been left. Rafael was hard put not to drag her from her chair and down the hallway to his bedroom as she smiled again in his direction.

"That was good. You were right, Rafael. Maria is a gem. I hope she will have patience with my blunders, but I will truly try to be a good mistress in this house."

His pleasure with her capitulation to his will fought with the desire he felt for the girl before him, and both emotions made his voice soft as he spoke her name and then let her know his pleasure for the evening hours.

"Would you enjoy sitting in the parlor for a while, Isabella? Or do you want to go with me to our room and ready yourself for bed?"

She seemed indecisive for a moment, and then she rose and stood beside her chair. "I think we may as well prepare for bed, Rafael. It has been a long day for both of us, and there may not be enough hours in the night to give you the sleep you need."

"I am used to short hours in bed, Isabella, but you

may sleep late tomorrow if you like. I'll be very quiet when I arise and leave you to your dreaming until you want to get up for your morning meal."

She nodded and stepped away from her chair, waiting while he joined her and took her hand. They left the dining room, and Rafael knew that Maria watched from the kitchen doorway, felt her approbation as her gaze warmed his back.

The corridor to his room seemed long as Isabella walked beside him, and he opened the door, then stood back as she walked into his room.

Our room. His silent correction made his heart leap with satisfaction as she crossed to where her clothing was stored, Elena having put every item in place in the low dresser Isabella would use. A drawer was pulled open and Isabella searched out a white gown, then closed the drawer and turned back to him.

"Where can I undress?" Her eyes telegraphed her confusion as she looked about the room for a place of privacy and found none to be had.

"Right here, where I can help you and take care of you, sweetheart," he said, his steps slow but deliberate as he approached her.

Isabella felt her breath catch in her throat as Rafael drew near, his hands outstretched to her. He grasped her shoulders and pulled her close, his arms enclosing her in an embrace that promised tender care. He turned her then, so that her back was before him, the buttons of her dress beneath his fingertips. His touch was gentle as he undid each button, allowing the dress to fall from her as he worked. She wore nothing beneath the bodice, a fact he had already determined, but her undergarments covered her from her waist to her knees.

He tossed the dress aside, after lifting her from its folds, then turned her again to face him, as her hands rose in an instinctive gesture to cover her breasts. He smiled down at her efforts and shook his head.

"Don't cover yourself from my sight, Bella. I want to see you tonight, I need to see your breasts and the soft curves that dress hid from me. Tomorrow you will wear your own clothing and it will fit you better."

He touched the drawers at her waist, his fingers finding the tapes that held them in place and swiftly undoing the fastenings, allowing the garment to fall to her feet. She flushed darkly in the light of the single candle burning at the bedside, and he took pity on her in that moment.

"Shall I blow out the candle?" he asked, lifting her chin with a long finger, the better to see into her eyes. She nodded her desire for darkness to hide her and he did as she wanted, leaning to one side to plunge the room into the black of night, the candle no match for his breath of air blown in that direction.

With an easy movement, he lifted her, placing her on the mattress. Then in the moonlight, his fingers deft and moving with assurance, he took his clothing from his body and dropped it at his feet, moving to lie beside her on the bed. He reached for her, his arms encompassing her, and she let out a small cry, as he smothered her against his chest. That the pressure of his masculine parts against her body had frightened her seemed to be a certainty, for she trembled in his arms, and he spoke softly, his words meant to soothe her apprehension.

"Do not fear me, Isabella. Let me hold you."

She relaxed in his arms, pleasing him, and he thought she was once more feeling anonymous in the quiet, dark room. "Dark or light, you will still feel soft and warm in my arms, Isabella. I will have you for my wife tonight, but if you will be happier with only moonlight to cast its glow over us, I will not complain."

"I thank you, Rafael, but I fear you are to be disappointed, for I cannot imagine that the part of you that is pressing against my leg will ever fit as you intend it to within my body," she whispered, and he knew a moment of compassion for her fears.

"You will see, Bella. I would not have you fear me, and though there will be a small amount of pain for you this first time we come together, I promise you it will never be so again. Just this once, Isabella," he said gently.

"Will I bleed?" she asked, and he silently castigated the creature who had so filled her mind with fear of his touch, yet he knew he could not assure her that such a thing might not come to pass.

"You probably will find a few drops of blood on the sheet tomorrow morning, but not enough to harm you. I will take care so that you don't find this painful, sweetheart. I want you to welcome my touch, and if

I hurt you overly much you won't want me to come to your bed tomorrow night or the next."

She was silent a moment, and then she whispered words that touched his heart and gave him the impetus to cherish her tender flesh. "I trust you, Rafael. I know you won't hurt me."

He swallowed the words that would have spewed forth, words that might frighten her, for he had heard from other men of women who bled copiously, of girls who gave up their virginity with cries and tears. He'd never had a virgin in his bed, for had he done such a thing, it would have been expedient that he marry the female, whoever she might have been. The name of McKenzie would not be tarnished by one of its lot damaging a woman's reputation in such a way, without offering marriage.

His mouth met hers then as he fought the need to take, the desire that ran rampant in his veins to conquer. Carefully, gently, he kissed her, fearful of her withdrawal should he rush her into this experience. His hands touched her body with care, her breasts were soft against him, her hips were lush in his hands, her arms timid as they encircled his neck, and he was gentle as he drew her ever closer to himself.

His arousal was fierce, pressing against her body, pulsing in its urgency. He feared that she would withdraw from him, but she let him do as he would and he lifted her a bit, holding her firmly as his tongue pressed for entrance against her lips.

She acquiesced, opening her own lips for his entry, docile beneath his kiss. But compliance was not what he wanted, what he ached for, and he touched her tongue with his, darting forward, then back in her mouth, in mute invitation of the other entry yet to come.

She met his thrusts finally, sensing the rhythm of his movements and joining in with an assurance he welcomed. Her mouth was open against his, her lips moving, her tongue tangling with his as he sought out the warm secrets of her mouth. She moaned beneath her breath and he withdrew from the kiss, touching her cheek with his lips, his mouth open against her jaw, whispering against her ear, telling her of her beauty, and his need for her.

She softened in his arms, her breath coming more rapidly as if his passion were contagious and she were the willing recipient of its power. Her hands left his neck to bless the hard muscles of his chest, her fingertips exploring through the curls that traveled in a long line to below his waist, where lay the source of his need. He held his breath as she allowed her fingers to touch his waistline, press into the shallow dent that was his proof of birth, the sensitive spot that made him shiver at her touch.

She smiled, for he felt the movement of her cheek against his as her lips lifted and curved. "Are you laughing at me, Bella?" he whispered, moving his hands in a leisurely movement against her back.

"No, only pleased that my touch makes you quiver, that your skin pebbles when I brush my fingers over it." Her hands moved lower then, but he halted her, grasping her fingers in his.

"No, don't travel too far, Bella mine, for I don't want this to be finished before it is barely begun. I am too needy for you tonight to allow your touch in such a private place."

She halted, and he felt her head tilt upward, knew she searched the darkness for his face. "I don't understand," she said finally.

"Ah, but you will. When you have learned what happens in this bed, between us, you will know of what I speak, what I fear will happen if I allow you to do as you were intending."

"You feel so hard, so urgent against my skin. I only wanted to know what it is that causes that part of your body to become so…"

As if she could not continue, as though the words were too private for her to speak, she halted, and he took mercy on her innocence.

"You will find out in due time, sweetheart. I won't have you frightened of me before you have knowledge of my body, before I take you as my bride."

"I know what is to happen, for Sister Ruth Marie told me of what happened when her husband forced her body to open for his male member."

"*That* is not what is to happen to you." As if he were angry, whether with her or the woman who had so frightened her, he spoke harshly and felt her cringe from him. "I'm sorry, Bella. I don't mean to frighten you. I only want you to know that although there are men who are cruel to their womenfolk, I will not be one of them, no matter what the good sister told you to expect."

Isabella relaxed then, her body seeming to become more pliant against his, and he breathed a deep sigh of relief that she had apparently believed his claim. He bent then to her breasts, his fingers molding them, his palms enclosing them, his mouth seeking out the tender crests that were firming beneath his fingertips. He opened his mouth over one, sucking the tender flesh against his tongue, playing gently with her, wooing her carefully, his eagerness stifled by the need to bring her to pleasure without damaging her trust in him.

He suckled gently, then more strongly as she twisted in his grasp, her body moving, pressing even closer to him. His hands were careful as he held her, his fingers brushing the tiny nubs that blossomed beneath his touch. He kissed her with skill, laved the pebbled surfaces with his tongue and murmured soft endearments against her skin.

Her hips twisted in time with his caresses and he felt a surge of triumph as he recognized her arousal, her willingness to allow him access to her body. His hands moved with care, down her ribs, past her waist and hips to where her thighs arrowed down from that place he craved to touch, the soft warmth hiding behind her curls.

His fingers parted her, felt the slick moisture that bathed her tender flesh, and he murmured his pleasure against her breast as he explored the soft tissue that hid her most treasured secrets from him. She twisted again beneath his touch, and her soft cry was almost muffled by her hand rising to cover her lips.

"Don't hide your pleasure from me, Bella," he whispered. "I want to hear the sounds you make, for it will tell me that I am not hurting you but bringing you joy."

She touched his head with her hands, her fingers making runnels through his thick hair, her palms holding his head against her breasts, lest he move from her and take away the source of her pleasure. "You are not causing me pain, Rafael. I have never had another person touch me as you are now. I can only wonder if it is right and proper for you to do these things to me."

"All that we do in this bed is right and proper, so long as we agree on it and neither of us is hurt or damaged in any way by it, sweetheart." He lifted his head and shifted his body up to cover hers. "This is all a part of loving and meant to be a joy to both of us. Will you trust me with your body? Will you let me touch you as I will and bring you the joy that is yours in our marriage?"

She lay beneath him and he hesitated, wondering if he had pushed her too rapidly toward the final movements in this dance they were to undertake. But her breath was expelled then and she whispered words that gave him leave to do as he would with her.

"I will not pretend to know what is ahead for me, Rafael, but I trust you to do what is right."

Her words made his heart swell within his breast and he lifted to her mouth once more, kissing her with a passion that he feared might bring fear to those dark eyes. But it seemed that Isabella was beyond that initial moment of dread, for she welcomed his caresses and offered her lips freely, her hands clutching at his head as if she were hungry for the taste of him.

He parted her thighs gently and settled between them, his arousal pressing insistently against her, and he fought the urge to thrust, to take, to conquer. Instead, his hand slipped again to where her soft flesh awaited his pleasure, and his fingers caressed her, setting up a rhythm she met with the movements of her hips. He was overjoyed at her compliance, at her ability to join with his efforts to please her in this manner, and his kisses once more swept to encompass her breasts, bending to suckle there and tug at the crests in a rhythm that matched that of his fingers.

She stiffened, then cried out softly and moved more rapidly against him, finding the release he had brought into being, her whispered cries pleasing to his ears. Without pausing, he positioned himself against her opening and pushed gently within, passing the stricture there and easing gently into the tight passage beyond. With careful nudges, quick withdrawals and then more flagrant, urgent movements into her depths, he found the warmth he had sought, and rejoiced that his wooing of her was a success, bringing her to this moment of surrender to him.

He felt the fragile tissue of her virginity give way

to his entry and heard her gasp of pain as her maiden-head was breached. He halted there, almost totally seated in her, until she was able to accept his length, until her flesh had softened and then formed around him, gloving him, giving him a joy he had heretofore not found in all of his years of seeking pleasure wherever it might lie.

"Ah, Bella, you are perfect, so tight, so hot, so right for me." His words were muffled against her skin as he settled over her, his mouth pressed against her shoulder, his lips opening to suckle at her tender flesh.

She lifted her hands again to caress him, her fingertips lost in the wealth of his dark hair, her palms filled with the lush, straight locks that covered his head. "Is there more?" she asked, her voice a whisper in the night.

"Much more," he assured her, lifting from her and then returning again to where her inner muscles gripped him tightly. "Just keep doing that, sweet. Just what you were doing then."

She clenched those muscles again. "Like that?"

His groan, it seemed, was answer enough for her, for she laughed softly and held him even closer. "Yes, just like that." His words were a moan, a supplication for more of the same and she responded, catching his rhythm quickly as he sought and found his own release within her body.

He relaxed then upon her, holding himself upright with effort, his forearms on either side of her shoulders, lest he crush her into the mattress. He would not have her feel trapped or suffocated because of his carelessness, and she moved a bit beneath him.

"I thought it would be painful, Rafael, but it wasn't. Only for a quick moment when it felt like something inside me gave way."

"It was your maidenhead, sweet. You are no longer a virgin, Bella. Now you are truly a wife. *My* wife. My own."

His eyes closed and he rolled to one side, taking her with him, arranging her in his arms, holding her close. She clung, not a shrinking female who had suffered at his hands, but a woman who had found the joy of loving with her husband, a woman who was content in his arms and ready for sleep.

CHAPTER FIFTEEN

WHEN THE SUN ROSE, it touched the windows on the other side of the bedroom, for Rafael's suite was on the back of the house, with windows on both sides of the room, both east and west. It was a large room, adjoined by a sitting room, and when she awoke, Isabella realized it was much more sizeable than she had thought before, the furnishings of rich mahogany, the four-poster bed, dresser and wardrobe. Now she saw it as if for the first time, the wide windows that looked out on the side yard of the house, there where the sun was coming up in fiery splendor, then across to the opposite set of windows where she could see the stable, where men rushed across the yard, hurrying as they prepared to go out into the fields and pastures to work with the livestock.

Behind her, Rafael was curled warmly around her body and she was glad that she was not facing him, for she knew that her cheeks were crimson, with memories of the night before alive in her mind. His arm lay over her waist, his warm hand pressed against her belly, and his thighs were cradling hers, the pressure of his arousal once more making her aware of its presence.

"Bella? Are you trying not to let me know you're awake?" he asked, his voice amused as he lifted to one elbow, the better to peer at her over her shoulder.

She lifted one hand to cover her eyes. "Don't look at me yet, Rafael. I need to prepare myself for this."

"For what? Surely you are not embarrassed, sweetheart."

"I don't know. Yes, I do. I am, for I'm not sure what you will think of me. I was not myself last night. You made me feel and do things I would not normally do."

"Ah, Bella. I only made you feel the joy your body was meant to feel. I know I hurt you when I made you mine, but I tried not to cause undue hurt. If I caused you pain beyond bearing, it was not meant to be, for I would not give you grief."

She shifted again, reaching for the edge of the mattress. "I think I want to get up now, Rafael. But I can't with you here behind me. Can you rise and find your clothing and leave the room, so I can dress and get ready for breakfast?"

"No, I won't do that." He slid from the other side of the bed and circled it until he was before her. She closed her eyes, but knew he did not move, that his body was directly in front of her and, should she open her eyes, he would be in the direct line of her vision.

"Isabella, look at me. Open your eyes. I will not hurt you or cause you to be frightened."

She chanced it, opening her eyes slowly, peering

up at him, her gaze shunning that place where she knew his male parts dwelt, there where she feared she might even now find traces of the blood from her body. She was aware then that he smiled at her, that he bent to her and lifted the sheet from her body, exposing her to his view, even as her eyes did not leave his face, and her voice was low as she spoke his name.

"Rafael?"

His smile was gentle, his hands careful as he touched her. "There now, that wasn't so bad, was it? Just slide out of bed and let me hold you for a moment, and then I'll help you to get dressed," he said, lifting her to stand before him. His arms circled her and she was drawn to him, her head against his chest, her arms sliding around his waist, while he held her in a tender embrace.

"Shall we get you dressed now?" His rough whisper was close to her ear as he bent over her and she only nodded, unable to speak aloud. He led her to the low dresser where her clothing was stored and waited until she pulled out clean undergarments, a chemise she hadn't seen before among the handful she brought forth. She held it up before her and looked at him questioningly.

"I had Maria get it from town for you, after you bought your gown," he said. "I told her to get a few more things so that you would have plenty of undergarments to wear. I wanted you to have pretty things, not just the usual, useful clothing you've worn before. You're a bride, Isabella. I want you to look like one, like a woman who is cherished by her husband. We will go to town today and buy more dresses for you. The things you brought with you are not fit for you to wear here."

"I have the things we bought in town the day I got my wedding dress, Rafael. I have plenty to wear now, enough clothing to only wash my things out twice a week. I'm not used to having a dresser full of things to wear.

"As to what I brought with me, I only have the homespun dress I wore at the convent, but there are also the dresses you bought while we were on the road coming here. You needn't buy me so many things," she said. "I feel that I've taken advantage of you with all the pretty things in my drawer."

"Bella, I remember exactly how you arrived in my home, and my memories of that day and those before it are stamped forever in my mind. There was much to enjoy about finding you and taking you for my own, holding you for hours atop my horse and listening to you speak of your life. I am sorry I didn't care for you better while we traveled, for you should have had shoes for your feet that would have withstood the journey. I was neglectful of you, but I will make it right for you now. You shall have anything your heart desires." He nuzzled her neck as he spoke and noted the fine shivers that traveled over and through her body, his mouth curving with the pleasure of knowing her senses were attuned to him.

"We will find an abundance of clothing for you in

the general store, for what you bought last week is but a small amount compared to what the wife of Rafael McKenzie should have available to wear. What they don't have in stock we will order from their resources back East. You will be dressed as befits my woman."

His words made her smile, and she stifled the chuckle that hovered in her throat, for he sounded as if he were making a vow, that he would dress her in finery such as she had never known. And indeed, her clothing for the past years had been only of home-spun, gowns that were formed after the pattern of the nuns' habits, loose and unfitting, made to hide the female form, not to enhance it.

"I want to see your curves a bit," he said, his hands sliding down her sides as he smoothed her chemise into place. He held the new drawers for her to step into, and she blushed, doing as he bid her, lifting one foot, then the other, until he tied the tapes at her waist. "Not too tight, are they?" he asked, and she shook her head, then glanced up to see his eyes, shining with a glow that she knew was matched by her own.

He walked with her to where his mirror hung on the wall. "I want you to look there, look at the woman who is in my mirror this morning," he said, standing her before him, pulling her back so that she leaned against his chest. "Do you see the bright glow in her eyes, the blush on her cheeks, the smile on her lips? That is a woman who has been loved and taught the ways of marriage by a husband who cares deeply for her."

"And do you? Care deeply for me, Rafael?"

His gaze met hers over her head. "Can you not see it in my face, the yearning I have for you, Bella? Can't you see the happiness you have brought to me in our bed reflected now in my eyes?"

She saw the heat rise in her cheeks again as he spoke and looked down at the top of his dresser. Her brush lay there and she picked it up. "I must put my hair in order before I'm ready to go to breakfast, and I haven't washed yet."

His fingers tightened on her shoulders. "Bella. Look at me. You haven't answered me. Do you see what you have given me? Do you recognize the feeling I have for you?"

She looked up, knowing that she must answer him, yet wary of the words he would have her speak. "I care for you, too, Rafael. I think I was right when I said that there must be at least a strong liking between two persons who would make a marriage and meet in the marriage bed. I hope we will be able to find a new depth of feeling for each other one day, that you will look at me with eyes of…of more than just a liking for my body and the pleasure it gives you."

"You will find that in me, Bella. My feelings for you are strong, and I only ask your patience with me, for I have never had a woman of my own, never had the privilege of having a wife of my own before."

"And I…I have never called a man husband, so we are on even ground, Rafael."

HE TOOK HER TO THE STABLES after they had eaten breakfast, a meal prepared by Maria, served to them with a great fuss, for, as Maria said, it was their first meal in this house as a *real* husband and wife. And what that meant, Isabella was too embarrassed to even speculate about. Apparently, Maria was privy to all sorts of information that Isabella had not thought to be her concern. And yet, Rafael and his happiness were high on the woman's list of priorities, and she no doubt made it her business to know all that went on in his life.

Or perhaps Maria had noted the look Rafael had mentioned earlier, the expression he'd seen in his bride's eyes upon awakening, the look he had bid her pay attention to in the mirror earlier. And at that thought, Isabella almost stumbled as she kept pace with him across the yard.

His strong arm came around her waist then, and he bent his head to look deeply into her eyes. "Are you all right, Bella mine? Am I walking too fast for you to keep up?"

She shook her head. "No, I just thought that Maria—"

"No, not another word, sweetheart. Maria knows nothing, only guesses what went on in our bedroom last night. What happens there, between you and me, is sacred to our marriage, and will never be known to another. What Maria may have guessed is that I am more than pleased with my bride, that she has given me all I ever yearned for in a woman. Now, don't fret over what Maria may be thinking. She cares for you and wants only the best for your life." He grasped her shoulders and she nodded quickly, knowing that he needed a response from her.

"Now, did I make you stumble when I dragged you across the yard?"

She shook her head, smiling, unwilling to have him guess the direction her thoughts had taken, making her miss her step as she reflected on the night just past. For she felt that any passerby would know by looking at her just what she had been occupied with in Rafael's bedroom.

But he seemed to accept her assurance of well-being, for he kept her close, but slowed a bit, speaking of the horses he would have her visit and learn to know.

"I have a mare for you, Isabella. She is small and easily led, and the younger children of the ranch have even ridden her. She is of finer blood than the mare you rode when you took to the trail with Matthew. I think she will do well for you, and if you enjoy her company we will consider her yours."

"I'll tell you the same thing I told Matthew, Rafael," she whispered and he halted his steps, looking down into her face with a puzzled frown. "I only was allowed on a horse a few times when I was but very young, and then not unsupervised. My father did not hold with girls being given any sort of freedom, and I was confined to the house most of the time. I used to yearn to ride the mare the ranch hands told me would be mine one day. She was so pretty and quiet and I loved to spend time with her when my father was not around."

"I can't imagine a woman being raised on a ranch and not riding a horse," he said in a low tone. "What was wrong with your father? Did he did not put you on a pony when you were but a small child? He should have known enough to teach you the skills you would need as a woman living on a ranch, where horses are the accepted means of transport. I'm surprised you had the courage to ride with Matthew when you left here."

"I rode, but not well, when I left. He had to ride more slowly than he would have done had I been better able to keep up with him. As to my father…" She lifted her shoulders in a shrug, unwilling to tell him more of the restrictions placed upon her by the man who had turned her over to the Sisters of Charity for the finishing touches. "Perhaps he felt there were no horses tame enough for a child to sit upon. I don't know the reasons, I only know that I loved to pet the animals and feed them when my father was not around, but I was never allowed to sit on a horse's back, except for those times when I went to the barns without his knowledge. I would ask the foreman to help me into a saddle and walk around the small corral with a man leading the horse they allowed me to use. I remember…"

Her voice trailed off and he looked down again, his words soft and encouraging. "No matter, Bella.

You will ride now whenever you please. You will have a mare of your own. If this one does not suit you or you see another you like better, you will make your own choice. I want you to enjoy riding with the wind, with me by your side, as we travel the miles of fields and pastures of this ranch. I want to show you my home. Your home now," he finished with a tender tone that couldn't help but catch her ear.

She looked up at him, noting the softening of his lips, the seemingly perpetual harsh frame of his jaw forming a more gentle line as he looked into her eyes. His hand held hers in a firm grip and she knew for a moment the strength of the man who walked beside her.

That he could crush her with those strong hands, that his arms could lift her high above the ground, making her helpless against his power, was a fact. But either of those things happening was beyond her scope of imagination, for he had proved over the night just past that his strength would not be used against her.

Confidence in him ran riot in her mind, for she knew suddenly that she was safe, here in the home, the arms, of Rafael McKenzie. No matter that they must forge a new path to follow, that their tempers might often conflict. For she was stubborn, Rafael arrogant. They were fated to live here, in this place, for the rest of their lives.

She felt her feet drag to a halt, knew his perplexity as he turned her to face him, and then saw the query in his eyes. "What is it, Bella? What's wrong?"

She shook her head. "Nothing is wrong, Rafael. Everything is right today. I am happy to be here with you, happy to be walking across the yard with you, content to be your wife."

His eyes lit with a familiar glow, one she had seen just hours past, and he clenched his jaw as if he were fighting off words better left unsaid for now. Then he bent to her, pressed his lips against her forehead and turned her against his body until she felt the lines of his chest against her back, the long length of his legs behind hers and the weight of his arousal that pressed insistently against her bottom. His hands met beneath her breasts, just at her waistline, and he spoke softly against her ear.

"Stand where you are for a moment, and look ahead of you, Bella. There where the corral fence turns to the south, there where that chestnut stallion is standing." He lifted his head and whistled, a low sound that she wouldn't have thought would carry so far, but the horse heard it, lifting his powerful head to seek out the source of the call that carried to his ears. He whinnied once, his ears twitching, his tail swishing the air, and trotted over to the nearby fence.

"He is the pride of my ranch, El Gordain. His name means 'hero' and fits him. For he has sired dozens of colts and fillies for us. His bloodline is strong and his line runs true. I want you to meet him and know him. And I want you to promise me that you will never approach him without my presence beside you. He is a wild card, a stallion of great independence, and cannot be trusted to always be calm and docile.

"You can meet him now, over the fence, but no nearer, for I would not have you put at risk. Do you understand?"

She nodded agreeably. "Yes. I've had dealings with stallions before. Not that I've handled them, but I've seen them throwing tantrums when the men tried to ride them, saw one almost kill a man when he went into the stall with the horse and made a false move. Our ranch foreman wanted to get rid of him, called him a monster, but my father said he was worth too much money to lose, that his get were worth much in the horse market."

"What happened to him?" They neared the fence and Rafael held out his hand, as if he beckoned the great stallion to come to him.

"He vanished from the ranch one day. My father threw a fit. In fact, I thought he would have apoplexy there on the spot. But there was nothing he could do, for the horse was gone."

"Did someone let him loose, or did he break down his stall door and leap the fences?" Rafael's hand rubbed at the long nose of the stallion who stood before him now, ducking his head to better allow the scratching fingers to reach a stubborn spot between his ears.

"No one knew. I suspect the foreman set him free on the back of the ranch and the stud just ran wild, gathering up a band of mustangs as a harem. He wasn't spoken of again, for my father was furious about losing him."

"Stallions are noted for their changeable moods, but this one is tame enough if he's handled properly."

"Do you ride him?" She held her breath, waiting for his reply, for she hoped he would deny such a thing. But it was not to be, for Rafael nodded, laughing a bit.

"He's a challenge, and I was never one to back away from such a thing. Yes, I ride him, but no one else is allowed on his back. He responds well to me, but I am careful not to trust him too far, for to let myself relax in his saddle would be to put myself at risk, and I'm careful not to do that."

"Will you ride him when we go about the ranch together?" She hoped he would answer in the negative, for the thought of that giant beast running beside her was frightening.

"No, when we are out together, I will ride my own gelding, a big, bluff fellow, who gives me no trouble. He is well broken, and I have had him for a number of years. My foreman calls him a pussycat, but he has spirit enough to suit me."

"And the mare you would have me ride? Is she well tamed?"

Rafael bent to her, his lips against her temple. "Do you think I would risk your neck on a horse that might turn mean or that would dump you in the dirt? The mare I have chosen for you is small and eager to please. She is the epitome of a female."

"Small and eager to please? Is that how you like your women, Rafael McKenzie?" Her chin rose as she spoke, and her eyes darkened.

He laughed. "I knew you would spit fire at me over that remark, Bella. No, I don't expect you to always be eager to please me, only when it involves our private life together. And then I will be just as eager to please you." He held her apart, his hands on her shoulders as he spoke, his eyes narrowed as he looked into hers.

"Didn't you realize last night how eager to please you I was? Couldn't you tell that I wanted it to be right for you, that you would not fear climbing back into my bed tonight and for all the nights ahead of us?"

She blushed, ducking her head, unwilling to look at him, fearing he might be laughing at her. But his mood was not triumphant or mocking, for her drew her closer and spoke soft words that were designed to aid his cause.

"I want you to be happy, Isabella. I desire above all else that you will fit into my home, my ranch, and take your place as its mistress, that you will find joy in your life with me."

She felt quick tears forming in her eyes and she would not shed them against his chest, would not let any onlookers think he had hurt her or wounded her feelings, so she blinked and brought them under control. But he was not easily fooled, for he tilted her chin upward with one long finger and looked his fill at the expression she wore, one that displayed the joy she found in his words.

"Ah, do not cry, Bella mine. This is a happy day for me, a day to show you the ranch I love and a day to spend time with my father, to let him know that all is well with us."

"I'm not crying, I'm only happy," she insisted, feeling a tear trickle down her cheek, and knowing that Rafael hid his smile from her. "The sun is bright and made my eyes water, that's all."

"As you say, Bella. As you say." He turned her toward the double doors of the stable and led her to where they sat open, the dim interior of the building quiet and cool.

"Come, let me show you the mare I spoke of." He led her through the doorway, down a long row of stalls, where horses stood in knee-deep straw, their bedding lush and clean. "It is time to turn these lazy beasts out into the pasture for the day, but I had them kept here, inside, until you had a chance to meet them."

He took her from one stall to the next, telling her the names of each animal, his hand reaching for the long necks that stretched out over the doors of the stalls. They all seemed to recognize him, whether by scent or vision, she could not tell, but his touch was impartial as he visited each stall.

Until he came to the last one in the line. There stood a small horse, a mare with a white blaze down the center of her nose, her ears perked high as if she had been listening to his voice as he approached her. She was pale, a color the men at the ranch had called buckskin, and her mane and tail were dark, both lush and clearly brushed by a human hand today. She was clean and long limbed, a horse to be admired, Isabella thought.

"This is Sheba, the mare we spoke of," Rafael said with pride. "I told Manuel to have her clean and ready for your visit. I see he did as I asked, for she has obviously been brushed and combed recently."

"She's a beauty," Isabella said softly, lifting a hand so that the mare could catch her scent. The nostrils flared and touched the fine skin on the back of Isabella's hand, then the mare stepped closer to the gate and leaned closer to the girl watching her.

"I think she likes me." Her delight was audible as Isabella smoothed the long nose and touched the spot between the mare's ears. "Look, she's bending to me."

"Let's take her out and see what you think of her up close." Rafael backed from the gate and unlocked the latch, opening it inward so that the mare had to move back and then around the barrier in order to walk out into the aisle. Reaching for a rope that hung beside the box stall, Rafael clipped it on to the mare's halter and handed the length of line to Isabella.

"She's yours. Take her out the back door into the corral."

She looked up at him quickly, knowing that the uncertainty she felt must be visible on her face. "Really? I can just take her out all alone? Will you go with me?"

"Of course I will," he assured her, giving a short tug on the lead line, urging the mare to follow their footsteps from the stall and out of the stable. "Just speak to her and touch her. Let her know where you are at all times. You know not to walk behind a horse without letting it know you are there, don't you?"

She laughed. "Yes, our foreman used to scold me for my lack of fear when I went into the barns. He feared that I would be kicked or walked on, but the horses seemed to like me well enough. I seldom had the opportunity to be near them, but when my father was gone from the house, I took every chance I could to visit in the barn."

She took up the slack in the lead line she held and walked beside Sheba's head, speaking softly to the horse, her tone that of a mother encouraging a child to do his best. "You're a beautiful girl, Sheba. Your coat is so shiny and your eyes are so dark and lovely."

Rafael stood to one side, aware that the mare was enthralled by the woman who walked beside her. The long nose nudged Isabella's shoulder and a soft whuffle of sound was spoken against her ear. As if mesmerized by the feminine tones of Isabella's voice, the mare kept pace, nodding her head and behaving herself as a lady.

"What shall I do with her?" Isabella asked, standing in the middle of the corral. The stallion who watched from beyond the next fence snorted then, the sound loud and harsh, and Isabella looked back at Rafael.

"He cannot reach you, Isabella. The fence is too high for him to jump without a head start and he hasn't enough room to do so. He just likes the scent of the mare, and is thinking of what he would like to do with her."

With that, the stud trumpeted loudly and the mare's feet danced against the bare earth. With a skittish look, her ears forward, she turned to the fence that held the large animal back from her and whinnied loudly.

"She is almost ready to be bred," Rafael said. "Perhaps she is thinking to entice him with her behavior. He has caught her scent, but he knows she isn't ready to be covered yet. It will be another couple of weeks probably before she is ready."

"I think she's flirting with him," Isabella said, her smile bright as she turned it in Rafael's direction. The mare was docile, but clearly interested in the stud who watched her so carefully. Isabella's brow furrowed. "When can I learn to ride her? Will you teach me?"

"You know I will, Bella. Not today, but perhaps tomorrow we can begin your lessons. It will help that you have done a bit of riding, even though you may not be adept at the skill yet. For now, I would like to turn Sheba loose in the corral and then take you in the house to see my father. I think Manuel and one of the men are waiting to turn loose the rest of the riding horses into the far pasture. They should be set free to graze for the day, and we have kept them here long enough.

"Come." He held out his hand and she took it, drawing the mare with her to his side. Rafael undid the clip that held the lead line in place and folded the length of leather in his hand. "I'll put this up near her stall," he said, looking to where Manuel watched from his spot on a bench inside the stable.

"We're going in now, Manuel. Thank you for cleaning Sheba for me. I think she likes her new mistress."

"*Sí.* She took to her right away. I noticed." He shot a look at Isabella, clearly not comfortable in her presence, as if he rued his part in bringing her here and was not certain of her response to him.

"Thank you." Isabella spoke the simple phrase softly. "I hope Sheba will let me ride her without tossing me to the ground too often."

"She will not, señora. I will speak with her and tell her the way of things." Manuel smiled then, his words teasing as he took the lead line and tended to it.

The return walk to the house was short, and upon entering the kitchen, Rafael spoke to Maria. "Is my father awake? Have you been to his room lately?"

"*Sí,* he is sitting by his window. He rose early and ate breakfast in his chair. I think he is feeling better today, more like his old self." She glanced at Isabella. "He wondered if his new daughter would be coming to see him. He has been worried about you."

Isabella blushed at Maria's words, knowing what had caused the older man's concern. "I'll go to his room now, Maria. We were just on our way there, in fact."

Simon McKenzie had a large bedroom, with comfortable furniture sitting about for any who cared to visit. But Isabella went to his side without delay, finding the words she sought as she touched his hand. "I see that you are weary, señor, and I fear I have added to your worry. I am sorry." She shot a look in

Rafael's direction but he was leaving her on her own in this, it seemed, for he did not speak.

With a smooth movement, she knelt at Simon's feet, as she had once before, and bowed her head against his knee, feeling the bones through the knitted covering that lay between her forehead and his leg. Maria may have thought he appeared more rested than other days, but Isabella felt the weariness expressed in his eyes, in the faltering touch of his hand as he lay his palm on her head.

"You are my daughter, Isabella. I cannot hold it against you for feeling stifled here. You are a stranger to my household and Lucia has not made things easy for you, but she is gone now and things will be back to normal soon. Maria has assured me that you have taken hold, speaking with her about the food to be prepared, and the girls have moved your clothing and personal things to Rafael's room. It is right that you spend your nights there in the place where his mother and I shared our lives."

Isabella lifted her head and held his withered hand in both of hers. Her head bent and she left a gentle kiss against his knuckles. "Thank you for your understanding. I will do as you have asked me. There will be no more running off or causing Rafael to worry about me. I swear this to you, for my heart is now set on making a success of my marriage to your son."

His hand trembled as he replaced it on his lap and his lips curved in a smile that made her think of Rafael. There was a strong resemblance between him and his father, and she saw it now as she had once before. In the long blade of his nose, the dark eyes so deeply set, the firm lines of his mouth and the wide, graceful look of his hands. Although his father's hair was white, where his own was still black as ebony, there was the knowledge that she could look upon this man and see what Rafael would be in another forty years.

If her own father had been but half the man Simon McKenzie was, she would have had a very dissimilar life to the one she had experienced as a child, she thought, rising to her feet and backing from Simon to stand once more by Rafael's side. If she had been given the understanding due a child from her father, she might be a different person than she was now. More able to understand Rafael and his ways, more sure of her place in his home, more able to accept the caring concern she felt from those around her.

CHAPTER SIXTEEN

THE DAYS WENT BY QUICKLY, each week beginning with
a quiet Sunday, the small church in the village being
filled on that morning of the week with an abundance
of the people who lived in the surrounding areas.
Isabella was taken there in the buggy early on the
first day, Sunday morning being a time of quiet,
Rafael driving the team of mares, who seemed to take
great pleasure in prancing and cavorting beneath his
gentle touch.

The village priest, the man who had conducted
their marriage, greeted them, looking upon Isabella
with a gentle smile as they left the church on a sunny
morning several weeks after her adventure with
Matthew. She looked back now on those days with
disbelief that she had been so foolish as to listen to
Lucia, to believe her words and listen to her sugges-
tions. Were it not that Matthew was an honorable
man, it might have ended differently.

For she had left Rafael so readily, without realizing
the dangers of the open road, the dangers Lucia's
machinations had put in her path. She wondered occa-

sionally what Juan Garcia was up to, whether or not he had given up his thoughts of gaining her in marriage, of taking possession of her father's ranch from her.

Rafael sent a message to her father's lawyer, asking specifics about the ranch, telling the legal representative that he had married Isabella and wanted to know the extent of her inheritance, so that they could plan for its future.

The answering letter came several weeks later, and he held it out to her. "You may read for yourself what the lawyer has to say, Bella. You are a rich woman, not in cold, hard cash, but in land and horses. Your father was a good manager and the ranch is thriving, according to the lawyer."

She took the letter, glanced at the first page, then handed it back. "I have no need to know about that place. It was not a happy home for me. I would rather hear about the convent where I lived the happiest years of my life. Though my days were regimented by the rules there and my hands knew hard work, I was treated well, and the sisters were good to me."

He folded the letter and placed it in the packet in which it had arrived. Then his eyes touched her, perhaps with a look of compassion, she thought, for he spoke words that were kind and meant to please her. "Wouldn't you like someday to take a trip to see your ranch, Isabella? Perhaps you might enjoy looking at the fields and barns and the big house and know that it is yours now and that you hold reign over it and the people who run it for you? Perhaps make changes if there are any that occur to you?"

She thought for a moment and then nodded. "If it would not interfere with the life here, if your being gone for some time would not play havoc with your own ranch, then it would be a trip I would enjoy. Perhaps I need to see the ranch through adult eyes, instead of remembering it as child might. I might find peace in my heart when I think of my father, if I see that he has indeed left me with a heritage I can be proud of."

"You are a wise woman, Isabella." His words touched her as if he had blessed her with drops of holy water, and she felt a moment of compunction as she wondered if her thoughts bordered on the blasphemous. Surely his thoughts for her could not be compared to the vessel of the sacred water that had sat on the altar in the chapel, the water that Father Joseph used to christen the babes brought to him by the families in the surrounding countryside, those who worshiped in the chapel and considered the convent of the Sisters of Charity as their own.

She knew that those simple folk were dependent upon the nuns for their children's schooling, such as it was, and for whatever nursing they might require. The convent was a haven for the young girls who considered the church as a future for themselves. The nuns were looked up to by the womenfolk as being above their own humble place in society.

Even now, with the happiness she had found with

Rafael, she thought with fondness of the time she had spent there, of the women who had taught her the ways of womanhood, of how to run a home, how to tend to a family. She yearned somehow to once more see the nuns who had been kind to her. Sister Agnes Mary, who had worked with her in the garden and the kitchen. Even Sister Ruth Marie, whose words of warning had frightened her from her early relationship with Rafael.

Now that she knew the man, now that his touch was no longer anathema to her, she wished she might speak to Sister Ruth Marie and assure her that not all men were cruel, not all men were so selfish as had been her own husband. Rafael was all that was kind and tender with her during those night hours in his bed. She rued the fight she had given him over her first experience with his loving, and thought often that she owed him an apology for those nights when she had cried off from allowing him to woo her, to put his hands on her body.

When she told him, late one night, about her thoughts, told him that she was sorry she had been so reluctant to accept his loving, he only smiled and kissed her, then carried her to their bed and held her close to his long, hard body.

"I knew you would come to accept me one day, Bella. I knew I could overcome your fears, your terror, if I was given a chance. I only wanted to take you as my wife, to give you the joys of marriage that I knew were possible for us."

She turned to lift herself over him, her mouth touching his chest, her fingers tangling in his hair. She pressed her fingers against his mouth, her fingertips sensitive to his needs, as she caressed his ears, his throat, then moved farther down to touch the flat expanse of his belly.

"Do not explore too quickly, Bella," he warned her. His arousal was rampant, surging against her belly, and she wanted badly to enclose it in her fist, to feel the silken flesh of his manhood, the steel beneath the surface, the hard length of it that pulsed against her body. But his words told her that he was too near the bursting point, that if she teased him in such a way, he would not be able to spend the time he wanted in wooing her body to his will. That he had no need to woo her, she did not tell him, for she much enjoyed the long hours he spent in giving her the pleasure of his touches, the kisses he spent on her breasts and belly, the taking of her body with firm thrusts of his manhood.

She laughed instead, lifting on her elbows over his chest, her fingers tracing circles around his flat nipples, feeling his great body tense beneath her. Knew the rush of air that he forced from his lungs, felt the power in his arms as they circled her and turned her to her back, then felt the strength of his will that kept him from taking her in a frenzy.

He would not invade her body until he knew she was more than ready for his possession, and his long nights of readying her for just that very thing made her aware that he was closer to the edge of violence than ever before. A primitive look had claimed his features, his lips thinning, his jaw hardening, as if he were reining in a powerful urge to have his way with her.

His eyes looked like midnight as he hovered over her, his cheeks ruddy with the passion that possessed him, and she moved beneath him, taunting him with her breasts against his wide chest, her mound pushing up against his groin, her arms and hands caressing him where she would. Her fingernails were short, but he felt them bite into his flesh as she held him, her hands on his shoulders, her mouth open against his throat.

"You will make me cruel in my needs, Bella. Don't push me so tonight." His words were raw and rough in her ear as he covered her, his body hard as he found his place between her thighs. He reached for her hands, pulling them to either side of her head, holding her prisoner, keeping her from the teasing ritual she had put into being.

"You are asking for trouble, sweetheart, with your pushing against me, your breasts warm beneath me, your warmth teasing me there between your legs. You will find yourself a prisoner to my passion in but a moment."

She smiled, a siren's look that he had seen but seldom on her lips, for she had only in the past weeks begun to entice him in such a way. He enjoyed her attempts at seduction, but knew she was still ignorant in some of the ways of loving that men enjoyed. She was too young, too fresh to be taught such things yet, but he yearned for the nights when he would show her the various ways they might find pleasure together.

"I need you, Rafael." The words were soft, spoken from lips that were swollen from his kisses, and he recognized her desire for him, felt a surge of pride that she was able to so speak aloud her thoughts. Without hesitation, he held her beneath him, his hands holding her hips fast for his invasion of her tender tissues, and then he surged forward as he took possession of the woman beneath him.

She lifted to him, her breath short as she whimpered at his taking, her eyes closing as she accepted his body into her own.

"Are you all right, Bella mine?" He halted, midway to paradise, and spoke the words softly against her ear, sensing her hesitation.

"Stay as you are for a moment, Rafael," she begged. "Don't move. Just let me rest." He felt her body relax around him, felt her muscles form to glove him and then the joy of her acceptance of his body. "I just needed to breathe," she whispered.

"I will not hurt you, Isabella. I told you weeks ago that I would not bring pain to your body, and if I have, I am sorrier than you know. I would not do anything to cause you harm."

She opened her eyes and he saw the soft promise in her eyes of what she felt for him. She had not told him of any great love in her heart, but he yearned nightly for her to give the words of her heart into his keeping.

That there was more than a liking between them he was certain. What a pallid word that was. *Liking.* He felt desire for her, a pride of ownership as he might for a prize he had earned, or a possession he had come to own by some great feat of strength and power.

And yet, there was, beyond that desire for her body, stronger than the primitive sense of owning this woman as his wife, a feeling he could not name. A warmth that encompassed his very being when he saw her across the room, when he held her in his arms, when he watched her kneel before his father and speak softly of her days to the older man, cheering his heart with her presence.

If this was the emotion known to women as *love,* he must own it, he decided. For he felt for her a need he could not describe, only feel in his depths, as he might feel a yearning for a drink of water on a hot day, or a meal when he was famished after riding the range for long hours without nourishment. Her very presence beckoned him with its soft, womanly form, her smiles luring him into her spell, her arms offering him a surcease from all the weary hours he spent away from her during the day. When he rode with his men, he thought of her, wondering what she was about, how she was spending her time. Thinking of his arrival home in the evening, of her welcoming arms when he found her in their room, of her kiss, her embrace.

And now, as she held him in that warmth, as her lips responded to his, he spoke the words that lived in his heart. "I love you, Bella mine. There is an urgency in my heart to speak these words to you. I want you to know how I feel, that there is more than liking between us, more than the urge to take your body on this bed, more than a hunger for you that cannot be sated no matter how many times we come together."

He waited as she seemed to accept his words, her gaze upon him, her mouth opening a bit as if she would speak, then the presence of her tongue as she swiped it quickly over her upper lip. She was hesitant, and he felt apprehensive. What if she were put off by his words, what if she did not feel this way toward him, what if she were unwilling to accept this declaration from him?

But his doubts were tossed into the dustbin as she spoke quietly, her hands against his shoulders, her eyes meeting his in the candlelight that glowed from their bedside. "I have felt a great love for you, Rafael. For weeks you have wooed me and loved me and taught me to crave your body. But it is not just your body that draws me, but the spirit within you, the great honesty of your heart, the kindness you bring to our bed, the tenderness you spend upon my body. You have given me much, the joys of marriage, the pleasures of loving you've taught me here in our bed, and the knowledge that I am a part of a great family."

He breathed deeply, aware that she had pledged herself to him in a new way, a way that superceded the marriage vows she had taken, that she had chosen a path that led into the future for them both. He held her close, rolling to his side, his arms filled with the soft, scented being who filled his thoughts both day and night.

His wife.

CHAPTER SEVENTEEN

THE WEEKS PASSED in a blur of activity out on the range, where horses roamed far and wide, where the ranch hands worked to gather the herd together in order that the young ones might be branded, the colts might be gelded while they were still less than a year old. The herd would be brought to the barns to be counted and sorted; the three-year-olds deemed ready for riding would be brought into the corral and readied for the men who would begin their training.

Isabella watched from the safety of the yard, the corral fence between her and the horses that abounded in the pastures and meadows. The stallion that Rafael had introduced her to was in great demand, for he was the sire of many colts and fillies, and those mares who had come in season this late in the year were ready for his attentions.

She watched the men with avid eyes, yearning for the expertise they demonstrated, wishing that she had been taught early in life to ride so well, to be a part of the raising and training of the magnificent beasts that had inhabited her father's ranch.

And she found herself on quiet afternoons walking the length of the stable, speaking to the horses who stood in large stalls, walking to the corral fence where others of the livestock waited to be claimed by the men who would ride them.

And always, her gaze was drawn to the stallion, El Gordain, Rafael's pride. She approached him with care, ever mindful of the warnings Rafael had delivered to her. Speaking softly, her words soft and lyrical, she uttered his name, praised him for his great strength and beauty, and gained a sense of security as the horse seemed to accept her presence before him.

It took long hours and several weeks of time before she touched his long nose, rubbed the spot between his ears and felt easy about being in his vicinity. But the stud began to welcome her with soft whuffling sounds, with arrogant tosses of his head, and allowed her close to him, without any threat of his strength being used against her.

She was careful not to press her luck, always keeping the stall door between them, or the corral fence a barrier, but the initial fear and apprehension she'd known in his presence gave way to a tacit understanding that seemed to grow between woman and horse.

On one placid afternoon, Rafael told her of his intention that she should be a larger part of his own operation, and began taking her on long rides, advising her on the details she was ignorant of, giving her praise when she performed well on her mare and teasing her when she was weary and ready for rest.

His big hands spent long hours massaging her sore muscles, rubbing liniment into the areas where she ached after the long hours of exercise. That he enjoyed his task did not go unnoticed by her, for he invariably ended the sessions with a gentle seduction of her senses, a tender taking of her, giving and receiving pleasure from her youthful body.

She rode well now, due to his tutelage, his patience with her attempts atop the little mare. Sheba had responded well to her, a most willing mount, and Isabella found that there was a bond between herself and the gentle mare. She took treats to her when she visited the barn, called her to the fence when the mare was in the pasture and petted her, speaking softly and offering her bits of apple or carrot on her palm. Rafael had bred the mare with his stud and Isabella found pleasure in the knowledge that in less than a year, the mare would drop a foal from the magnificent stallion. Rafael said it would be hers to care for, to train and perhaps one day she would put her own child upon its back.

But of her interaction with his stallion, she did not speak to Rafael, for the knowledge that he would not approve of the risk to her safety was strong in her mind.

Life progressed at a pace she enjoyed, and to her delight, Rafael decreed she had progressed enough to ride with him on the range, to be with him as he helped to herd the horses. Lest she be in danger, he made her promise to do as he said, to be ever careful of exposing herself to an animal that looked to be mean or wilder than was to be expected.

She rode beside him, sitting in her saddle as might a man, astride, rather than using a lady's sidesaddle, for he had said that she could not control her horse properly from that vantage. She wore a split leather skirt that he bought in the general store for her use, and a wide-brimmed hat that she had chosen from those offered there. Her boots were new also, carved leather, pale in color, matching the buckskin mare she rode. And she rode with pride, that this man loved her and wanted to share every part of his life with her.

For his pride in her was absolute, his joy a viable thing when she neared him during the day, and if his men noticed and smiled knowingly as they watched the actions of their employer and his lady, he did not care, for his heart was involved now in the relationship he had formed with Isabella. That Manuel spoke occasionally of his employer mooning over the woman he had married was of little account to Rafael, for the man was ever respectful of the woman he spoke of.

To Isabella's mind, it seemed all was well, that her life was on an even footing finally, that she was beloved by the man she had married and their future seemed assured. Her monthly cycle was disturbed, for she had not had her normal flow for several weeks, and she had begun to sense changes in her body, when Maria called to her one morning after breakfast.

"Señora, will you stay and speak with me? After the men go out to the range to work?"

Isabella nodded, speaking her farewells to Rafael as he left the house, waving her hand as he turned back to look at her before he entered the stable, noting the smile he wore, the look of contentment that seemed to be his over the past weeks.

"What is it, Maria? Is there something wrong I need to tend to?"

She spoke from the doorway, her mind still on Rafael, her smile tender as she felt the touch of his hand against her back in memory. That he could not keep from laying his hands on her was an affliction she cherished, for she had learned to crave his nearness, to reach for him when he had not approached her for more than a day or so. And his pleasure at her somewhat aggressive behavior pleased her, luring her into more adventurous delights in their bed.

Now, she suffered the long look of teasing Maria bent in her direction. "You are indeed a woman who loves the man who she has married," Maria said softly. As if she had planned for such a thing all along, she nodded her head and went to the table, drawing out a chair for Isabella to sit on.

"Come, join me," she offered. "We have much to speak of, señora."

Isabella did as she was bid, settling on the chair and picking up a last piece of bread from the plate still on the table. She tore off a piece and put it in her mouth. "I'm hungry all the time, lately," she mused, watching as her fingers tore the bread into small pieces.

"And do you know why?" Maria's query was gentle, her eyes dark with a question Isabella did not understand.

"Perhaps I'm happy and my appetite has increased to fit my mood." She ate another piece of the bread and leaned back in her chair, waiting till Maria should speak the words that were obviously on her mind.

"Do you not know that you are with child, Isabella? That you are carrying Rafael's baby in your womb?"

The piece of bread she was chewing slid down her throat and Isabella choked on it, coughing it up and spitting it out onto a handy napkin. "How do you know such a thing, Maria? Is there a way to tell for certain?"

"You are filling out a bit, in your breasts at least, and your eyes are bright with knowledge. I knew there was something different about you, and when I saw the face you made yesterday at the coffee Rafael was drinking, I recognized it for what it was. I, too, had problems with coffee when I was carrying my children," Maria said with a definite air about her.

"I've only begun to think I might be in the family way," Isabella said slowly. "In fact, I haven't even told Rafael yet, for I wasn't sure."

"I think you can be certain of it, since I have not seen any trace of your monthly flow for over eight weeks."

As the one who was responsible for wash day, for the scrubbing out of the clothing and assorted bits of linen used by the household, Maria would have knowledge of such things, and Isabella blushed as she realized that her every move was taken into account by the woman.

Maria's smile was soft, her voice a whisper when she spoke again. "When will you tell the señor?"

"I think it had better be soon, for he will surely guess for himself if I wait much longer," Isabella said, thinking ahead to the night to come when she might share her news with the man who would no doubt be happy over the news. "Tomorrow we can tell his father if Rafael thinks it is time to do so."

And with that, she left the kitchen to walk alone in the yard, to sit beneath a tree as she thought of the months to come, of the child she would carry and nourish within her body. Rafael was not due back in the house until suppertime, for the men were riding the fence lines today, making repairs and watching out for strays as they did so. Maria had packed them a generous repast to carry with them, and only two men remained in the barn to watch over the house and the women while the rest were away.

She walked to the stable then and approached Jose, who was busy at cleaning stalls. "Do you think you would have time to saddle my mare for me?" she asked as he paused in his work to smile at her.

His mouth drew down in a grim look and he shook his head slowly, regretfully. "I cannot do that, señora, for Rafael has said you are not to ride alone unless he tells us otherwise. I am sorry I cannot do as you ask, señora, but I would not give him reason to be angry with me."

She was stunned, her eyes wide as she considered the words she had just heard. Rafael had said she could no longer ride alone? Why? What reason could he have to keep her here unless he provided otherwise?

"I don't understand," she said quietly, thinking of what his reasons could be. "Does he think I am going to run off again and so he will not let me ride alone?"

Jose shrugged and leaned on his pitchfork. "I don't know, señora, only that he has given the order and I cannot disobey it without making him angry with me. And I can't do that."

She nodded and left the stable, walking back slowly to the hacienda, where she sat on a bench near the door. Maria found her there a few minutes later when she brought a pan of beans out with her, ready to snap them and take off the stems in preparation to cooking them.

"What are you moping out here for?" She settled on the bench, Isabella moving over to make room for her. "Here, take some of these beans in your lap and help me get them ready for the kettle," she said, settling herself in place.

"I just asked Jose to saddle my mare for me so I can ride and he refused. He said Rafael told him I was not to ride out alone, and I can only think he does not trust me, that he fears I will run off from the ranch while he is gone."

Maria laughed. "I think it is more likely he suspects you are carrying his child and he wants to protect you from accidents, and so does not want you to ride without him by your side."

So readily she spoke, Isabella was stunned. "How could Rafael know? Why would he suspect such a thing?" She had been quietly snapping the beans, holding a handful of the ends to be tossed aside and pausing as she considered such a thing as Rafael knowing her thoughts almost before she did.

Maria laughed, gathering up her pan in one hand, holding the corners of her apron with the other, where the snippings from the beans were gathered. "You don't give him credit enough, Isabella. He is a man, yes, but also he is a smart man, and he knows your body perhaps better than you do. Don't you think he might have already figured out that you have not been on a regular schedule of late?"

Isabella followed her into the kitchen, where Maria dropped the bits and pieces of her chore into the bucket they kept aside for feeding the pigs. She went then to the sink and worked the pump handle, until water flushed into the bowl of beans. She rinsed them well, changing the water twice to be sure the bits of soil were washed from the vegetables they would eat for supper.

Isabella found an onion in the pantry and brought it to her. "You will want some of this cut up into the beans, won't you?" she asked, and at Maria's nod, Isabella found a small knife and cleaned the onion, then cut half of it into small bits, before adding them to the pot. "What else can I do to help?" she asked, looking about the kitchen as if she would recognize any other food preparations Maria had set into motion.

"We'll need to have some carrots scrubbed clean and then cut up to cook," Maria said, frowning as if she considered what her menu should be. "I thought to chop up some beef for a meat loaf with tomatoes and onions in it. You can cut up the rest of the onion you began for the beans and make it ready for me to use. Then tear up some bread to put in it, too."

Isabella did as she was told, more than familiar with the ways of cooking from her long years at the convent, a fact which she spoke of often to Maria. Now they worked together in harmony, the older woman taking on the form of a mentor for the girl who had taken on the duties of wife to the man who reigned here.

They worked throughout the afternoon, taking time out for tea at the big table, Maria making bread, Isabella helping to form the loaves, then mixing the ingredients for pie crust, a task she was more than familiar with. A custard that was Rafael's favorite was cooked and placed in the pie crusts, in preparation for suppertime, and then it was time to peel potatoes to be cooked and mashed for the meal.

It was an enjoyable way to spend her time, Isabella thought, working side by side with the woman who had been kind to her, who now gave her leave to work in the kitchen as though it were her right. And indeed it was, for she was the mistress of this home, and as such Maria deferred to her. Isabella had a problem with such an attitude, for she was but a novice, with years of practice at being a kitchen helper, but only months at the helm of a home such as this.

"Thank you for allowing me to help you today," she said as they put the final touches to the supper preparations, and Maria looked up at her in surprise,

"You are the mistress of this home, and as such, you may do anything you please," she said firmly.

"But it is your kitchen, Maria, and you have far greater knowledge than I as to what must be done here in order to feed the household."

"You are learned in all ways of preparing food, Isabella, and I find you a worthy helpmate to me." Maria brushed aside her words easily, smiling in a generous manner as she brought the meat loaf from the oven and then drained the potatoes into the sink.

"Will you go out now and ring the bell, so the men will know that it is time to come into the house for the evening meal?"

Isabella did as she was bid, standing on the small covered porch, pulling on the rope that allowed the bell to swing back and forth, sounding the gong that would call the men in from the barn. They came quickly, six of them in all, including Rafael, stopping at the horse trough to wash in the water that poured from the pump, manned by Jose so that the others could have fresh water.

They hurried, apparently lured by the scent of food from the kitchen, then, laughing among themselves, they approached the house. Rafael was in the lead, his figure taller than the rest but for Matthew, who stood as tall as his employer. His booted feet stepped onto the porch and Rafael looked down to where Isabella waited for him.

His smile was warm as he encompassed her in a welcoming look. "You have been busy, haven't you?"

he asked, holding the door open for her to enter the house before him.

"I helped to get supper ready," she said, making little of the work she had done during the day. But it was not to be, for Maria heard her and spoke to Rafael.

"Your bride has done more than her share in the kitchen today, señor. She has made your meal ready for you with my help." She picked up a tray and headed for the hallway. "I will take Señor Simon his meal, for he is weary. I'd hoped after the wedding that perhaps…" Her words faded and Rafael nodded in understanding.

At the words so blatantly complimentary spoken by Maria, Isabella turned, opening her mouth to speak, only to have Maria's index finger silence her with its appearance on her lips. "Hush, little one, for you have no notion of how much you have done today, and it is only right that your husband should know that you are capable of working hard and making ready for his evening meal."

Rafael slid his arm around Isabella's waist and tugged her against his side. "There is no need to try arguing with Maria, you know, for she is the head of this household. She allows me to think otherwise, but I am wise enough to know where the authority lies." His teasing words made Isabella smile and she looked up at him, eager to find time with him alone, anxious to speak her news to his listening ear.

"Later I must speak with you," she whispered, her words carrying easily to him.

"Is there a problem?" he asked, immediately alert to her tone.

She shook her head. "No, just something we must speak of."

He nodded then, and sat her at his side at the head of the table. His words of grace were spoken as the men bowed their heads, and his hand lifted to sketch the sign of the cross on his chest as he finished. Isabella felt a sense of pride as she watched him, knowing that Rafael took his position as head of this house seriously, no matter his teasing words to Maria. As the leader of his home, he spoke words of thanksgiving daily at the evening meal, unashamed of his faith, willing to show his men his thoughts in such a way.

Now she ate, her appetite good, as, around her, the men spoke of their day's work on the range, of the fences repaired, the horses gathered up and brought back to the stable. She heard them as a buzzing of bees, her mind on the conversation she would have with Rafael later on; and before she was aware of the passing of time, they were being served the pie as dessert, and Rafael was voluble in his words of praise to Maria for the food she had prepared.

With the finish of the meal, Elena and Delores stood and cleared the table, freeing Maria from the evening work, and Rafael took Isabella's arm, leading her to the parlor. They sat on the sofa there and he looked at her inquiringly. "Do you want to speak to me now?" he asked, and only smiled when she shook her head.

"No, later, when we go to bed." She took up a

scarf she had been working on for several days, embroidering flowers on a length of linen they would use for a covering on the library table that sat before the big front windows. Her needle was quick as she plied it in the fabric, and she changed colors of thread twice, then worked at the pattern she had established while Rafael watched.

After a long thirty minutes had passed, he touched her hand and halted her work. She looked up at him inquiringly, her cheeks flushed a bit as if she knew his thoughts, and he coaxed her gently to put away her work for the night.

"It is time for us to go to bed," he said. "Maria has gone to my father and brought back the dishes from his meal. Now she's gone to her room and our part of the house is empty and waiting for us, for the girls have retired, too. Will you come with me?"

He stood and held out his hand to her and she smiled eagerly, knowing that the time had come to speak her secret aloud to him.

Rafael closed their bedroom door, watching as Isabella began to take down her hair. He sat on the side of the bed and drew his boots from his feet, then stood and stripped off his clothing, tossing it into the basket Maria had provided for their soiled garments.

Isabella had stripped off her clothing and donned a robe, allowing it to swing freely, the belt undone as she climbed into their bed. And Rafael could no longer refrain from his curiosity. "What is bringing this blush to your cheeks, my love?" he asked, smiling at her as he stood before her, his form naked, his eyes intent on every nuance of her expression as he prepared to wash up before joining her in the bed.

Filling the basin with warm water left for them by Elena or Delores, whose task it was to do such things, he picked up a cloth, then rubbed the bar of soap on it, using it to cleanse himself, from the top of his forehead to his waist, the suds standing out on his flesh as he worked the cloth over his skin. He rinsed it out then and returned on the same path, taking the perspiration of the day from his body, then completed the ritual by washing the lower half before he toweled himself dry.

"I like to watch you prepare for bed." Isabella sat in the middle of the mattress, garbed in her white robe, her hair flowing down her back, the brush she had been using still in her hand. He turned to her and his heart seemed to turn over in his chest, his eyes seeking the soft smile she wore, the slender lines of her body beneath the encompassing folds of fabric.

"I enjoy watching you no matter what you are doing," he said, walking to the bed, rubbing the towel over his chest as he moved across the floor. He watched her eyes widen as he approached, then in a swift move, cast aside the towel and reached for her. She was lifted into his arms, her knees on the edge of the bed and his hands were deft as he pulled the robe from her, removing it in a flurry of dark curls and waves, her hair floating down once more to cover her breasts and shoulders.

Holding her at arm's length, he allowed his warm gaze to roam where it would over her body, settling finally on the nest of curls that hid her femininity from him. He saw the quick blush that rose to cover her cheeks as he gazed his fill, knew that she was flustered by his actions, and blessed the innocence that she still wore as a cloak of beauty about herself.

"What do you have to talk to me about?" His gaze was warm, verging on the heat of desire and passion, and he didn't know how long he could wait for her to speak her mind.

Her eyes widened as he spoke and as though she sensed his patience, she tilted her head and spoke with a distinct air of pique. "If you have other things on your mind, then I will keep it to myself, Rafael McKenzie. I thought you'd be interested, but if you only seek to pacify me, then I will be silent."

He softened, recognizing that he had insulted her by his words, and he lifted her to himself, until her round breasts were pressed to his chest, her belly rubbing against his own, the warmth between her legs cradling his arousal, for he was already hard, his manhood seeking out the place where he would take his pleasure.

She stiffened a bit, shoving against him, her mouth a pout as she peered up from beneath her lashes. And he was moved to appease her, his head bending to drop soft kisses on her lips, across her cheeks and settling finally on her temple, where the beating of her heart touched his mouth.

His whisper was soft and languid. "Tell me, Bella mine. What news do you have for me tonight?"

She pulled at him, her arms around his neck, and she touched his ear with her lips, her murmur warm against his ear. "I think you will be a father before too many months have passed, Rafael McKenzie. I am sure I am carrying your babe."

He stiffened, his hands curved to hold her against himself, his mind racing with the speed of lightning as he considered the words she spoke. And then he held her away, looking down into the dark eyes she offered him. "Are you sure? How long have you known? Have you said anything to anyone else?"

"To Maria," she told him haltingly. "I wouldn't have, but she seemed to know already, for she spoke of it today when we were working in the kitchen. She had noticed…certain things."

"Like the times you should have had a monthly flow but have not?" His smile was wide, for he could feel it stretching his mouth as he inspected her face. He held her farther from him and looked closely at the lush lines of her breasts. "I think your breasts are larger than before, Bella. Do you agree?" He knew his face was set in lines of pride, that his joy must surely be apparent to her, for her smile matched his own as she reached up to kiss his lips.

"I have blossomed where I had not thought I would," she agreed. "Maria seems to think I am over two months along in this pregnancy."

He swept her close, his arms enclosing her then as

if he could not hold her tightly enough to himself, as though he wanted to mesh their bodies in such a way that they would be as one. "I am proud, Isabella. My heart is singing with happiness that we will have a child of our own. I have long wanted a family, boys and girls to fill these rooms with their shouts of laughter. My father will be so pleased. I know he has wanted this, too, for his house, and he will die easier knowing that our family will live on in the place he leaves for their comfort."

"Oh, Rafael. Don't talk so of your father's leaving us. Surely it will be a long time yet before he is taken away from us."

He shook his head, looking down at the quick tears that had sprung to her eyes. "There is no promise for any of us for one more day or week or year, Isabella. And for a man such as my father, who has been ill for so long a time, a man whose heart is becoming weaker day by day. There is even more reason to know that his days are measured. He will not live much longer. It saddens me, yet it makes my heart sing, knowing that his joy will be great at this news. We will tell him in the morning and make his day a good one."

She nodded, burying her face against his chest, her mouth open against the brown circle that lay against his left side. She touched it with her tongue, then turned her head to listen intently to his heartbeat, there where it kept a steady pace beneath the muscular surface.

"You have a strong heart, Rafael, a heart that will

love our child. I cannot ask for more in my life than what you have given me." She melted against him, and he felt a rush of warmth steal through his veins, a heated need to hold her close to his body, a steadily building flame that threatened to burn them in the fire of their mutual passion. He toppled her to the mattress, following her down, careful not to let his weight smother her.

For suddenly, it seemed that his care of her must be greater than ever, more tender, more careful that she not be overtired, that her body get enough rest, that she be protected from all harm that might threaten. For he knew, deep in his heart, that the threat of Juan Garcia was not gone from their lives. He was ever watchful that she not be left alone, and when Jose had refused to saddle her mare today she had been upset, not understanding the edict he had put in place that she not ride out alone. He felt that he must speak to her of it now, for she was in a mood to understand his concern for her.

"Jose told me that you wanted to ride today and he would not saddle Sheba for you." He looked down at her, at the puzzled look she shot in his direction, for she had been deep in thought even as he stretched out over her. Now she opened her eyes wide and awaited his words.

"I told the men that so long as there was any chance that Juan Garcia might be out and about I do not want you alone on your horse. I will be with you when you ride, and Maria will watch over you when you are in the house. I will not take a chance with your safety again, Bella. I'm not trying to make a prisoner out of you, and I don't want you to feel that you are being spied upon, but I don't want you out of sight or hearing of someone at all times."

She looked up at him, her mouth set in a rigid line, and he wondered what his punishment would be for this edict. She was silent, her mind seeming to be sorting through his words, and he only watched and waited. Her eyes were dark with an emotion he thought might be anger, and yet she was not pushing him away or asking him to remove himself from her.

"Am I not to ride anymore? Or will you still take me out on the range on occasion?" She asked the question soberly, as if the answer was more than important to her.

He breathed a short sigh of relief and was quick to answer her. "When I am able to do so, I'll take you anywhere you want to go. But we will carry a rifle with us and never will we leave without the men knowing which way we are heading and how long we will be out of sight."

"Do you think that Garcia will come after me? Can he possibly want me that badly, or is it just my inheritance he is after?"

Rafael bent to touch his lips to hers, a soft caress that spoke of his concern and caring, and then he spoke words that were frightening, even to himself. "Juan Garcia wants *you,* Isabella. Not just your property, although that is a big drawing card. But he wants the woman your father promised to him. He would use you as a possession, hold you prisoner in his home, treat you without the respect due to you as a woman, and in all ways he would not be a good husband to you.

"And the only way he could claim your inheritance is if he kills me first, for I stand in his way when it comes to his ever being able to become your husband. For as it is now, I hold the deed to your father's land and belongings. You know I would not take it from you, sweetheart, but legally it is mine, as your husband."

"I don't care about the inheritance. If it would mean his absence from our lives, I would give it over to him, for if he killed you I would not want to live, Rafael." Her words were spoken in a hesitant whisper, but the strength of her convictions was strong and her jaw was set in a stubborn line.

"He will not kill me, Bella. I am watchful and he will get no closer to me than my men allow. And they are all to be trusted. Even Matthew." As he spoke the man's name, he smiled down at her. "You may have yourself a real champion there, Bella mine, for he would have given his life for you had Garcia threatened you with bodily harm."

"Matthew is a good man," she agreed. "I'm glad you didn't punish him for what he did. He said that if he hadn't taken me, Lucia would have found someone else, and he would not trust my safety to any other of the men."

He bent low and kissed her again and this time his mouth lingered long upon hers, his hands slid up her body to seek the soft curves of her breasts and he rolled to one side, pulling her into his embrace. "Enough of this talk of other men. I am the one you should concentrate on, Bella. I am all the man you need to make you satisfied and content. And if you have a problem with that, I'll see what I can do to make things more conducive to your happiness."

She fitted her hands about his face, holding him before herself in a captive grip he did not argue with. Her eyes had softened, her lips had formed to his and she was all that was warm and womanly in his arms. She kissed him eagerly, whispering words that spoke of what her body yearned to receive from his touch, and he felt the heat of passion fill him, readying him for her taking.

He reached between them, his hand careful as he let his fingers slide through her curls and the slippery petals of her womanhood. He found what he sought there, and his movement against her tender flesh brought a quick moan of pleasure from her lips. His hips nudged her legs a bit farther apart, and then he found the warmth of her, his male arousal sliding without hesitation into the hot channel he had readied for his taking.

She clung to him, murmuring words that only served to encourage his movements, her arms around him, her legs and body forming a cradle for his use, and he was caught up once again in the thrill of loving the woman he had married.

The woman who had become the center of his life.

CHAPTER EIGHTEEN

RAFAEL CHERISHED EACH DAY that passed, spending all the time he could with his father, speaking with him of many things both past and future, hoping to gain some small amount of time in which to store up memories that would sustain him in the days to come.

But to no avail, it seemed, for he woke with a start early one morning, his senses warning him of sadness to come.

"Señor, I have sent for the doctor." Maria had rapped sharply at the bedroom door and now she spoke words that brought a chill to Rafael, and he shivered. "His nurse is worried, for he is not responding this morning."

Within the hour the doctor had arrived and with great care had examined Simon, standing erect to motion Rafael from the room. The shades were drawn, the room darkened and the household was quiet, as if they were already in mourning.

"SIMON MCKENZIE IS DYING." The words that would forever change his life resonated in Rafael's mind, the doctor who spoke them standing before him.

"How long?" Rafael voice was low, harsh, as he

asked for a reply he hoped would give him the time he needed to speak with the man who lay, even now, in his bed, his body growing cold, his mind fogged with the tendrils of death that threatened to carry him from this life.

"Hours, Rafael," the doctor said, the words uttered in a tone that conveyed his sympathy with the younger man. "You would not wish him to linger, for he is in pain. His heart is struggling to perform as it should, and my medicine is no longer strong enough to help him. Say your goodbyes to your father and know that he is ready to close his eyes for the final time. He is weary."

Rafael stood tall, his strength equal to the task before him, but his sorrow was deep and he yearned for the touch of Isabella, for her presence at his side. "Where is my wife?"

Maria heard his query and murmured a reply he barely heard, then bustled down the corridor toward the dining room and kitchen. In mere moments, Isabella followed her back, retracing the path the housekeeper had taken. She stood before Rafael and looked up into his face, her eyes glazed with tears, her mouth trembling.

"What can I do?" The words were a promise of her support and he reached for her, his hands clutching her shoulders as he brought her up against his chest, holding her fast, lest she not linger there where he would have her be.

He felt the warmth of her breath against his chest, in

the opening of his shirt, where she had buried her nose, where her mouth touched the patch of skin that covered his throat. "Maria said that your father will soon breathe his last, Rafael. He will want you by his side."

He nodded, unable to speak, for his throat seemed to have closed, his heart beating more rapidly than was its wont, and he could only clutch this woman close as he inhaled deeply and tried to shutter his mind against the hours to come. "Will you go in with me and stay there, Bella?"

Her head moved against him and her single word of acquiescence told him all he needed to know. His wife would not fail him, she would stand by his side and bear his grief as her own. His eyes seemed almost blind as he opened the bedroom door and stepped over the threshold, Isabella at his side. They went to the bedside, there to look down upon the wasted figure of Simon McKenzie, the man whose wisdom and strength had made his name synonymous with that of the man who ruled the area from Santa Fe.

Rafael's cheeks were wet with hot tears, his hands trembled with the grief that filled his very being and he sensed the support of the woman who stood beside him. And then she knelt at the bedside, taking the already cool hand of his father, holding it against her lips.

"We are here, Papa," she whispered, and Simon's fingers moved against hers, his hand locking about her more slender fingers, and a murmur from his lips became her name.

"Isabella. My child. My daughter." The rheumy eyes opened and for a moment Rafael saw a hint of his father's former strength there in the dark orbs. "My son, Rafael." With a whisper of his dying breath, the old man spoke the name of his child and sent a message of love that was unmistakable to the man watching.

"Papa." The word was broken as Rafael knelt beside Isabella. His hand covered hers, there where she held the long fingers of his father in her grasp. Together, they touched. Pale, slender fingers, longer, darker, stronger digits and those of a man who was breathing his last, held between them.

"God's blessing...on you both. May He...give you...children to fill your lives." As if he offered his own blessing on them and yet placed them in the hands of the Almighty, Simon spoke the words that seemed to forecast the future, and Rafael leaned closer to speak more directly into his father's ear.

"He has already done so, Papa. For Isabella is to have my child, my son. Our fondest wish is that you might be here with us to greet his birth, but barring that, I will name him for his grandfather, and tell him stories of Simon McKenzie and his life. Of the man who was his grandfather, the man who would have loved him beyond all else."

Simon nodded, his eyes closing, a smile of perfect peace touching his lips. "Thank you, my son. Thank you. When I meet your mother again, she will be glad to know this news." His words were but a murmur, barely heard by the two who watched and waited, but understood as a message from his heart.

They knelt by his side, his hand clasped between theirs for long minutes and then his breathing ceased, slowly and gradually as life left his body. The doctor neared and Rafael looked up to see the man shake his head in a slow movement that told of life passing and death taking hold.

"He is gone, Rafael." The hand he touched grew even cooler against his palm, and Rafael drew Isabella from the bedside, lifting her to stand beside him as they looked down on the shell of the man who had founded this dynasty, this oasis in the desert where Diamond Ranch gleamed like a rich jewel.

"Come, Rafael." Isabella took his arm and led him from the room, down the corridor to where their own rooms awaited their presence. They went in, closing the door quietly behind themselves, settling on the wide sofa that sat before the window looking out upon the courtyard. She held him as he slouched beside her, and then leaned heavily upon her, his head on her breast, his body limp with the pain of his grief.

Her hands were firm against him, her mouth warm against his face, his hands, his throat, wherever she could reach in order to bless him with her lips, speaking softly the words of comfort that warmed his heart.

It was there that Maria found them an hour later, an hour in which Rafael knew the people of his ranch had been told of the death of their employer, the man who had devoted himself to making their lives more than just an existence. For Simon McKenzie had run his ranch as a small city, where each individual had his own place, where even—in fact, especially—the children were respected and honored as members of the community.

Maria called upon the foreman's wife, Luisa Gomez, to come into the house and help her prepare the elder señor for his burial. The priest was sent for, the kitchen set into motion with Elena and Delores beginning preparations for the food that would be needed to feed the community after the burial.

Now, Maria came into their private sitting room where Isabella held her husband. In the midst of death's presence, it was time for him to face the future, and the changes in his life that began in this moment.

He stood, drawing Isabella up beside him, and faced his housekeeper. "I will speak to the people, Maria. Have they gathered?"

"Even now, they are in the yard at the back of the hacienda, Señor Rafael. They are waiting for you."

He nodded and walked from the room, stopping for only a moment in the kitchen to wash his face at the sink, Isabella using a clean towel to dry his cheeks and her long fingers to comb back his hair, before they went to the door and out onto the porch.

"You have been told that my father is dead. Simon McKenzie has gone to his rest." The words were only a confirmation of the news the people had already been aware of, but they sounded as a solemn phrase upon the air. The assembled crowd murmured only a moment before they stilled and then faced their new employer. He did not disappoint them, for his mind had already formed the words he would speak to them.

"He was a good man, a man who always had your interests at heart, and he would want me to continue on in the path he walked. I vow to follow his footsteps, keep this place a haven for all of you, where you may raise your children and be a part of Diamond Ranch all the days of your lives. We will bury Simon McKenzie in two days' time, but he will live on in your hearts forever."

Rafael bowed his head, unable to speak longer, and the men who would serve him on the ranch moved forward to lend him their support. They came, one at a time, to the porch where he stood, shaking his hand, offering warm words of sympathy, their presence an unspoken vow of support for his leadership.

Isabella stood beside him, a slender figure in a dark dress, her hair pulled into a long braid that hung down her back, her face that of a girl, too young to be faced with the task of being the matriarch of this family. But the determination on her face, the strength of her features, gave assurance that she would support Rafael in all that he did. She was drawn from his side by the womenfolk then, those who were wives to the men who had worked on the ranch for many years, whose children swarmed around them now.

"Señora McKenzie." One of the women addressed her and Isabella looked up into the kindly face of a white-haired lady, a woman who was easily the age of the man who had just died inside the hacienda.

"Yes. You are the mother of Manuel, aren't you?" Isabella asked, recognizing the woman as having been pointed out to her days earlier by Maria.

"*Sí.* I am Manuel's mama," she said. "I will help your girls in the house to prepare the meal, leaving Maria free to tend to all the other things she will be doing tomorrow and the next days."

"Thank you," Isabella said, recognizing that she would be swamped with offers of help by the women before her. "Thank you, one and all, for I know nothing of such things, and I will depend on all of you to help me take my place here in the days to come. I will listen to what you tell me and pay mind to what you advise me to do, for this is a new role for me to play, truly that of the mistress of Diamond Ranch. I need help if I am to be a success at this."

With murmurs of support, the women circled her and spoke of their places here on the ranch, of what they might do to lend a hand in the days to come.

"Isabella." Behind her, Rafael loomed, a dark figure who seemed somber and without the good humor she was so accustomed to seeing on his face. "Come now, Isabella. We must go in and speak with the priest. He has come to speak the last rites over my father and then to talk to us about the burial in the family cemetery."

She turned to him, offering her hand and following him to the house, walking through the back rooms into the parlor where the Father waited for them, his gentle demeanor fitting for the occasion.

The next hour was one of planning, of messages written and sent to relatives and friends, of writing down the facts of Simon's life as Rafael recalled them. He spoke to the priest of his mother, of the life she lived before her death, of the love her people felt for her, and of the great love shared with her husband.

It was a time of revelation to Isabella, hearing of Rafael's mother and father during the early years of their marriage, of their vision for this place and the years of hard work it had taken to make Diamond Ranch the prosperous, thriving empire it now was.

The priest took his leave, promising to return early the next day, and Maria appeared in the parlor, coaxing the two of them into the kitchen, where she had set places at the plain wooden table, pulling out two chairs for them to use, as they ate the simple meal prepared.

It was food meant to be nourishing, a hot stew, fresh bread and mugs of coffee, laced with rich cream. Fresh butter appeared, the result of Elena's time spent with the churn just an hour before, and honey from the hives at the northernmost part of the ranch was brought to be spread on the soft bread.

They ate, allowing the food to nourish their bodies, unaware of the flavor of the mouthfuls they ate, only intent on sharing the time together, soft whispers flowing between them, Isabella comforting her husband, Rafael finding strength in her warmth, finally, by the meal's end able to cope with whatever would come to pass.

THE BURIAL WAS QUICK, for the heat of summer would not allow the body to linger longer than a day or so without becoming dark. Rafael wanted his father to have the dignity left him, with the villagers and the outlying community gathering to offer their final words of respect for the man who was a legend in the territory.

The relatives who would gather in from farther away would not be in time for the funeral, but there would be days of family gatherings, perhaps a week or so of guests coming at all hours of the day and night to visit with Rafael and his bride.

And among those was the family that included Lucia, whose father allowed her to come with the family, but kept a stern eye upon his daughter, and offered apologies to Rafael for the damage she had done. Lucia watched with sullen eyes, and Isabella was fearful of her interference in the rites of mourning.

But Lucia only watched and stood back, as if she were unwilling to cause problems.

But miles away, a man held a note that had come into his hands by way of a young man from the household in which Lucia lived. A note that told of the death of an acquaintance named Simon McKenzie, of the gathering at Diamond Ranch of many friends and relatives, a gathering that would last for at least a week, and at which there would be many people, enough to perhaps shield his presence from Rafael McKenzie.

Juan Garcia rolled up the paper that promised him another chance at the woman he had lost to the younger McKenzie, and set his plans.

IT WAS THE SECOND DAY after the burial and still the ranch teemed with relatives who had arrived from afar, with neighbors who came with food and offered to help handle the overflowing crowd of those who would pay their respects to the family of Simon McKenzie.

Rafael was tired, weary to the bone, his sleep interrupted often by the voices of those who slept in the hacienda and the barns. It was common practice, Rafael knew, to gather to give support to those grieving, and yet he wished vainly for the week to be finished, so that he could get down to the business of running his father's ranch, of spending time with his wife, of caring for her needs as she had cared for his.

Now, he stood at his bedroom window, looking into the night, aware of the fires burning in the yard, where men sat around with guitars, playing the music his father had loved, watching as the younger women danced, coaxing their counterparts to join them. And his lips lifted in a smile, knowing that his father would have wanted his family to enjoy their time together, no matter that the occasion was one of sadness.

For out of death came life, Simon had said long ago, and though Rafael had not understood his words then, now they came back to him as clearly as if his father said the words in his ear. On that day long ago, Simon had spoken of the details of his own father's death and the days of reunion he had spent with scattered members of his family.

And as he had predicted, now those same families had gathered here, and Rafael could not regret that they were renewing old ties, finding old friends because of the gathering at Diamond Ranch. His father's memory was being honored by their presence.

CHAPTER NINETEEN

THE NEXT DAY FOUND Rafael walking from group to group, meeting anew with relatives he had not seen in years, recalling his childhood memories with aunts, uncles and cousins who remembered him from childhood. The support of these friends, gathered in one place, was precious to him, and he heard their words and stored the memories in his mind to be spoken of later when he and Isabella lay in their bed at night and talked of this time.

And later on, when his own children were born and asked the questions that children asked, about their families, their grandparents and what would then be in the past, Rafael thought of lifting small boys and girls to his lap and speaking to them some of the same words his own father had used, so long ago. The thought cheered him, for as his father had said, *"From out of death, comes life."*

Unknown to Rafael, a group of men was gathered behind the barn, their watchman keeping track of Rafael and his wanderings. Their leader was Juan Garcia, wearing a large hat, with a broad brim that partially hid his face, his guns covered by the jacket he wore. He walked among his men, his orders to them given in an undertone, his plans in place.

They kept apart from the family members, seeming to be a group from far off, and one of the uncles, who apparently thought it was his place to approach them, broke off from those with whom he was speaking and walked behind the barn, his steps sure, his mission one of friendship.

His words were unheard to those gathered in the yard, for the building that separated them was large, the doors closed, and in a matter of moments, the spokesman who had thought to extend the hand of friendship had disappeared.

Instead, the form of Juan Garcia appeared at the corner of the barn, his movements closely watched by the men who followed him. And when he saw the now delicately rounded form of Isabella McKenzie come from the house, crossing the yard to where her husband stood within a group of men, he turned a possessive gaze upon her, his eyes darkening with fury that would not be quenched except by her capture and her presence in his own hacienda. For her waist seemed to have thickened, her form was more womanly, as though she might carry a child beneath her heart.

He spoke in an undertone, his words carrying only as far as the men behind him, but his message was clear. "That is the woman I will take back with us. The wife of Rafael McKenzie. The woman who was promised to me by her father many years ago."

His men did not speak aloud, but murmured among themselves, and Garcia looked about the group, knowing that his face was hidden by the low-riding hat he wore.

Rafael sensed the approach of his wife and turned to her, holding out a hand to catch hers up and bring it to his arm. He held her there, a possessive gesture that served to tell all watching that she was his, a precious belonging he was proud of. His woman, his wife.

To the man who watched from near the corral, the sight did nothing but hone his anger to a fine pitch, for the surge of wrath and envy he felt was almost overwhelming. He'd been robbed of Isabella's inheritance, for his plan to snatch up the woman and leave with her was of necessity being thwarted by Rafael. Taking her from the man's side would not be possible. Unless Rafael were killed first, and then the woman taken quickly, which would neatly solve the problem that had cursed Juan Garcia for months. For once he was wed to Isabella, her inheritance would be his.

He backed from his stance and spoke rapidly to the men with him. His plan was made quickly, but was no less lethal for its swift inception. He would kill Rafael. Then, with two men he would ride into the open and, taking advantage of the crush of the crowd, take Isabella up onto his horse and they would ride from Diamond Ranch. Quickly and safely.

His horse pranced beneath him as he set his plan in motion. In moments he was before the barn, his mount pressing its way past numerous family members, all of them waiting for the dinner bell to ring, calling them into the house for the meal even now being prepared.

From her place next to Rafael, Isabella looked up at the melee that stirred the dust in the yard near the barn, and her quick eye caught sight of a familiar face, a young man who had ridden with Juan Garcia during the time she'd been captured by him. She turned to Rafael, unwilling to interrupt his conversation, but aware that danger lurked close by.

"Rafael, there is trouble," she said beneath her breath, and the words caught his ear immediately, turning his attention to her.

"Where? What is it, Isabella?" He looked up, his gaze touching the groups of people near him, then moving on to the scattered relatives standing farther off. In their midst rode a dark horse, its rider seeming intent on pushing his way through the throng, and in an instant, his instincts told him that this was the danger Isabella spoke of.

Before he could do more than push her behind him, before he could reach for the gun he realized too late he had left in their bedroom, he saw the man before him level a gun at him.

In that moment, he rued the day he had left Juan Garcia alive on the trail, knew that he should have put a bullet in the man then and there, and was now facing the results of his own softhearted neglect. For the finger on the trigger was a message of death, and if the man who sat atop the horse had his way about it, Rafael McKenzie would meet his maker, here in the courtyard of his own home.

A shot rang out, catching the tall man, the impact throwing him to the ground. Before the onlookers could do more than shout out vain orders to catch the gunman, the horse and rider broke through their midst, and the wife of Rafael McKenzie was grasped and pulled up on the horse, tossed carelessly across the saddle and the horse pivoted and was sent into a flying gallop by its rider.

Isabella twisted in Garcia's grip, watching the men running for their weapons, the women seeking out their children to hide them from danger and Rafael's men running to his fallen body, the horse jumping the corral fence and, followed by several others, running the length of the pasture and then north to where the open range held the cattle and horses of the Diamond Ranch.

"Rafael!" Her voice ringing out loudly from the porch, Maria, who had seen the bullet hit her employer, ran from the porch to where he lay, kneeling by his side and turning him to his back.

"He has been hit in the side, but I think it is not a fatal wound," she said quickly, tearing aside his shirt, the better to see where the bullet had creased his flesh. "Quickly, you men carry him into the house so that I may wash his wound and dress it. He will awaken very soon, and it is better that I do this while he is still unconscious."

She looked around at the men who hovered over her kneeling form. "The rest of you get mounted and follow the *bastardo* who has taken the señora. Quickly, catch them and bring her back. Do not spare your bullets, but at all cost, bring her back with you."

If they resented the orders being given by a woman, the men did not show their feelings, but instead ran as a group to the barn, saddling horses quickly, gathering their guns and mounting for the ride ahead of them.

Four men picked up Rafael's form and carried him into the house, finding a flat surface in the parlor upon which to place him, his head atop a small cushion. Maria knelt by the sofa and used her apron to stanch the flow of blood, then quickly gave orders for water and clean rags to be brought to her. Elena and Delores ran to do her bidding, and she made haste to wash and bandage Rafael's wound before he awoke.

From the depths of darkness that had enfolded him in its embrace, Rafael heard the hum of voices around him, knew he was being tended, handled by caring hands, and murmured the name that came quickly to his mind.

"Isabella." The voices around him ceased their murmuring and he heard Maria's soft undertones whisper words he rejected.

"Señor. Just lie quietly, so that the bleeding does not begin again. You must be quiet, Señor McKenzie."

"Where is Isabella?" he asked, his lashes opening a bit to better judge whose hands touched him, whose voice he heard. "Where is she, Maria?"

The woman who bent over him was ashen, her face awash with tears, and he reached for her hands, which were busy with white strips of fabric.

"Put that down and tell me where Isabella is," he demanded, his voice stronger than he'd hoped.

He struggled to sit up, and as if she knew he would not be thwarted, Maria helped him to sit erect, then took advantage of his position and wrapped the soft lengths of fabric around his body, securing the bandage she had applied.

"Señor, you must be still. You must rest for a bit, and then you will know all that has happened."

He pushed her aside, his legs swinging over the side of the sofa, his head spinning as he attempted to hold himself upright, and again spoke the question that begged to be answered. "Where is Isabella?"

He looked around at the assembled crowd in his parlor, seeking the beloved face of the woman he feared for, and his heart sank as he realized she was missing from the room.

His cousin, Ernesto, a man from three villages away, knelt by his knee. "Rafael, listen to me. Your men are already mounted and armed. They have followed the man who stole Isabella from the yard. They will catch them, and bring her back. Maria told them not to spare their bullets, but to do all necessary to gain her release."

Rafael focused on the young man who spoke, a man he trusted, his uncle's son. "I must go. I'll follow them and be there when they catch up with him," he said. "I must ride to find her. If Juan Garcia has her, he will harm her, and I will not rest here while Isabella comes to harm."

"You are not able to ride," Ernesto said quickly. "You have been wounded, and though your life is not at stake, you have lost a goodly amount of blood, Rafael. Let the men do this for you, for they are trustworthy and will do their best to get their mistress from the intruder."

Rafael caught his breath, and his words were coated with hatred. "The man who took her is determined to have her as his own. He is Juan Garcia, an evil man. Not just a bad man, but a man driven by hatred, and anger toward Isabella. We have no concept of the sort of things he may be driven to do, the crimes he would commit upon her body."

Ernesto surveyed his cousin, his thoughts apparently in turmoil. Then he turned to Maria. "Find Rafael a clean shirt and help him to dress. Be certain his wound is tightly bound. I will have his horse saddled, and I will ride with him. He won't rest so long as his wife is in danger, and I cannot expect any less of him than that he join in the hunt for her.

"If any of the rest of the men want to go along, I'm sure there are horses aplenty to hold them."

A murmur arose from those watching, for the parlor was filled with the men of the family who had followed Rafael's stricken body into the room. Now they milled as one toward the parlor door, flowing out through the kitchen and into the yard as a stream of humanity bound to set right a great wrong.

The stable was cleared of horses, both the stock from Diamond Ranch and the animals belonging to the friends and relatives of Simon McKenzie. In but a few minutes, the men had gathered up tack from the barn and located as many mounts for their use as they could find.

"I will ride my stallion, El Gordain," Rafael said firmly, standing on his feet, reaching for the holster Maria brought to him. With help from that quarter, he found it buckled around his waist, the familiar weight of his gun against his leg in moments. Ernesto walked with him, his arm firm around Rafael's back.

The stallion was saddled when they reached the barn, and Rafael stood by his head for a few long seconds, speaking to the animal in a low voice, his hands touching the great head. Then in a swift movement, and with the aid of Ernesto's strong arm, he was astride the giant horse, the reins in his hands, his jaw set firmly as he looked about at the group of men who stood ready to ride with him.

"You will have to keep up as best you can," he told them.

"El Gordain is a fast horse," Jose said, his hold on the bridle still holding the stud in place, and speaking to the men who would join in the chase. "You will be eating the dust from Señor Rafael if you do not mind well your riding skills."

"Release him," Rafael said to Jose, his smile a grim expression of his thanks. As the young man took his hand from the bridle, the stallion whipped around and headed for the pasture fence, sailing over it with but a single leap, his sturdy haunches providing the pivot for the movement, leaving behind him a group of men who mounted and headed their horses on the path of dust that followed him.

Jose held the open pasture gate in one hand, seemingly stunned by the rapid exodus of the men who rode past him. Ernesto rode at their head, astride one of the best horses on the ranch, following Rafael. And behind him, the rest of the men pushed their mounts to keep up with the two who led them.

The trail they followed was well marked with hoofprints aplenty, and Rafael had no difficulty in recognizing the path the riders ahead of him had taken. Their path led due north and across the open range to where the mountains hung against the horizon.

His side was aflame with the pain of his wound, but he put it from his mind, for the pursuit of Juan Garcia was uppermost in his thoughts. If the man thought he had killed Rafael, it would be to the advantage of those following, for he would not expect the man he had shot to be hot on his trail.

ISABELLA RODE UPRIGHT NOW, the man who held her having hauled her from her ignominious position sprawled across his saddle, to sit before him, his arm holding her against his body. She trembled with fear, not for herself, but for the man who had been sprawled in the dirt in the yard of the Diamond Ranch.

The man she loved better than life, the man whom

Juan Garcia had shot in cold blood. If Rafael lived, if the bullet had not taken his life, she would be forever grateful. But the memory of his broken body lying before her claimed her thoughts, and she sought in vain for some thread of hope.

Fighting off the grip of the man who held her was of little use, and she vowed to save her strength should she be given a minute's opportunity to escape his hold later in the day. Or during the long night to come.

"I would not cause you pain, Isabella." The words were spoken in the guttural tones she had come to despise, and she ignored his vow, sitting even straighter in the small space allowed her. She felt the rumble of laughter in his chest behind her, and lifted her chin even higher, determined that he would not find her to be frightened, quailing before him.

"You are a brave woman, señora." He spoke her title in a fashion designed to insult her, as though he mocked her marriage and the man who had given her the right to use the name of Señora McKenzie.

"I am only a woman stricken by fear that her husband is lying dead on the ground behind her, and my bravery is but a sham," she said quietly. "I do not fear what you can do to me, Señor Garcia, for what you have already wrought is guaranteed to kill the spirit within me. I am but a shell, a woman bereft."

His arm tightened beneath her breasts, and he inhaled sharply. "You will learn to be the woman I need with me, by my side, Isabella. Your days spent with Rafael McKenzie are at an end. From now on, you will be my wife. We will stop at the convent to speak our vows, for with Rafael out of the way, you are free to be my wife."

Darkness threatened to engulf her and she fought the encroaching gloom that would take her consciousness, vowing silently to remain strong, so that Rafael would have been proud of her, of her resistance to the man who had taken her captive.

Her head swam, her limbs becoming limp as she found herself fighting the pain of her loss, for the sight of Rafael on the ground, the blood staining his shirt and spreading on the ground beneath him, was a memory she could not shift from the forefront of her mind.

They rode on for what seemed like hours on end, and her body grew weary from the tension of holding herself upright and away from the powerful man who held her. The miles that separated her from Rafael served only to stiffen her resolve that Juan Garcia would not be the victor in this battle, for she vowed silently that she would never speak words before a priest that would bind her to this man. No matter the damage Garcia might do to her person, he could not force her to utter the phrases of the marriage ceremony in his ear.

The sun had set and their mad plunge from Diamond Ranch had settled into a steady pace that took them miles from any rescue attempt made on her behalf. Isabella knew a sense of despair that seemed to grip her in talons of pain and grief. The slowing of the horse she rode touched upon her consciousness and she felt the tension that gripped the man who held her.

"We will halt here for a few hours to rest our horses," he said against her ear. With quick movements, he dismounted and then brought her from his saddle to stand before him. "I am going to tie you, Isabella, for I cannot trust you to remain here with me. You will not be hurt, so long as you obey and remain where you are told."

"I must relieve myself," she whispered, unwilling that the men who surrounded them should hear her need spoken aloud.

"Come with me," her captor said, drawing her from the group of men into the wooded area where they would set up camp. He took her beyond the sight of those who might catch a glimpse of her and set her loose from his hold. "Go over there where the brush is high. I will give you two minutes to tend to your needs, and then if you do not come back to me, I will find you and your punishment will be severe."

She bowed her head, aware that she was at his mercy, and did as he bade her. In minutes she was back at his side and, with tears in her eyes, she watched as he tied her wrists firmly before her, the bonds too tight for her to pry apart.

"I will help you to eat," he said, leading her back to where the men had built a small fire and set a coffeepot atop a tripod to heat. Bread and meat was brought to her as she sat on a small blanket, and Garcia lifted a bit of bread to her mouth. She bit into it, chewing and swallowing, with the knowledge that she must keep up her strength. For it would not be to her benefit to refuse food, lest she be faint and unable to think properly once they were on their way again.

She settled once more on the bit of blanket that offered her a place to rest, and lay on her side, her neck twisting in discomfort at the lack of a pillow of sorts beneath her head. With a grunt of aggravation, Garcia lifted her head and stuffed a rolled up shirt beneath her, supporting her from contact with the hard earth.

"Now, rest. For we will only be here for an hour or so," he said, settling beside her and allowing her no chance to look about or seize upon an opportunity to flee his presence.

RAFAEL FELT THE PAIN in his side as a flame that would not cease its burning. The bandages held firm against his ribs and he was thankful for Maria's skills in binding him so tightly, for it enabled him to hold himself upright in the saddle as he rode. Their pace was by necessity slower than he would have liked, but he knew that without care, his weakness would soon put him on the ground, unable to keep up a faster pace, so he held his patience firmly and did as Ernesto bade him, knowing that his cousin had his best interests at heart.

"We will find them, Rafael. Perhaps not tonight, but surely tomorrow our horses will be fast on their trail."

"I fear what he has planned for Isabella." Rafael spoke aloud the words that spun in his mind, for his delicate wife would have no defense against the bulk of Juan Garcia. She would be a victim to whatever cruel punishment he dealt to her, and a knowledge of his helplessness washed over Rafael, the thought of it a pain he could barely contain.

They rode at a steady pace, then pulled their horses into a walk for fifteen minutes or so before they once more set them into a ground-eating gallop. Not only the horses needed the time of rest, but Rafael also felt the pain of his injury and knew that the weakness would overcome him if he did not pace himself.

The sun sank in the west and still they rode, only halting when Ernesto decreed they must rest their horses for longer than half an hour or so. Dismounting, they sat to rest, one of the ranch hands quickly building a small fire, the other men seeing to their horses, tying them where there was grass for their evening meal.

Rafael lay upon the ground, aware that he must rest in this brief time of respite, that he could not push farther on the trail they followed without some time in which to replenish his strength. In less time than he physically needed, but not quickly enough for his impatience to handle, they mounted once more and put out the fire that had provided them with a pot of coffee, riding again, but at a slower pace, lest they lose the trail.

The moonlight was good to them, and the men at the forefront of the group watched carefully that they not stray from the path of the horses they followed. With so many riding ahead of them, it was not difficult to see the trail they left behind, and they rode late into the night.

His fear for Isabella's safety nagged hard at Rafael's mind, only the knowledge that Garcia would not damage her fatally keeping him sane. For the man wanted her as his wife, and if he thought he had indeed killed Rafael, he would not be in any great hurry to seek shelter, for his one thought would be to speak vows of marriage with Isabella.

In order to do that, he would no doubt make his way to the convent where she had spent long years with the Sisters of Charity, there to seek the presence of Father Joseph to do his bidding and speak the vows of marriage over them.

For the convent sat in a direct line between the ranch of Juan Garcia and the enormous acreage of Diamond Ranch, a matter of fifty miles or so. It was there, Rafael was certain, that Garcia would take Isabella, and to that end he formed a plan.

CHAPTER TWENTY

"COME. WE WILL ride now." Juan Garcia tugged Isabella to her feet and she swayed, her mind foggy with the tendrils of sleep that clung tenaciously until his grip on her arm woke her to his voice.

She lifted her hands, attempting to brush her hair from her face, aware that it had fallen from the arrangement Delores had formed early that morning. The girl had pinned it in place atop her head, but now the strands had come loose from their anchoring and she felt their length streaming over her shoulders and down her back.

She looked to where Garcia watched and spoke words that galled her. "Please, Señor Garcia. Untie me that I might repair my hair. My fingers are numb from—"

She halted, frustrated by her helplessness, and he merely grunted impatiently, then bent to her and loosed the bonds, releasing her wrists. She gritted her teeth, feeling the blood flow to her hands and rubbed them together a moment before she lifted them to form three long hanks of hair, then made an awkward attempt to braid it. But it seemed Juan Garcia had other ideas.

"Leave it loose. I like to see it flowing down your back." With harsh words of instruction, he pulled her hands from their task and forbade her to tend her grooming. She only nodded, knowing that to argue would do her no good, for he was determined to have his way with her, and she would not waste her energy in fighting him now.

With swift movements he tied her again, then lifted her to his saddle and stepped into his stirrup, swinging his leg over his horse and mounting behind her. She held herself stiffly and he growled words of warning, pulling her against his chest.

"Do not fight me, Isabella, or I will stop my horse and take time to tame you to my will. I would not insult you by subduing your struggles before my men, but if you insist, that will be the result of your challenging my power over you."

She nodded, aware that she could not win a battle against him, felt a tug against her scalp as her hair flowed again over her shoulders and down her back, his fingers catching a strand. She felt his hand brush its length, heard the faint hiss of his breath as he pressed her head against his chest, and knew a moment of terror as she thought of what he might have planned for her.

The discomfort of bonds that were too tight for her to free herself angered her, and she twisted her arms in a futile effort at loosening their grip on her skin.

"Do not fight the ropes, Isabella, or you will only hurt yourself," he said warningly in her ear. Settling her closer to his body, he wrapped her tightly in his right arm, holding the reins in his left hand and nudging his horse into a faster pace.

"We will ride to the convent, and there you will marry me," Garcia said, his tone harsh and unforgiving. "You will not cause a problem there, or I will make short work of the priest and the sisters. Don't think to have them help you in escaping me, or I will make you responsible for their deaths. Do you understand?"

She nodded and then spoke quietly, words that were meant to shame him. "I had not thought even you would threaten the lives of a man of God, and of the women who have given their lives to His service. You should hang your head, Señor Garcia, for you have spoken words that will come back to haunt you when you face your Maker one day."

"Ah, but before that day arrives, I will find much pleasure in you and the joys of your body, Isabella. It will be worth the price I pay one day, the time of having you in my home, sleeping in my bed, keeping you as my own."

The shiver that passed through her body made him laugh aloud as he obviously felt the spasm she could not control. "That excites you, Isabella, doesn't it?" he murmured, taunting her with words guaranteed to anger her.

She subsided against him, not willing to allow him

the joy of forcing her to his will, intent only on loosening the bonds that held her wrists so firmly. She slept after a while, her body unable to hold itself upright any longer.

The sun was high when she awoke, the horse beneath her moving quickly, the men surrounding them with a security she could not argue with. Perhaps when they arrived at the convent, she thought. Perhaps then she would find a way to escape his presence. And to that end she put her thoughts and mind, escaping in the only way she knew in order to combat the feel of his body behind hers, his arms surrounding her.

They rode on for another hour and then he called a halt, once more lifting her from his horse and following her into the nearby patch of bushes and rocks, where he untied her hands and left her alone for a few minutes. She hurried to relieve herself, pulling her clothing back into position and smoothing down the wrinkled dress she wore. She felt soiled, not only by the touch of his hands, but by the dust that had covered her and her clothing during the long ride.

"Can I wash, please?" she asked, her tone low, lest she be overheard by the other men and then be a source of their laughter should Garcia refuse her request. But it was not to be, for he looked at her carefully, apparently aware that she needed a cloth and clean water.

With a lifting of one hand, he called a man to himself and issued clear orders that resulted in

Isabella being handed a damp cloth and a clean bit of toweling. She took both and, turning her back on the assembled men, washed her face, and then her arms, undoing the sleeves of her dress and drawing the wet cloth over her skin.

The towel was rough against her skin, but she dried herself off and turned to Garcia, returning the cloth to him. "Thank you." It was the least she could do, for if she expected him to give her the courtesy of privacy when needed and the time to refresh herself as required, it would be well to placate him in such a small way.

His mouth curved upward in a smile as he accepted the fabric from her hands, and he nodded, then tossed the bits of toweling to a waiting hand. "You are learning, Isabella, to behave as you should. I will not harm you needlessly, but your safety depends on your behavior."

They mounted and rode again, the horses being ridden hard as Garcia pushed forward on the trail to the convent. He told Isabella that they might even reach its gates by nightfall, if their route was uneventful, and she only pressed her lips together and held her silence. Surely Rafael's men would be tracking them even now, and somehow would effect her release from the man who held her life in his hands. It was the only bright spot on the horizon of her mind, for the thought of Rafael's condition was too dire to dwell on.

It was very late, long after midnight, when they approached the gates of the convent, and she watched as two men dismounted and rattled the iron gates, calling out in strident tones for the watchman to heed their summons. It was almost ten minutes before the convent doors opened and a garbed figure stood in the aperture, speaking in a low voice to the man who hurried across the courtyard toward the gate.

"Who are you?" he asked, peering at them in the light of the lantern he carried. "The sisters must know your identity before they will allow me to open the gates for your admittance."

Juan Garcia spoke loudly, so that the woman waiting in the doorway would hear his words. "I have Isabella McKenzie with me, and I seek shelter from the night for her and for my men."

"Is it truly you, Isabella?" the nun called out loudly and then waited.

"Answer her. Give her the assurance of who you are," Garcia said forcefully, gripping her tightly, and Isabella did as he told her, aware that he might harm the man standing by the gate if she did not do as he commanded.

"It is indeed Isabella, Sister Agnes Mary," she called out, and in moments the gate was opened and the group of men rode within the walls.

"I will speak to your priest," Garcia said, his words harsh and his countenance forbidding as he dismounted and approached the sister who waited in the doorway.

"Father Joseph is asleep," she told him, and stood her ground.

Juan Garcia lifted a hand, his fist clenched, and

she only watched him, her expression stoic, her eyes unblinking.

"If you think to persuade me to your will by force, you may continue," the sister said firmly. "My body is mortal, but my soul and spirit are eternal, and I do not fear your might."

Garcia laughed aloud. "Perhaps not, but the pain I am capable of bringing to bear would not be pleasant, sister, and it is my suggestion that you awaken the good priest."

"If you desire rooms for the night, I will show you to a series of cells you may use, and I will put Isabella to rest in her old room. Father Joseph will appear at breakfast as is his usual practice. You may see him then."

At the nun's quiet defiance of his orders, Garcia hesitated, and then, as if he thought it of little matter, he nodded. "All right. We will rest for the night, but I will keep Isabella in a room with me. She will not be out of my sight."

Sister Agnes Mary looked dubious at his declaration, but finally nodded and reached to touch Isabella's arm. "Come with me, child," she said kindly, leading the girl inside the walls of the convent proper and down the hall. It was the same route Isabella had taken months before when Rafael had taken her from this place and she yearned now for his presence to be with her, fearful of what Garcia might do to her in the privacy of her cell.

They halted before the door and Sister Agnes Mary

opened it wide, ushering them within. She cast a long look at Isabella, her eyes tender with a pain she could not conceal, and with a trembling hand she made the sign of the cross against her breast as Garcia led Isabella into the room and shut the door.

It was fully dark in the cell, and though Isabella knew where the small bits of furniture were located, Garcia did not, and she heard his oath as he stumbled against a chair. "Where is the bed?" he asked, his voice a harsh growl.

She stepped away from him and he followed closely as she sought the narrow cot she had slept on for so many years. It was beneath the window and the light from the moon shed an eerie glow upon her as she turned to him.

"It is here, Señor Garcia. Must I share it with you?"

"We will both sleep there, Isabella. I have not decided yet if you will be mine tonight, or if I will wait until the priest speaks the wedding ceremony tomorrow."

She did not argue with him, but sat on the edge of the cot and took her shoes off, then lifted her legs to the cot and rolled to face the wall. His weight pulled her back against his body and she clung tightly to the edge of the mattress, lest she be molded against his form behind her.

He laughed at her efforts and simply flung his arm over her and held her fast. She felt the heavy beating of her heart, knew a fear more terrible than any she had ever faced in her life, and prayed silently for the mercy of God to shield her from the man who held her prisoner.

It seemed her prayer would be answered, for his grip, though firm, was not hurting, and he did not force her to turn toward him, but held her a prisoner between his body and the wall.

"Sleep, Isabella. I will not harm you," he said, and she swallowed the tears that had formed in her throat, only nodding as he spoke. It seemed that she would lie awake, for she could not envision sleeping with his hands upon her body. But the long hours of the day, the events that had combined to tire her and cause her to be weary, overcame her and she felt her eyes close in sleep.

DAWN WAS BUT A pale shadow in the east when Rafael and his men succeeded in catching up with the earlier contingent from the ranch. Now they greeted each other silently, lest the sound of their voices allow them to be found there, the smiles of those who had feared for his life relieved at Rafael's appearance.

The convent loomed before them, and together, the two groups formed as one, Rafael leading his men into the wooded area just in front of the gates. They were silent, keeping their horses quiet so as not to be heard by the men who slept in the courtyard, for apparently there had not been enough rooms to house all of Juan Garcia's men inside the building.

Manuel removed Rafael's dressing from his wound and applied a soothing salve sent for that purpose by Maria, then applied clean pads of soft fabric and tied long strips around his chest to hold them in place. His assurance that the wound was clean and already appeared to be healing was a comfort to Rafael. Though he cared not about himself, he knew he must be able to fight should the time come, in order to defend Isabella.

The light was turning from gray to a pink glow from the rising sun when a man appeared by the gate, motioning at Rafael, who watched from a vantage point.

"See what he wants," Rafael told Manuel, who had approached and stood next to him. Without a word, Manuel made his way to the gate, watching as the man held up his hand in a bid for silence. Their heads were close on either side of the iron gate, and in moments Manuel came back to where Rafael awaited his return.

"He said that Garcia brought Isabella here long after midnight and they are still sleeping inside. He told me that Isabella was safe and he saw no signs that she had been harmed."

Rafael breathed deeply, a sigh of relief that his wife was not broken and bleeding after contact with the man who held her prisoner. Perhaps they could effect this rescue without direly affecting Isabella. And he breathed a silent prayer to that end as they turned back into the trees.

Before them, the man quietly undid the locks that held the gates fast, and then disappeared once more into the door of the convent.

In less than an hour, the bells rang for the nuns to

arise and take their place in the chapel, and the waiting men watched as Father Joseph walked across the courtyard, picking his way among the half-dozen men who slept soundly on the ground. As if he had been made aware of the night visitors to his holdings, he showed no surprise at their presence, but ignored them as he walked on to the chapel.

A long line of sisters exited the convent doors then and followed his path, careful to skirt the men who were now rousing from their sleep, sitting up to watch their silent figures as they went into the chapel for morning mass.

Behind them came another group, this time of men, six or eight of them, followed by the figure of Juan Garcia, who turned back to reach for the woman who reluctantly followed in his path. His hand snatched at her arm and drew her from the doorway, pulling her up against himself.

Rafael watched as Isabella winced at the contact, and then her gaze flew to the iron gates, as if she sought some sign that he was nearby. Or perhaps she sought the presence of his men, for he was certain she thought he had died from the bullet that Garcia had fired at Diamond Ranch.

He moved from his hiding place amid the trees and stood where she could see him, and was rewarded by the look of relief that washed over her face as she fastened her dark eyes on him. She lowered her head then, as if fearing that Garcia might notice the half smile that trembled on her lips. With dragging footsteps, she followed his lead to the doors of the chapel, the awakening men in the courtyard trailing behind them, still caught up in the dregs of an uncomfortable night.

"She is well," Rafael murmured to the man who stood behind him, and Manuel muttered words of agreement. "Now we move," Rafael said, motioning at the men who waited behind him, a sizeable number, representing a formidable presence.

Mounting their horses, they went toward the gates and Matthew dismounted, swinging them wide so that the men could pass through and make their way to the walls of the chapel, halting before the doors.

CHAPTER TWENTY-ONE

"YOU WILL SPEAK the words of the marriage ceremony for me and my bride." Juan Garcia spoke loudly as he stood before the altar, his men ranged in the back of the chapel, Father Joseph standing before him, prayer book in hand. The sisters were arranged in the pews, heads bowed in prayer, awaiting the words of the mass that was scheduled to begin, and as one, they turned to the group that had assembled silently at the front of the small church.

"It is my understanding that this woman is already married, to a man named Rafael McKenzie. Is this true?" Father Joseph asked, turning to Isabella.

She nodded. "We were married over four months ago in the village church near Diamond Ranch, south of here."

Father Joseph frowned. "Then how can you become the bride of this man, Isabella? I cannot do this thing."

"Her husband is dead," Garcia said harshly. "I saw him fall when he was struck with a bullet the day before yesterday. He had stolen my bride and I went to retrieve her. The man is dead, and Isabella is no longer his wife. She is a woman without a husband and I will make her my wife. Now, speak the words that will bind her to me."

Father Joseph shook his head. "I cannot do this thing without thinking of the effect it will have on Isabella. She has not had time to mourn her husband and you would rush her into another alliance, one which she may not desire."

"She has no choice," Garcia said harshly. "Do as you are told, or my men have instructions to dispose of the nuns."

Father Joseph looked at him with eyes that promised vengeance. "You would threaten the lives of women who are committed to serving their God?"

"If that's what it takes to make this ceremony go forward, then that is what I will do." His mouth twisted in a grimace that promised peril to the nuns who watched from the pews behind him, and Garcia turned to cast a long look at the men who were waiting at the back of the chapel.

"I must think on this for a few minutes." Without pause, Father Joseph knelt at the altar before him, and his lips moved as he prayed, his hand lifting to touch the crucifix he wore about his neck.

As if he were stunned by the turn of events, Garcia's face darkened and his jaw tightened, as if he gritted his teeth.

"Do not harm him," Isabella said quietly. "Or the nuns, for they are women innocent of guile, and they offer you no threat."

"I will not be halted in my plans, Isabella. If the priest will not do as I tell him, I will take the lives of those women. By the time my men have killed one or two of them, he will come to his senses and do as he is told."

"I will not do as you tell me, Señor Garcia," she said firmly. For this was as far as she was willing to go. To speak the words that would bind her to this man was not to be considered. Her spirit ached with the pain of the certain knowledge of Rafael's shooting and the injury his body had suffered, yet she could not find it in her heart to despair overmuch, for the sight of him outside the convent walls had lifted her spirits.

Likely the shot had not wounded him deeply, or he would not be able to ride and give chase as he had. She felt encouragement, knowing that even now he was nearby, that he would rescue her from the man who stood beside her. And to that end, she allowed her body to slump against Garcia, lifting a hand to her forehead, as if she felt faint.

"What is wrong? Are you unwell?" Garcia looked down at her and she closed her eyes for a moment, lest he see the thoughts she held within her.

"I am weak, and I fear I will faint if I cannot sit down for a minute," she said, allowing her bones to remove their support and feeling herself falling to the floor.

With an exclamation of disgust, Garcia stepped backward with her to the front pew and with a harsh hand, pressed her onto its seat. "Sit, then," he said, standing over her and keeping a close eye on the man who knelt before them at the altar.

Behind her, Sister Agnes Mary reached to touch her shoulder and bent to whisper a word of courage in her ear. "All will be well. You will see."

And as if she had been given new strength, Isabella nodded, a barely perceptible movement of her head. A sound from the back of the chapel caught her ear and she stilled, her hearing quickening as she listened to the whisper of men, the brush of the heavy door against the tiles of the floor.

Beside her, Garcia uttered an oath and stepped away from her. Then, looking down to where she sat, he spoke an order that fixed her attention on him.

"Do not move, Isabella. Stay where you are."

She nodded, turning her head a bit to look back to where his men waited, only to see a general exodus of those same men as they went out the door that had been opened into the courtyard. With an oath that sounded loudly in the chapel, Garcia made his way down the aisle and threw the second door wide, looking out to where his men had gone.

From the open space beyond where he stood, she heard voices, loud and distinct, and with a sudden flare of excitement, she ran through the chapel's back door. The path led to the front of the chapel where men were gathered, most of them on horseback, milling about in the dusty courtyard.

She hesitated by the corner, fearing to be seen, peering to find the location of the man she sought, finding him astride his stallion, slouched a bit, his features pale but determined. He dismounted, drawing his gun and approaching the chapel, walking out of her sight.

Before she could catch a breath, pandemonium erupted and she heard the voice of Juan Garcia, his words loud, calling his men to his side from where they were being held prisoner by the ranch hands from Diamond Ranch. Apparently drawn from the back of the chapel by armed men, they stood now in a tight knot at one side of the mounted horsemen, unable to do as Garcia willed them.

Isabella stepped around the corner and saw him then watched as he drew his gun and took aim at Rafael. "You are supposed to be dead already, Señor McKenzie. I will make that a reality now, for it seems I did not aim as well as I should have the first time."

Rafael stood before him, a look of dark intent on his face, his own gun already pointed at the man who threatened his life, and without hesitation, he pulled the trigger on his weapon, firing twice.

Garcia slumped to the ground, his own gun shot from his hand by the first bullet fired, his arm damaged by the second, blood flowing freely as he lay on the ground, his eyes filled with hatred as he looked up at the man who stood before him.

"I have held her in my arms all night long," he said, his voice filled with a dark satisfaction as he spoke words that guaranteed his death, for Rafael took aim once more.

Isabella ran then, crying out loudly. "Don't kill him, Rafael. Let the law handle him, for he is not worth the stain on your soul if you shoot him where he lies."

She stood to one side, and the big horse that had carried Rafael long hours atop his back whinnied sharply, catching her attention.

"Back up, Isabella. El Gordain has caught sight of you. Get away from him." As if he feared mightily for her life, Rafael lifted his gun at the horse who had recognized the woman whose soft tones had lulled him over the past weeks, whose almost daily visits to the stable had lured him into her spell.

Now he lowered his head and offered it to her, silently begging her touch, and Isabella reached for the stallion, careful not to move too quickly, lest she startle him. Her voice was soft, her words crooning as she spoke carefully, words that only the horse heard, so quiet were they. She stood by his head, then moved to the shelter of his side, leaning against him with a trust gained from long hours of coaxing him to her will.

"Get Garcia on his feet." Rafael's gaze left his wife and he spoke the words to his men, watching as they hauled the form of Juan Garcia erect, then bound his wounded arm with a kerchief torn from his neck. "Tie his hands and get him on a horse, and watch those men of his."

But it seemed Garcia's hired hands were not willing to shed their own blood for their employer's cause, for they put up their hands and made a great show of surrendering to the men who threatened them.

"We will find a lawman nearby," Rafael said, looking at the chapel door as the sisters passed through it, followed by the stout form of Father Joseph, who had left his prayers to seek out the source of the hullabaloo in his courtyard.

His wide grin was proof of his happiness as he caught sight of Juan Garcia bound, obviously wounded and a captive of the band of men. "I see I will not be performing a wedding this morning," he said loudly, turning to where Isabella stood by the stallion. He made as if to walk toward her and she held up a hand.

"Come no closer, Father Joseph, for this horse will not allow a stranger to approach him." With the safety of the priest uppermost in her mind, she grasped the reins of the stallion and held him quiet by the force of her will, for her strength would not have been ample to do the trick.

"You had better do as she says, Father," Rafael told him, smiling at the picture of his wife controlling the massive horse that elicited fear in the hearts of his ranch hands. "I don't know how you managed it, Isabella, but it seems that you have my stud at your mercy," he said with a smile that gave her his blessing.

"I have only spent time with him, befriending him," she said quietly, waiting till Rafael should draw near. And then he was there, his hands on her, his arms around her, his breath in her ear as he held her against himself.

"Ah, sweetheart. I feared for you. I was so worried that he had hurt you." And then his eyes fell to her wrist, where bruises had formed due to the rough treatment she had suffered under Garcia's touch. "Are you bruised elsewhere?" Rafael asked, his voice harsh, his look flashing her length as if he would see through her wrinkled clothing to the tender skin beneath.

"No, I am safe and untouched," she said softly. "I am well, Rafael. I knew you would find me in time." Her eyes felt the first sting of tears as she knew the wash of relief that engulfed her, and she leaned against him, willing him to take her weight.

He bent low, his mouth touching her forehead. "Do not cry, sweetheart. We are going home now, and Garcia's men can leave and return to his ranch, there to await news of his fate."

He turned to Manuel. "Take this man to the village and find the lawman who tends the sheriff's office there and give him the prisoner. Tell him I will file charges as soon as I locate a place for Isabella to rest before we return home."

He turned then to the men who watched and awaited their fate, the men who had ridden with Garcia. "The lot of you, mount your horses and go home. Garcia will pay for what he has done, but I do not hold you responsible for his acts. Find your way back to his ranch and do as you will. He will not return there."

The men did as they were told and in minutes, they had found their horses, gathered their belongings and left the convent walls. Garcia did not speak, did not look at them, only sat slumped in the saddle and waited for his captors to escort him.

IT WAS LATE AFTERNOON before the paperwork had been completed, and Juan Garcia was in a cell awaiting the U.S. Marshal who would be coming to get him within days. Now it was time for Rafael to gather his wife from the small hotel and make his way home, and he was more than ready to do just that. His side pained him, but the thought of Isabella's presence drew him to the hotel and he fought off the throbbing that would have forced him to rest at another time.

In the hotel, he climbed the stairs to the second floor, to the room where his wife awaited him. When he found the door behind which she was waiting, he knocked once, then opened it and entered. From the bed where she had been lying, she rolled to her feet and stood waiting for him to draw near.

His hands went out to her, his left arm slower than the right, due to the pain that surged through it at his movement, and she saw his wince of pain, and drew him to the bed, pushing him to sit on the edge of the mattress.

"We will stay here overnight, Rafael," she said forcefully, determined on her course. "I will have Manuel find dressing for your wound and hot water to bathe you and a bathtub for my use, for I feel the stains of the past days deep upon my body and spirit. I need the cleansing effects of a bath, and I think it would be good for you to be clean and refreshed before we try to make our way home again."

He did not argue, apparently willing to do her bidding in this, for he only nodded and watched as she went to the window and looked down into the street, where his men were waiting, having tied their mounts to the hitching rails and resting for the return journey home.

She leaned from the open window and called out to Manuel. He responded quickly to her summons and in moments, he was at the door, awaiting orders. She told him her needs and he nodded, smiling as he caught sight of his employer on the bed, his shirt off, his bandages loose, in preparation for Isabella's ministrations.

"I will return in a short time," he said, tipping his hat to her in a salute of appreciation, then vanished down the stairs.

It was late in the day before Rafael awoke, his wound newly bandaged, his body clean and dressed in clothing found at the general store. Beside him, Isabella lay quietly, her eyes open on his as he lifted his lashes and sought her face.

"You have slept well," she said softly, lifting a hand to his jaw and touching the whiskers that grew there. "Perhaps you will be able to shave before we go downstairs to the restaurant to eat."

"If you can find a razor for me, I'll do that." His smile was wide as he turned his head to kiss the palm of her hand.

"Manuel brought one up with the bath earlier," she said, pointing toward the commode where a basin and pitcher sat awaiting their use. "I think we will rest here tonight and go home tomorrow. Most of the men have gone, but four have stayed to ride with us. Will that plan suit you?"

He smiled, catching her hand again and drawing it to his lips. "Whatever you have planned for tonight is fine with me, love."

She turned her eyes upon him, her smile brilliant, and her words teased him as she offered him the bounty of her love for the hours to come. "If you feel well enough, I will claim you as my husband tonight, Rafael. For I am ready to once more be the wife of Rafael McKenzie, in every way. You need only lie with me and accept my kisses and the love I will devote to your pleasure."

His gaze told her of his joy in her offer and she bent to him, her mouth blessing him with the proof of her devotion. "I knew that somehow I would return to Diamond Ranch, Rafael. I was not sure if you were alive or dead, and I feared the worst when Garcia took me away. But I knew that I would live through whatever happened, and that I would end my days at Diamond Ranch. My prayer was that you would share those days with me."

"We will ever be together, Isabella. For all the years to come, we will live in the house my grandfathers built, raise our children in the rooms that were made for their use, and our lives will be as I have already planned. For the day that I first saw you in the chapel, when you bowed your head to pray on that morning months ago, I vowed that our lives would be intertwined, that you would be mine, that we would share a lifetime of loving together at the ranch."

"I have been the captive of two different men, Rafael. And I am so happy that you were the victor in this struggle, the one who loved me enough to come to my rescue, that you wanted me as your wife, that you made it possible for us to share our lives."

His arms were warm about her then and he pulled her close to lie beside him in the bed. "I am willing for you to be in charge tonight, Isabella. But, do you think you could change the schedule just a bit?" he asked. "Perhaps we could share the loving first and then go down to the restaurant for our evening meal later on."

She laughed softly beneath her breath and her fingers grew busy with the buttons of his new shirt. "I think that is a remarkable idea, Rafael McKenzie. And if you will allow me, I'll be very careful in removing your clothing, so that I don't hurt your wound."

He smiled, allowing her touch, giving her leave to do as she would, and then lay back to revel in the woman who was his whole life. His love for all time.

His wife.

It was early in the year, when the mares had dropped their foals, when the cattle had come back to the barns with their new calves, when the time of new life was apparent all over Diamond Ranch, that Rafael stood by the side of his wife and welcomed the son she had promised him into the world.

He held the tiny mite in his hands, amused at the doctor's description of him as a big, strapping boy, for anyone could see that he was but about seven or eight pounds of infancy, completely dependent on his father's hands to protect him, upon his mother's milk to nourish him, and the women who ran the kitchen and supervised his coming and going at Diamond Ranch to watch his every move over the years to come.

"He is Simon Rafael McKenzie," Isabella said softly from her resting place beside him. "Your father would be pleased if he could see him, wouldn't he?"

Rafael nodded, unable to speak for the tears that threatened his dignity. He lifted the tiny babe to his face, kissed the wrinkled forehead, then placed him in his mother's arms.

"He is a fine son, Isabella," he managed to say, his voice rough with the emotion of a new father. "Thank you for giving him to me. Thank you for being my wife and the mother of my son."

"I can think of nothing else that could make my life complete, Rafael," she said, her eyes filling with tears to match his own. "You are the center of my life, and I will love you for all the years to come."

He simply bent then and touched her lips with his, a soft blending of two people who had come a long way, whose lives had meshed into one, who faced a future that beckoned them into a bright tomorrow.

REQUEST YOUR FREE BOOKS!

2 FREE NOVELS
FROM THE ROMANCE/SUSPENSE
COLLECTION PLUS 2 FREE GIFTS!

YES! Please send me 2 FREE novels from the Romance/Suspense Collection and my 2 FREE gifts. After receiving them, if I don't wish to receive any more books, I can return the shipping statement marked "cancel." If I don't cancel, I will receive 4 brand-new novels every month and be billed just $5.49 per book in the U.S., or $5.99 per book in Canada, plus 25¢ shipping and handling per book plus applicable taxes, if any*. That's a savings of at least 20% off the cover price! I understand that accepting the 2 free books and gifts places me under no obligation to buy anything. I can always return a shipment and cancel at any time. Even if I never buy another book from the Reader Service, the two free books and gifts are mine to keep forever.

185 MDN EF5Y   385 MDN EF6C

Name	(PLEASE PRINT)	
Address		Apt. #
City	State/Prov.	Zip/Postal Code

Signature (if under 18, a parent or guardian must sign)

Mail to **The Reader Service:**
IN U.S.A.: P.O. Box 1867, Buffalo, NY 14240-1867
IN CANADA: P.O. Box 609, Fort Erie, Ontario L2A 5X3

Not valid to current subscribers to the Romance Collection,
the Suspense Collection or the Romance/Suspense Collection.

Want to try two free books from another line?
Call 1-800-873-8635 or visit www.morefreebooks.com.

* Terms and prices subject to change without notice. NY residents add applicable sales tax. Canadian residents will be charged applicable provincial taxes and GST. This offer is limited to one order per household. All orders subject to approval. Credit or debit balances in a customer's account(s) may be offset by any other outstanding balance owed by or to the customer. Please allow 4 to 6 weeks for delivery.

Your Privacy: Harlequin is committed to protecting your privacy. Our Privacy Policy is available online at www.eHarlequin.com or upon request from the Reader Service. From time to time we make our lists of customers available to reputable firms who may have a product or service of interest to you. If you would prefer we not share your name and address, please check here. ☐

BOB07